TAINTED TIES

TETHERED FATES
BOOK ONE

GHEETI NUSRATI

Editing by Emma Jane of EJL Editing
Cover Design by Daniela of Ever After Cover Design

 Created with Vellum

AUTHOR'S NOTE

Tainted Ties contains mature and graphic content that is not suitable for all audiences. Reader discretion is advised.

I trust that you know your triggers.

PLAYLIST

"Here With Me"—d4vd
"Those Eyes"—New West
"I Wanna Be Yours"—Arctic Monkeys
"unless you leave"—Chase Elliott
"No Time To Die"—Billie Eilish
"Shut Up and Listen"—Nicholas Bonnin, Angelicca
"Shameless"—Camila Cabello
"lovely"—Billie Eilish, Khalid
"Million Dollar Man"—Lana Del Rey
"eyes don't lie"—Isabel LaRosa
"Daylight"—David Kushner
"Work Song"—Hozier
"love notes"—Alexa Cirri
"A Little Death"—The Neighbourhood
"Die For You-Remix"—The Weeknd, Ariana Grande
"Set Fire to the Rain"—Adele

For those who seek the light.
Embrace the dark.

PROLOGUE
AURORA

Ten Years Ago

Italy. My home country. A place that once brought me joy, but now left painful memories in its wake.

"Aurora, it's past noon." Chiara opened the curtains in my room, blinding me as the sun blazed in.

"Too early," I groaned, my voice coming out muffled through the pillow on my face.

"Your *papà* has asked for your presence today. Come on, up you go," she sang, pulling the pillow away from my face.

Sheer panic seized me in a vise. My father was one of a kind and not in the way a daughter hoped. Yet a part of me yearned for his love even now. Even after he neglected me in the years since *Mamma* passed away.

The cancer slowly spread throughout her body until it reached her heart. We all knew what was coming, but no amount of time could've prepared me for losing her. Not a day went by when I didn't think of her. The emptiness in my chest grew with each passing minute and I didn't think anything, or anyone, could ever fill that void.

"It'll be different this time, *figlia mia.*"

Chiara was more than our head housekeeper. After the passing of my mother, she made me her only priority.

I wasn't the easiest person to be around. Some days were harder than others, but she was patient and held me when I couldn't contain the pain that consumed my body and soul. She was the closest thing I had to a mother now and I was grateful for her.

The wrinkles around her brown eyes were more prominent today. My heart twisted with guilt. "You can't care after me forever, Chiara."

I knew she was tired, but the mere thought of her absence sent my heart racing with anxiety.

"Nonsense, I love you like my own." Her smile erased any doubts I had mere seconds ago.

Jumping from my four-poster bed, I kissed her on the cheek. "I love you more."

When I entered the bathroom, I stripped off my sleepwear and hopped into the warm shower.

As I shaved my legs, the realization of seeing my father today settled in. I wondered what he wanted from me. I hadn't done anything to disobey him, so I knew it couldn't be for punishment.

A stinging sensation zapped me out of my thoughts.

I peered down, watching as blood trailed the side of my leg onto the shower floor.

The pounding of my heart rang in my ears as oxygen ceased to enter my lungs. I grabbed the acrylic wall with shaky hands, steadying myself before losing all sensation in my knees.

As an eighteen-year-old, you'd think my childish fear of blood would diminish as time passed, but no, it kept getting worse.

Darkness was near, threatening to consume me if I tried to move. In an unsteady voice, I called for the one person who always showed up. "Chi- Chiara."

A second later, the glass door of the shower slid open and Chiara stood there with furrowed brows as she took in the scene.

The cut on my leg continued bleeding. "Not again," she bemoaned, reaching over to shut off the water.

"I wasn't paying attention." I let out a tight laugh. If it were anyone else seeing me naked, I'd be embarrassed, but this was normal for us.

She carefully cleaned and bandaged the cut. Then she grabbed my cotton robe and helped me put it on before bringing her delicate hands up to cup my face. Chiara's face was wet with tears as she whispered, "If I don't care after you, who will?"

As I descended the grand staircase, my stomach churned, the smell of fresh pastries and coffee overwhelming my senses.

I walked through the dimly lit corridor, pushing the kitchen doors open.

Amaretti, cannolis, sfogliatella, and frittelle covered the marble island. I licked my lips and reached over to grab a cannolo when a hand smacked my own. "Not for you," Gaia scolded.

"If not for me, then who?" I asked, crossing my arms.

Gaia and I had never gotten along. Our relationship consisted of bickering back and forth till one of us stormed off. She was a grumpy old lady, but I'd be lying if I said arguing with her was for practical reasons and not for my amusement.

"For the guest," she responded with her head held high. She always was confident in everything she did. I couldn't blame her; the woman was the best cook in all of Italy.

"You work for me, which means you can't deny me what I want." I raised a dark brow challenging her.

She leaned back, letting out a vehement laugh. "I don't work for *you*; I work for your *papà*."

I never was comfortable treating the staff as anything but family.

When I turned to leave, Gaia grabbed me by the wrist and placed a cannolo in my palm.

"Ah, she does have a heart," I drawled playfully.

"Don't push it, *ragazza*."

Pulling out an island stool, I sat and ate the cream-filled pastry, savoring each bite. Gaia moved to the other side of the island and started rolling out dough.

"This cannolo is the best I've ever had... also, I didn't know we were expecting guests tonight," I said nonchalantly. I knew she wouldn't give me details if I sounded too eager.

Gaia eyed me for a moment with a smirk. "Your manipulation skills need some work."

I sighed, assuming my inquisition had failed, but when she focused back on her task, she continued, "It is a business party. Now, go away. I need to work."

A business party, one that I wasn't allowed to be a part of, undoubtedly.

My father never permitted me to be around the men who occasionally occupied our mansion and if they were anything like my father, then I was better off not attending.

A trickle of doubt washed over me as I walked out of the kitchen.

If my father was attending to business today, why did he want to see me?

Uneasiness formed in the pit of my stomach.

"Aurora," a commanding voice interrupted my thoughts, rendering me still.

My father stood a few feet away from me, wearing a black coat and boots. His demeanor was cold and calculated, wearing his Mafia *Don* expression, even with me.

"*Papà.*"

"Good, you're already dressed for the occasion." He glanced down at his watch. "We're going to the stables today."

My attire was simple, jeans, a white sweater, and knee-high black boots.

A heaviness settled onto my shoulders as he draped my black faux fur coat around me. "*Grazie,*" I thanked him with a small smile.

Maybe I misinterpreted the situation; *maybe* this would be a genuine moment for us. He knew my love for riding horses, and *chose* to spend time at the stables today, showing me that he was trying. After all this time, he was trying, and I wondered what changed.

As we made our way across the snow-covered field, I wrapped my arms around my torso to block the cold wind.

Security guards were covering every inch of land we owned. It should've been unnerving seeing them armed, but given my childhood, it wasn't.

The drive to the stables was quiet and short, the awkward tension slowly suffocating me.

I stole a glance at my father, who wore an aloof expression. His blue eyes were dark and distant, as if in deep thought. I swallowed hard and looked away. I wished he would show more interest when spending time with his only daughter.

We walked to the stables in silence, the only sound coming from our boots crunching against the thick snow. "Where are the horses?" I asked, my face twisting in confusion.

When I received no answer, that's when I heard it.

A muffled sound coming from somewhere in the stables, as if someone were struggling to speak. My heart dropped. "Who is that?"

My question went unanswered.

"Come, Aurora," he ordered.

His calmness infuriated me but had my skin crawling with fear. I knew I couldn't escape when his hand circled my elbow, pulling me inside.

The muffled sounds grew until I found a man shackled to a chair. His mouth was gagged by a piece of brown cloth, diminishing his screams. Instinct took over and I moved toward the man. "Let him go!" I panicked.

I didn't make it far before I was yanked back by my coat. "I will, eventually." A sinister expression took over my father's face.

Disgust brewed in me as I unleashed myself from his grasp. "I don't want to watch you kill him," I spat out.

An amused chuckle escaped his thin lips. "You don't even know this man. Besides, I'm not killing him."

Relief washed over me as I inhaled deeply. But the next two words that followed paralyzed me. "You are."

Nausea rolled through me, drying out my mouth. I backed away as my vision turned hazy from unshed tears. "I- I'm not. *I won't.*"

I turned to run but found the entryway of the stables blocked by three men. That's when the first tear fell down my face.

A heavy hand dropped onto my shoulder. "This is for your own good, *mia cara*. It's time to get over that stupid fear of yours." He exhaled obnoxiously, his voice dripping with distaste as his grip held firm.

Stupid fear.

I was naive to think today would be different. He wanted to break me, my morals, and what was left of my heart.

Puffs of air were visible as I steadied my breathing, blinking back the tears threatening to release and faced my father. "*Mamma* would be disgusted by you," I seethed through gritted teeth.

I knew I had taken it too far when the back of his hand connected with my cheek. The slap was forceful, sending me to the ground.

Absently, I palmed my cheek to relieve the sting.

When the metallic taste of blood settled on my tongue, I knew he had split open my lip.

An object dropped in front of me with a thud. *A gun.* "Pick it up," he commanded bitterly.

When I didn't show any intention of moving, he tried another tactic. "Pick it up, or Chiara will pay the price." The weight of his threat settled between us, churning my stomach in knots.

I hesitated for a moment before wrapping my fingers around the cold metal.

"Now, get up and walk to him." Another command from my father that I couldn't resist.

My legs were restless as I tried to hold my balance. The resentment I felt for my father intensified as I took in his stoic expression and the small amount of love I had left for him withered with each step I took.

The sight of the shackled man caused the bile in my throat to rise. His forehead was dripping with sweat and his eyes were rimmed red with tears. I couldn't help but look away as I pointed the gun at him with shaking hands.

"Look at him when you do it."

The tears streamed down my face uncontrollably when I opened my eyes again to the helpless man. The front of his pants was a shade darker than before, and I realized he had peed on himself.

I caught his fearful eyes and whispered, "I'm sorry."

My rapid heartbeat drowned out his groans as I pulled the trigger.

Bang!

The gun slipped from my trembling fingers as the floor

shifted beneath my feet, the ringing in my ears consuming me.

The body slumped forward, blood dripping on the white snow, marking it red—the proof of what I had done.

Gaping down at myself, I wanted to scream in horror. I was covered in blood.

The roiling in the pit of my stomach rose to the surface before I lurched forward and retched.

"You were doing so well." My father tsked, making his disappointment evident.

I felt lightheaded as the shock of what I had done covered me in a thick blanket. I whimpered, covering my mouth to contain my sobs. *I need to get out of here.*

A rush of adrenaline coursed through me, and I ran. I ran as fast as I could until I reached the car before fumbling with the key in the engine, cursing until it roared to life.

Backing away from the field, I let the sounds of my sobs fill the small space.

Through the short drive, I pulled the blood-soaked coat off me, weeping as the stench hit my nostrils. "Oh God, *please,*" I said thoughtlessly, not knowing what I was pleading for. Forgiveness? Death?

Staring at the multitude of cars that now surrounded my house, I knew my poor excuse for a father had done this on purpose. He never did anything without thinking it through.

What was his intention? I couldn't go inside covered in blood and he knew that.

Remembering there was a secret side entrance to the house for emergencies, I ran to it.

Tapping in the security code, I slipped inside.

Soft Italian music mixed with masculine voices buzzed in the air.

The corridor was dimly lit as I cautiously walked through it, hoping to avoid any wanderers.

Rounding the corner, I collided with a hard surface, causing me to lose my footing and stumble backward.

An arm circled my waist, steadying me. "Careful," the mysterious man said, his voice deep and solemn.

The small amount of light from a wall lamp illuminated the space between us.

My breath caught in my throat.

A pair of eyes as black as the midnight sky trailed the length of my face. Eyes that carried underlying danger and dominance.

His gaze settled on my busted lip, an expression dark enough to conjure up a storm.

That single look from him burned my skin, causing me to remove myself from his grasp.

Avoiding his searing gaze, I excused myself, my voice barely a whisper.

As I ascended the stairs, I felt his eyes touch every inch of my body, igniting a burning heat within me. The sheer awareness of him watching me slowed my breathing until I shut my bedroom door.

I leaned my head against it, trying to cool myself down.

Who the hell was that? Surely no one good if he was in my father's house.

A few moments passed before I heard a knock. "Who is it?"

"Open up, *figlia mia*." Relief flooded through me at Chiara's voice.

I opened the door and when she took in my appearance, a horrified expression masked her soft features. "What happened to you?"

"This time would be different, huh?" I snapped at her with the words she told me this morning. She knew my appearance had everything to do with my father.

When she tried reaching for me, I inched back. "What do you want?"

Hurt flashed across her face at my tone of voice. I knew I was taking my anger out on her, but all I wanted to do right now was scrub my skin raw.

"Your *papà* has asked you to come downstairs." He never deserved to be called *Papà*, especially not after what happened today. When I called him that, it was endearing and showed my love.

A humorless laugh escaped me as I shook my head, the sting of tears pricking my eyes. "Of course, he did."

I turned and left Chiara standing in the middle of the room, while I entered the bathroom.

Avoiding the mirror, I peeled my clothes off in revulsion before stepping into the shower. As soon as the water touched my skin, I scrubbed myself till my skin became red and painful.

This was a sick game that I didn't want to be a part of. I needed to leave this awful life behind and start over. I knew I couldn't do it alone and the one person who could help me was across the hall.

"Please, Enzo, help me," I pleaded, my voice breaking.

My brother knew of the pain I endured these past few years because of our father and how I faded away day after day.

We weren't close, and I almost couldn't blame him, considering he was my father's right-hand man. *Almost.*

For a moment, I thought he would slam the door in my face, but then the furrow between his brows eased. "He'll come after you."

I knew the risks. I knew my father might come after me, but this was the only chance I had at starting over. I held onto that sliver of hope that anchored me from losing myself completely.

"I'm aware and I'm not afraid."

He waited for a beat before nodding in understanding, opening the door to his room wider.

The plan was simple; leave the house without being seen while Enzo distracted our father. A helicopter would be waiting for me a few miles away from the house.

Back in my bedroom, I quickly stuffed my duffle bag with my necessities.

Grabbing the photo on my nightstand table, I stared at the smiling faces. Chiara had captured the moment when we weren't aware. I was ten in the photo, perched atop my mamma's thigh. She was smiling down at me as I showed her my drawing. My father was seated beside her, gazing at her with something I hadn't seen since she passed away: *love.* Enzo wasn't in the photo, but he was there laughing at my drawing. I sighed as I shoved it in my bag, zipping it closed.

A gentle knock came through before Enzo stepped inside. "Ready?

I gave a nod, swinging the duffle bag over my shoulder.

The music sounded distant, coming from the other side of the house as we slowly made our way downstairs.

Once we reached the bottom steps, Enzo glanced back at me, and his eyes spoke volumes. *I'm sorry it came to this.* I gave him a brief hug before parting, appreciating the fact that he did this for me.

Walking down the corridor alone, I became jittery. I was close, *so* close to leaving this life behind me. I would finally find peace and build a life filled with joy.

I hadn't heard the footsteps behind me until it was too late, and a hand covered my mouth.

Thrashing against the strong arms that hauled me away, panic overtook my senses. I bit down on the hand covering my mouth, loosening the attacker's grip long enough for me to run.

I didn't get far before I was yanked back by my shirt and pushed against the stone wall, the impact of it disorienting me.

"Your father is waiting," the man hissed, his breath hot against my cheek.

The last bit of energy and hope slowly dissipated as I was dragged away.

When the sound of music and voices became louder, I knew death would be better than what awaited me.

I stood in the middle of the room with male eyes on

me. Their arms were outstretched, pointing guns at one another.

Small beads of sweat caressed my forehead from the scene.

"I don't know what you're talking about; I did no such thing." The voice belonged to my father.

I gaped at him and then at the man standing across from him.

My eyes widened when I found familiar obsidian eyes on me, piercing me with a deadly stare.

"I did no such thing," my father repeated, his voice slicing through the thick tension in the room. "My daughter did."

The air dropped ten degrees. I flicked my gaze back to him. "*What?*" I asked.

"Ignorance doesn't suit you, Aurora."

When I didn't respond, he continued, "You put a bullet through the head of Roman's underboss, did you not?"

The earth crumbled beneath my feet, ready to swallow me whole. My throat tightened, forbidding me from talking, *screaming.*

An ear-splitting pop went off somewhere before someone shoved me behind them. *Enzo.*

"Go!" he shouted, pushing me toward the door.

Everything moved in slow motion after that. It took immense effort for me to run from the living room and out the front door.

The shouts of men grew louder and closer as if they were right behind me.

I made it through the main door, the night breeze jolting me to run faster.

As I approached the car, I glanced back without thought.

Standing on the front porch, dressed in all black, like a fallen angel, was Roman. His hand was up, halting his men from approaching me.

"You can run, but I *will* find you," he said with no mercy in his voice.

His promise seeped into me, causing me to shiver in fear. I climbed into the car and drove away, never looking back.

CHAPTER 1
AURORA

Ten Years Later

"Did you wrap up that case?" I asked my best friend, Irina, who sat cross-legged on the sofa beside me.

Irina and I had met in a coffee shop shortly after I had arrived in New York. She had one of those infectious personalities that allowed you to be comfortable enough to share anything with her.

Without the blonde Russian, I wouldn't have been able to enroll in a university or find a full-time job, even if it was a waitressing position.

Now years later, we were both successful attorneys with a partnership firm and clientele.

Irina knew the gist of my life in Italy; I could never go into too much detail without breaking down and she never pushed me on it either.

Starting a new life in a new country had been difficult, especially with little money.

Enzo had left me an envelope containing a few grand to help me on my journey, but I only managed to secure a small apartment then.

"Yes, thank God. It was extremely tedious," she answered, wiping her mouth with a napkin.

After Raphael and I had broken up two weeks ago, Irina slept over intermittently to make sure I was okay. We were now sharing our last meal before she went back to her house, indefinitely.

Raphael and I met in my second year of law school. To say I was head over heels for that man was an understatement. The first few years of our relationship were pure bliss, until they weren't. If I thought about it for too long, guilt washed over me because deep down I knew we wouldn't last. Raphael was good to me, he was nice, but the spark faded as the months passed. At least for me, it had.

A warm hand covered my own, pulling me out of my head. "I can stay for another night."

I saw the sincerity in her ocean-blue eyes. "You've done enough, Rina."

The clock hit twelve when I leaned back in my chair, exhausted from the bulk of paperwork I'd read through.

Becoming an attorney was something I hadn't planned, but I thought it fitting when I wanted to diminish the injustices of the world and feel a sense of security.

I will find you.

A shiver ran through me as I recalled the moment that

had taken away my sense of peace and put me on high alert for fear of being found. That same moment haunted my thoughts every single day.

But I did it for me. It wasn't easy by any means; some nights I wanted to give up and most nights I was close to doing so. I had come a long way to get to where I was now. Passing my bar exam was one of the best days of my life.

I stared at the picture sitting atop my desk. *I hope I made you proud, Mamma.*

My stomach grumbled, reminding me of the lack of food in my system. I was never skipping breakfast again.

I stood and made my way down toward the lobby, where I spotted my partner. "Irina, I'm grabbing lunch. Do you want anything?"

"Is that even a question? Get me a slice of Joe's." She winked.

"You got it, boss lady."

Pushing through the double doors, I was met with the first few drops of rain. The darkening clouds overhead indicated that it wouldn't clear anytime soon.

The streets were crowded with people who had the same purpose as I did, trying to avoid the unforgiving rain and reach their destination.

As the rain picked up speed, I cursed myself for not bringing an umbrella. I had been too eager and hungry to care.

The fast-paced crowd caused me to stumble over a puddle on the caved-in pavement.

I accepted my fate of pummeling to the ground face-first, when an arm shot out and circled my torso, catching me in a firm hold.

Blinking through the rain, I felt the blood drain from my face as I came face-to-face with my worst nightmare. *It couldn't be...*

Eyes black as sin, bore into me. "Careful," he drawled, voice laced with danger.

The world stilled around us as the rain picked up speed, neither of us breaking eye contact.

It'd been ten years since I last saw him, and he'd aged dangerously beautifully.

Terror gripped me in a vise as I took in the sharp angles of his bronzed skin. His raven black hair glistened with rain, a few wavy strands falling over one of his thick eyebrows. And an aristocratic nose that peered down at me with dominance.

Thunder boomed in the distance, pulling me out of my horrific trance.

The sounds of New York City came blaring in, causing me to step back from his searing touch.

I took an uneven breath. "Excuse me." I moved past him, fear gnawing at me slowly until it was all I could feel.

The urge to turn back was compelling, forcing me to pick up my pace.

"Irina, my office. *Now*." I walked through the lobby and up the glass staircase, nausea churning deep in my stomach before I entered my office.

Soon after, I heard the door click shut. "Is everything okay? You're back ear—"

"*He* is here," I strangled out.

Her face twisted in confusion. "Who?"

I pulled the neckline of my white blouse, gasping for air. "I- I can't..."

Then understanding dawned on her when she took in my panic-filled form.

Irina immediately reached for me, cupping my shoulders. "Rora, he's not going to hurt you. I won't allow it."

Everything I had worked hard for would be taken away from me. I thought I could escape and start over. Start over and close the wound that was ripped open today.

The cold marble bit into my skin as I lost sensation in my legs and crumpled onto the floor.

"Take deep breaths. Come on, inhale... now exhale."

We repeated this multiple times until the trembling in my hands stopped and my sobs faded into hiccups.

After a few minutes of utter silence, I explained what happened.

"Do you think he recognized you?" she asked, concerned.

"I don't know."

When I arrived in New York City nearly ten years ago, I dyed my hair blonde to avoid being recognized in case I was followed. My facial features became prominent with age and my body filled out to become curvier. Most importantly, I changed my name.

"It could be a coincidence that he's here." Considering Irina had a habit of being a pessimist in every situation, I knew she didn't believe the words that came out of her mouth.

Before I could comment on how low the chances of

that were, my phone rang, causing my heart to pick up speed again.

I grabbed it from where it sat atop my desk, the screen displaying a number I didn't recognize.

I had a feeling in the pit of my stomach; my day was only going to get worse.

With trembling fingers, I answered, "Hello?"

The line was silent for what seemed like an eternity, heightening my anticipation.

"Aurora."

Cold sweat broke out in hives on my body at the voice I hadn't heard in a decade.

I couldn't process what was happening, and it must've been evident from my silence because the voice came through the line again. "Aurora, are you there?"

"Enzo." My heart was in my throat, unsure of why he was calling me after all this time.

"It's good to hear your voice, *sorella mia*." His voice came out constricted, as if he wasn't calling to simply to catch up. As if his phone call had *nothing* to do with being a concerned brother.

Closing my eyes, I ripped the band-aid off. "What do you want?"

His silence was all the confirmation I needed to know his intentions.

"That's why you're calling, isn't it? You need something. Why else would you call me after ten years?" I couldn't hide the maliciousness from my voice. "I don't even know how you got my number."

He laughed bitterly. "The phone works both ways," he retorted.

"I'm not interested in what you have to say or need."

"If you're as good an attorney as those New York reports say, then I do need your help."

The phone in my hand grew slick in my palm from sweat. "How do you know that?"

"Just because I never called, doesn't mean I forgot about you."

I bit my lip, willing myself to be immune to his words. Despite this new information, a sliver of pride rooted in me that he knew how successful my career as an attorney was—even all the way from Italy.

After everything I went through, I wanted them to know I didn't need them or anyone else to survive—never did and never would.

"Then you should know I'm not in the business of committing illegal acts," I pointed out. I would not get involved in anything that would jeopardize my career or myself.

"I need you to come to Italy and create a contract for me." He sounded confident, as if I would agree to it, which deepened my anger. Then he cleared his throat gruffly. "It's been years since the Mancini family took over our businesses and seized our accounts, Aurora. Our night-clubs, trades, and connections are all gone. They're finally willing to give them back."

My brows furrowed in confusion. "Who is the Mancini family and why would they do that?" I asked, unsure of what my family had done to put themselves in that position. "Years, Enzo? When did this happen?"

"I know you're not familiar with our line of business, but I'll explain in simple terms. There are four crime organizations in Italy, Cosa Nostra, 'Ndrangheta, Camorra, and Sacra Corona Unita. The Mancini's run the Cosa Nostra, we run the 'Ndrangheta, the Camorra is run by the Canaveri's, and the Sacra Corona Unita is run by the Amato's, but they're more secluded.

Oh shit.

I knew the gist of what my family was capable of, but this was another level of power.

"How were they successful in overtaking your organization then?"

"The Cosa Nostra and 'Ndrangheta conspired against us. They somehow infiltrated our enterprise and took everything."

"Again, why would they do that?"

He disregarded my question completely. "The contract will specify that the Mancinis will hand over what's rightfully ours, the Bianchis. Can you do that?"

"If this is an order from our father, then no. I'm sure there are lawyers in Italy who could do that for you," I deadpanned. He called me for *this*. It was laughable.

"There are, but after the feud, our family lost respect and status. Plus, I don't want them in my business."

It made sense. If they lost their status, then they must've lost employees. Regardless of where I stood with the family, he *needed* me to carry out this contract.

"You wasted your time by calling. I'm going to hang up now."

"*Don't.*" His voice boomed through the phone, strong and purposeful. "I helped you when you needed me. Consider it a debt owed."

His words sliced through me, rendering me speechless.

Irina squeezed my shoulder, reminding me that she was in the room and pulling me out of my shock.

My vision blared red; I was done being civil. "How *dare* you. How dare you say that to me. You are a pathetic man, Enzo. If this is the debt I must pay, so be it, but after this, you will delete my number and stay the fuck out of my life. Forever." I didn't give him a chance to respond before hanging up.

Irina's concerned face came into view, and with a blank expression, I told her something I never expected to leave my mouth, "I'm going back to Italy."

CHAPTER 2
AURORA

As I sat in my living room, reeling from the events of the day, my phone pinged, cutting through the silence.

See you soon.

Like clockwork, I had summoned my brother.

There was an attachment connected to the text and when I clicked it, I found my flight details, indicating that I was flying first class at five in the morning, tomorrow.

Wait, that can't be right...

I'm billing you for my services, especially now that my flight is tomorrow. Also, first class? How did you afford that when everything was taken from you?

My phone pinged a second later with my brother's reply.

Because I didn't sit on my ass and made a living for myself.

I groaned into the palms of my hands as I laid back on my plush couch. Tomorrow was too soon.

I considered how fast this was happening, but knew I had no choice but to take that flight.

The only good thing coming out of this was that if Roman was in New York, I'd be far away from him until I figured out why he was here.

Leaping off the couch, I headed toward my bedroom to scavenge my closet for the only suitcase I owned.

Then, I mindlessly grabbed clothes off the racks and shoved them into the suitcase.

If I sat and pondered on what to take, then I wouldn't be able to escape the intrusive thoughts that would surely end with me having a full-on mental breakdown.

"If you need me to fly to Italy to kick some ass, call me." Irina's eyes filled with sympathy as I lifted my bag up my shoulder.

Forcing out a small smile that I knew didn't reach my eyes, I waved my phone in front of her. "On speed dial. Anyway, I'm boarding soon, so I guess this is goodbye." I didn't want to leave, but if I didn't put up a confident front, Irina would drag me out of the airport without hesitating.

"Yeah, yeah, *okay*. Text me when you land?" I wouldn't necessarily call this parting awkward, but it was close to it, considering we both had never been apart from each other longer than a day. We were terrible at goodbyes.

"Of course, I will." Closing the distance between us, I wrapped her in a tight hug. "I'll only be gone for a few days."

Most people feared flying, but I had never had a problem with it. In fact, the window seat was my favorite. The view was captivating, and no number of pictures could accurately capture its beauty.

After putting away my carry-on bag, I settled into my seat and peered around my cubicle. There was enough space to make this nine-hour flight bearable and a door to provide me privacy.

"Can I get you anything to drink, ma'am?"

Turning to my left, I saw a flight attendant smiling down at me. Her blonde hair was pulled high into a bun, accentuating her cheekbones.

I smiled back at her. "A mojito, please... go heavy on the alcohol."

"For good reason, I'm sure."

"You've no idea."

CHAPTER 3
AURORA

When I stepped off the plane, Enzo's driver greeted me. He was a broad-shouldered man who was old enough to be my grandfather, minus the fragility.

As I sat in the back seat with my windows down, I allowed the warm air of Italy to envelop me.

I almost felt a sense of home, but it wasn't home—it hadn't been for a long time now.

There were many emotions coursing through me, many things I could say to the ones who hurt me, but was that worth it? I was here for only a few days and then I'd return to my life.

I had two goals for this visit; finalizing the contract and avoiding my father at all costs.

The family house came into view and it appeared the same as it had ten years ago.

Memories swarmed in, my mind yelling at me to turn back.

"I've got it, *grazie*," I thanked the driver, grabbing my luggage from him.

Instead of walking through the front door, I sought out the secret entrance on the side of the house.

Every step I took caused my heart to beat faster. The last time I went in through this way, all hell had broken loose.

"Front door is over there."

That voice stopped me in my tracks, and I cursed myself for getting caught.

Just because I never called, doesn't mean I forgot about you.

There was before my mother's death and then after. As you can guess, the after was when everything in my life crumbled to pieces, including the relationship between my one and only sibling.

I'd be the first to admit that my brother is on my list of people I'm not fond of, but I couldn't help the smile that slowly spread across my face.

I turned to find him staring at me with an amused expression.

He never was fond of suits. Even now, he had on a black fitted t-shirt and pants.

"I knew you still had an ounce of love left for your big brother," he teased.

I strode toward him; a sense of nostalgia overcoming me. "Ha! You wish. I'm here to pay my debt."

Enzo always had a ruggedness to him and over the years, it had grown tenfold. His full beard and man bun were only the tip of the iceberg.

Although he had helped me escape, he hadn't

protected me from our father when I needed him to. It was hard to forgive him, even if my father was ultimately the one to blame.

"Debt or no debt, it's good to see you, *sorella mia*." His voice came out soft as he embraced me.

I avoided seeing anyone else and headed straight to my room.

I was shocked to find it untouched, as if I had never left.

This must've been Enzo's doing, because my father would have demolished this room the minute I ran away from home.

There was no time to dwell on the past. Reliving memories usually ended up with me in a fetal position, heaving from crying too much.

The fact of the matter was, I hadn't been involved in the family business for a decade now—not that I ever really was—and I needed to prepare for tonight's meeting.

I didn't know what to expect except for arrogant men fighting over superiority.

A knock came on my bedroom door, pulling me away from my thoughts, and I hesitated for a moment before opening it.

A petite young woman, dressed in a housekeeper's outfit entered my room. "Enzo sent lunch."

She was young, too young to be working here. Her youthful red cheeks told me she must be in her early twenties.

I wondered how she ended up here.

Smiling, I took the tray of food from her. "Thanks."

When she turned to leave, I grabbed her arm. "Is Chiara here?"

The one thing that plagued my conscience heavily was that I had never contacted Chiara after settling in New York. Even though I had no way of reaching her, I felt guilt chipping away at me constantly.

It didn't matter though, because now that I was here, I would make it right. She was the only person in this family who loved me as much as my mother had.

The girl put her hand over mine and before she had a chance to speak, I could tell by the way her face masked a pitying expression that Chiara was gone. *Dead.*

A loud shatter startled me and when I searched around, trying to find the source of the sound, I found the tray I had been holding seconds ago scattered across the floor.

It was an out-of-body experience as I knelt, frantically picking up pieces of glass. As if I weren't even there. Unwilling to accept the brutal reality.

"I'm sorry," I whispered to no one.

"Stop! You'll hurt yourself!"

The voice sounded distant, as if I was in a trance, unable to stop. I needed to clean up the mess I had made.

Chiara was dead. She was dead and I'd never see her again.

"Ouch," I yelped when a piece of glass sliced my palm.

The housekeeper reached for my hand, but I turned away from her touch and got up before walking the few steps into my bathroom.

The rush of blood pounded in my ears as I slid down the door and clutched my wrist, watching the crimson liquid pool in my palm.

Hot tears sprang from my eyes as I breathed—*in* and *out*—slowly like Irina had taught me.

When the room stopped spinning, a grunt escaped my lips as I held in my sobs.

Chiara always tended to my wounds; she knew my fear of blood. And here I was in my childhood home, alone. *So alone* that being in my own skin felt foreign.

The small amount of energy I had left was drained on the bathroom floor.

I wasted time that I had meant to use toward meeting preparations.

However, I couldn't bring myself to care, not even the slightest, not even as we drew closer to the nightclub where the meeting would be held.

I wasn't sure what I expected, but I had hoped for something less sweaty and loud.

"Are you feeling better?" On my right, dressed in all black with a gold watch around his wrist, sat Enzo. He appeared the part of a mobster determined to take power.

I matched his appearance, wearing a short black dress with a deep neckline stretching to my naval.

It was a risky dress with the amount of cleavage shown, but risky business called for risky attire. "Not one bit," I sighed. "I wish you had told me about Chiara."

Enzo had found me curled up on the bathroom floor

and carried me to my bed, where he sat next to me as I dozed off to sleep.

"If it brings you an ounce of peace, she died painlessly in her sleep."

It didn't. It still hurt the same, if not more.

"Have you seen our father? I know you're avoiding him. He know's it, too. That's why he's not here." He paused for a second. "And I think he's avoiding *me*. Has been the whole day, now that I think of it."

The mention of him sent me into a hand-trembling rage. "I'd rather talk about the young housekeeper you've hired," I scoffed. "Who is she?"

Enzo's eyes narrowed in displeasure. "No one."

His reaction to my question didn't go unnoticed, but I already had enough to think about.

The car pulled up to a dimly lit street, filled with people mingling as the night grew darker.

"Is there anything else I should know before we go inside?"

He pinned me in place with a fierce stare. "You're safe with me. Remember that."

It was odd to hear those words coming from him, but as the car came to a slow halt, I hung onto them.

Shaking my head to get rid of the feeling, I pushed up my breasts and grabbed the paperwork.

I turned to Enzo again and found him scowling at me. "Real classy," he grumbled.

I flashed a fake smile. "One of us has to convince them to sign."

CHAPTER 4

AURORA

The smell of undesirable aromas invaded my nostrils; body odor, alcohol, and scents I couldn't decipher were not a pleasant combination.

The nightclub's sultry interior created an intense but classy environment. Shades of vibrant red lit up the space along opaque black walls.

Enzo grabbed me by the arm and led us through the pool of people on the dance floor. I tried not to gag as I felt sweaty skin touching my own.

I had never found the club scene appealing—I mean, besides it being unsanitary, who wanted their eardrums blown out by horrible music?

We stopped in front of a black door, but before Enzo opened it, he peered over his shoulder at me. "Remember what I told you."

I gave a slight nod because I didn't know what to say. This was the first time he had verbally expressed his concern for me.

As we descended the stairs, I felt my heart skip beats as if something might truly go wrong.

I didn't realize how tightly I was gripping my brother's arm until he looked back at me with concern.

All I needed to do was present the contract, have the opposite party sign it, and leave. Easy enough, I hoped.

I let out a heavy sigh. "I'm ready." *I had no other choice.*

There were five men with their backs to us as we took the last step down the basement.

Either they were ignoring our presence, or they were waiting for us to present ourselves.

Enzo had the same thought because he cleared his throat, resulting in four of them to turn our way.

They all appeared identical, causing me to laugh internally. Some were bigger, some thinner, but essentially, they all had the same features: brown eyes, olive skin, and groomed beards.

The last thing I wanted to do was show any sign of weakness, so I showed my dominance by slowly letting my attention fall on them.

One of the larger men eyed me predatorily and whistled. "You've brought a plaything."

Snorting in disgust, I spoke, "If you're insinuating that I'd even come within five feet of you, you're not only mistaken but brainless too."

He took a step forward, face twisting in anger. "Put a leash on this *puttana*," he growled, glowering at my brother.

There was a beat of silence before a rough laughter

broke the tension, coming from the man whose back was still to us. "You will do no such thing."

That voice...

Sometimes I thought the world was against me, and this moment proved it true when the man turned.

Standing before me was someone who had haunted my existence since I left Italy a decade ago.

If I could have dug my own grave right now, I would have.

Sweat coated my back and I felt exposed, bared on display as Roman's jaw tightened, his bewitching eyes raking down my body.

Unsettling fear formed in the pit of my stomach at his lack of surprise at my presence.

He was clad in all black. The top buttons of his dress shirt were open, chest hair peeking through across his golden skin.

When I brought my gaze up to his face, he was already staring at me with narrowed eyes, cold and flinty. It became unbearable to hold the intensity of his stare.

I broke eye contact and stared at Enzo next to me.

I ran my tongue across my teeth, shooting daggers at him with my eyes.

This was why he avoided my question. He knew the mere mention of Roman would eliminate any chances of me coming to Italy. I could have *murdered* my brother right now.

Instead, I focused on surviving and leaving this room as fast as possible.

We had been in this polished basement for almost an hour —to say it wasn't going in our favor would be an understatement.

In conclusion, my breasts were not winning material.

Not only was I uncomfortable with how I was dressed, but a particular pair of eyes had been glued to my form since I arrived.

"I don't understand the problem here," I uttered with exasperation. "You gave your word to the Bianchi family that you would hand over their assets. Sign the contract and both parties can part ways without bloodshed."

The only reason I had a firm grip on my senses and hadn't tumbled into a fit of fright was because I had gone unrecognized. It seemed that my change of appearance had worked after all.

I scanned around the table and set my eyes on the leader.

It was only fair to stare at him when he had been unashamedly gawking at me for the past hour. Had no one ever taught him that staring was disrespectful, or was Mr. High and Mighty immune to such mundane manners?

He tilted his head to one side, and I swore I saw the slightest hint of a smirk playing on his lips. Before I could register it, his face had gone flat again.

To my dismay, Roman began to speak, "And I will." He waved a hand in the air swiftly. "Once I'm given what I've been promised."

His voice was silky smooth as words rolled off his tongue like liquid gold. He was the epitome of danger and seduction.

If I were to come out of this meeting unscathed, I needed to get ahold of myself.

"Promised?" Enzo asked, his eyebrow lifting in confusion.

A slimy feeling crawled up and down my body as the air charged with something sinister.

Roman stared at me with an eerie calmness that made me want to peel my skin off.

I swallowed thickly. "I'm not sure what you mean. We've brought this contract to you to create a semblance of peace. We haven't promised you anything else," I muttered the last part menacingly.

"On the contrary." Leaning back in his chair, Roman rubbed a hand across his jaw, scrutinizing me in place with his unrelenting stare. "I've been promised a valuable... object."

Suddenly, he stood from his seat, the chair scraping against the tile floor in a deafening screech. "Your father has made a trade. His daughter in exchange for his fortune." Inhaling deeply, he sighed in feigned wonder. "It's quite poetic if you ask me. He offered *you* many times over the years, but the timing wasn't right."

I almost thought I heard him wrong, but power dripped from his voice, loud and clear.

He recognized me.

The room spun as I blinked away the sudden light-headedness. My father had offered me up as if I wasn't a human being, *his* flesh and blood.

Enzo stood from his seat, stepping closer to me in a protective stance. "Those weren't the terms we agreed upon."

Inevitability, fright tumbled into me, freezing me in place like a statue, *lifeless.*

It was my worst nightmare, except this time, I couldn't wake up.

"Your father and I agreed on other terms. *My* terms." Roman threw a wad of papers on the transparent table, where it scattered before me. "The man was pathetically desperate to gain his belongings that he didn't even read through the contract before signing." He shrugged a shoulder. "Either that or he didn't care to tell you. However, I can understand his conflict. It seems that you have a sweet spot for your sister."

Survival instinct surged me forward on my feet.

I made it to the bottom of the stairs when a calloused hand wrapped around my elbow, pulling me back with a force that had me grunting in pain.

A bite of electricity shot up my arm from where flesh touched mine.

I glanced between Roman's face and his hand that dared to touch me. Now, I was furious. "Get your hands off me."

He took a step toward me, invading my space with his suffocating presence.

We were mere inches apart and it all felt too familiar. His aroma beckoned me to come closer and yet run far away.

"Sit down, *anima mia,*" he commanded in a low growl, using a nickname that sounded more threatening than loving.

If I couldn't escape now, then I would be trapped in the same past I had worked so hard to escape.

He might be used to having everyone surrender to him within seconds, but I wasn't just anyone, let alone one of his puppets.

I steeled my spine. "I'd rather not," I spat out. Within seconds, the hand that held my arm snaked around my throat before he slammed me against the wall.

The unexpected impact knocked the breath out of me, forcing me to gasp for air.

"Enzo, don't move, or my men will shoot you dead on the spot and we all know you don't want that. Besides, I would hate for this contract to be void so soon."

We were outnumbered.

Oxygen ceased to exist altogether when Roman leaned in, his lips brushing my ear, causing my skin to prickle with nerves. "Little do you know, your rebelliousness turns me on," he whispered to my ears only.

I knew the traitorous blush had crept along my skin when his eyes scanned my chest all the way up to my face.

A bead of sweat formed above my brow from his scurrility, and I clamped down the urge to wipe it off. I had gotten this far without showing any weakness and I would not start now.

My act of self-determination had gone to waste when he nodded to himself, certain he would get his way.

I turned my face away from him, wanting him to get off me.

He grabbed my chin, forcing me to look at him again, and without breaking eye contact, he said, "Enzo, when Aurora satisfies me by being a good little wife, I will see to it that your assets are yours again. Until then, tell your father not to sweat it."

My mind spun, unable to comprehend the words that leaked from his mouth.

Obsidian eyes searched mine. "After all, you were the one who killed my kin, though your family bore the brunt of it when I took everything from them. Seems fair that you also suffer, yes?"

Dread flooded my senses, drowning out all other emotions.

Everything clicked into place.

Roman in New York wasn't a coincidence. It was part of his grand scheme.

Bringing my face close to his, I shook off that dread and replaced it with wrath. "Fuck. You," I seethed, spitting on the floor in disgust.

CHAPTER 5
AURORA

I ascended the stairs hurriedly and opened the door. Immediately, the pounding of my heart clashed with the pounding of the music.

Mindlessly walking through the crowd of people, I replayed the last few seconds of conversation as I made my way through the exit.

"Over my dead body will I let this contract carry through!" I was no longer calm.

"Necrophilia isn't my thing," Roman said, his mouth set in a thin line.

How could this have happened? Enzo didn't know about our father's secret contract and now I was the one being tortured.

If my father thought I would sit pretty and accept whatever came my way, he was in for a rude awakening.

I built a life for myself back in New York and I would destroy anyone who tried to take it away from me.

The tightness in my chest was excruciating. *Inhale. Exhale. Repeat.*

I couldn't possibly marry Roman, let alone a Mafia *Don.* I would become physically ill if I witnessed their cruelty. I didn't leave this life behind to be sucked back into it because two men said so.

I would not rest until I was back in New York.

The door of the club opened and closed. Turning, I found a furious Enzo walking toward me.

"Dammit!" He paced back and forth, body tense with frustration. I realized then he truly didn't know about this.

"How does it taste to be a pawn in our father's game? Pretty fucking bitter, huh?"

Enzo pulled me a few feet away from security. "If I had known our father's true intentions, I would have *never* asked you to come back home," he spoke quietly.

"You brought me here knowing Roman would recognize me!"

"I didn't think he would! You almost fooled me in that photo in the news report. The one where you received the Super Lawyers award."

My head shook at the horrific turn of events. "Enzo, he can't force me to marry him. It's *against* the law."

"The *law* doesn't matter to us Made men. You bring legality into this, and you're fucked."

He was right. They would come after me and anyone I had ever cared about. I would rather endure this than put my loved ones at risk. I felt defeated and helpless.

My brother palmed my face with both hands. "I will get you out of this, I *swear* it," he whispered.

The irony of this moment was that all I ever wanted

was to be protected by my brother, but now that he was trying to, it was impossible.

"No, I won't have your death on my conscious too."

I glanced over at the security guard who was standing by the door, eyeing us skeptically, and my brother's gaze followed mine.

We looked back at each other before I embraced him in a hug and whispered in his ear, "We must pretend that we agree to this, for now. I won't resist and you won't start another problem."

"Keep the shots coming," I yelled to the bartender as I sat on a stool.

After my conversation with Enzo, we went back inside to show our compliance, even though my fingers were itching to suffocate the bastard who thought he held power over me.

My brother returned to the basement to discuss business details while I went to the bar to drown out my thoughts. To forget that I needed to act like I was okay with this arrangement. If it meant that my father and Roman would be brought down, then I was willing to suffer.

Six shots appeared before me in a row. I wasted zero time and downed three back-to-back, welcoming the burning sensation in the back of my throat.

I thought the alcohol would calm my nerves, but it only fueled my anger.

"Surely, the news of marrying me hasn't caused your

soon-to-be drunken state." *That* voice slid down my spine in a rough caress, causing me to stiffen.

For a brief second, I glanced over my shoulder before turning away. "Better get used to it. Being around you sober would be a suicide mission." I downed another shot, surprised he hadn't asked me to stop.

He could try, but I'd tell him to go to hell if he did.

Roman moved to my side, brushing against my bare skin, and smothering me with his devilish presence. Not only did he have a staring problem, but he also didn't understand personal space either.

"And here I thought you were celebrating."

I caught his eyes through my lashes, hoping the expression plastered on my face was one of annoyance. "You're forcing me to marry you. I'm not celebrating; I'm *mourning*."

When he said nothing, I used his silence to my advantage. "When we ran into each other back in New York, you knew who I was."

He leaned against the bar, eyeing me with curiosity. His relaxed demeanor irritated me, as if I wasn't a threat to him.

The sheer touch of him made my body buzz with anger as he took the shot glass from my hand. He tipped it back, never breaking eye contact and it might've been the sexiest thing I'd ever seen if I didn't hate him with every fiber of my being.

Placing it on the bar's island, he made a show of leering at my cleavage. "I did. Although from our last encounter, you weren't dressed like a whore."

Boiling rage heated the blood pumping in my veins. "You're a pig."

"I've heard worse." Suddenly, he gripped my jaw, digging his fingers into my flesh. To everyone around, it would've appeared affectionate. "If you're to be my wife, you better play the part right." His anger was palpable, causing me to shiver.

"I'm not your wife. And if I'm *dressed like a whore,* I might as well act as one." Fury vibrated through me as our harsh breathing synced in unison.

His smile was deviant. "You'll learn what kind of man I am soon enough, Aurora."

It couldn't be worse than what I already knew.

"And *you'll* learn what kind of woman I am."

He stared at me for a long beat, his eyes dark, boring into my very being before breaking the silence. "I hate to put an end to your celebration, but we're leaving. *Now.*"

"Yeah, I think you're right. *It is* time for me to leave. Back. To. New. York." I enunciated the last part.

"You can run, but I will find you."

I stared at his blank expression. He knew that was exactly what he said to me all those years ago. Though he was right, he found me.

"You'll come to find your worst nightmare if you continue commanding me left and right."

He was done with the conversation. I knew because he didn't utter another word and grabbed me by the arm, pulling me after him.

"Let go of me!" I thrashed against his back with my free hand. This man was made of steel, my efforts rendering useless.

He ignored me. "Where's Enzo?" Tears threatened to spill from my eyes. I didn't want to go anywhere with Roman. Not when I was drunk. *Not at all.* I didn't trust him.

As we stood outside the club, panic filled me, clawing its way up my neck.

He eyed me with cool indifference making my hate for him intensify. "I sent your brother home. I assured him you'd be safe. Stop acting like a child."

Before I could respond, a black Audi pulled up by the curb.

Roman gripped my arm once more and pushed me into the backseat of the car.

The alcohol buzzing in my system made me feel like I was floating, lightweight and free. Dozing in and out of sleep, I couldn't remember where I was.

Slowly coming to consciousness, my heart thrashed against my chest. I searched around frantically, blinking rapidly to get rid of my hazy vision before it cleared. I was in a car. *Alone.*

Anxiety gripped me in a vise, clawing at me viciously.

Then it hit me all at once—the meeting, the contract, and *Roman.* My head pounded furiously, causing me to squeeze my eyes shut.

When I opened them again, I peered out of the car window. It was hard to make out what was concealed in the darkness, but the silhouette of a large arched door came into view.

A chill went through me, raising the hairs on my body. I slumped back on the leather seat as realization dawned on me. Roman brought me to what I assumed was his house and left me in the car.

The silence was eerie as I contemplated my next move.

I pulled out my phone and cursed at the black screen. *Great*, I couldn't even call Enzo.

This place must have been gated with security if he had trusted me to be all alone.

Anger bubbled inside of me into something feral. He could've at least woken me up. I didn't expect to be carried inside bridal style—not that he was the type of man to do that. No, Roman was the type of man to take and do what he wanted regardless of the consequences.

As I thought about it longer, the urge to rebel against him grew.

I bet he hoped I would wake up and come searching for him like a frightened little girl. Well, there was no way I was going inside of his house. If he wanted me inside, he could come get me himself.

Time passed as I sat in the chilled car, my eyes growing heavy.

Leaning my head against the window, the last thing I heard before I fell into a heavy slumber was the click of a door.

CHAPTER 6
AURORA

I could've stayed in bed forever had it been my bed.

A wave of nausea passed over me as I jerked upright from the sudden movement.

I pressed my fingertips to my forehead; I didn't remember falling asleep in a bed last night, which meant someone had come to get me from the car. *Was it Roman, or did he have one of his bodyguards do it?* Both scenarios repulsed me.

I gazed down at myself and exhaled shakily. I had on a black silk nightgown.

Warmth spread across my face at the thought of someone having seen me naked. Not just someone, but Roman.

I tried to slow my breathing down even though my heart picked up a dangerous pace.

When I heard the door of the room open, I covered myself quickly as an older woman came walking in. She resembled Chiara so heavily that I almost thought I was dreaming.

"Mrs. Mancini, you're up," she said in a motherly tone. Her hair was gray and in a low bun that made the hollows of her cheeks more prominent. The wrinkles around her mouth weren't from old age, but from smiling constantly and her warm brown eyes were inviting. She wore a yellow dress with white flowers and sandals that showcased her painted toes. "Mrs. Mancini?"

Mrs. Mancini? I opened my mouth to correct her mistake. That I was not married, nor was that my last name, but nothing came out. Instead, I kept repeating a name in my head. *Roman Mancini.*

"Your presence is requested downstairs. Anything you should need is in this room."

Ignoring her command, I asked, "What's your name?"

A warm smile adorned her aging face. "Gianna."

I nodded, giving her the cue to leave and when the door clicked shut, my eyes wandered around the room.

It was bigger than average, and dimly lit by small twinkling lights in each corner.

Dark colors and rich textures with vintage décor covered every surface, creating a surprisingly welcoming environment.

I got up from the four-poster bed, made my way to the dark gray curtains and pushed them open. I put my hand up to my face as light seeped into the room.

There was a small opening across the room, with two doors on either side of it. I hesitated before walking toward it and opened the left one. It was a walk-in closet.

There were racks of clothing on each side with

columns in the middle. I dragged my hand across the fabrics, touching the rich material of each item.

I stepped outside of the closet and took a few steps toward the other door.

Once opened, the first feature I noticed was the black marble floors. It was a massive bathroom with two sinks, a huge bathtub in the middle, and a shower next to it.

Both the closet and bathroom resembled the main room with neutral off-white shades mixed with earthy tones.

After going through my hygiene routine, I settled on a green dress with a square neckline. It was the most appropriate attire considering the summer heat.

The dress fit me like a glove, and it should've been a little alarming that Roman knew this information, but it was instead unsurprising.

Taking a last look in the mirror, I noticed despite my dampened mood, my cheeks had a healthy glow, and my lips had a natural tint to them.

Not bothering to put on makeup, I turned on my heel.

I almost backed out of going downstairs, knowing *he* was the one who summoned me, but I remembered I had made a pact with Enzo. I needed to be obedient until we found a way out.

Closing the door behind me, I stepped into a long hall. The only source of light came from cylindrical lamps hooked on each side. A double staircase cascaded down to the main floor and I slowly descended from the right, one step at a time.

My palms grew clammy, sticking to the rail. The thought of seeing Roman during the day seemed far more terrifying than seeing him at night. At least in the dark, one could conceal things they didn't want to be seen.

The main floor was magnificent. Chandeliers dangled high above, shining as the sun came through the tall windows that were decorated with velvet curtains draped to the side. Wooden bookcases, ornate gold frames, black leather couches, and bold marble tables decorated the space beautifully.

I didn't expect someone as cold as Roman to live in an environment warm and inviting.

Crossing the corridor, I entered an arched doorway to my right and stopped in my tracks when I spotted him.

Luckily, my bare feet against the solid floors didn't elicit any sound to make my presence known.

Roman's blue-back hair glistened as a ray of sunshine came through a window on our left. While his back faced me, I wondered if it was too late to walk back up to my room. *What was the point of eating when I would surely hurl it back up from this encounter?*

There were only two chairs, one of which Roman's large body occupied. His broad shoulders laid back against his chair, power rippling off him. The second chair was to his left.

I cursed myself because it was one thing having breakfast alone with him and another having breakfast alone with him *while* being seated that close in proximity. With a huff, I diverted my attention to the main attraction.

A long oakwood table had all manner of breakfast foods laid out: pastries, fruit, poultry, and dairy. My mouth betrayed me as it salivated at the sight; I was famished.

"I don't mind you staring at me all day, but the

rumbling from your stomach is quite irritating. Sit and eat, Aurora."

His voice startled me, causing me to jump at his amused but demanding tone.

Pursing my lips together, I entered the dining room.

Ignoring him wholly, I grabbed the empty chair and dragged it to the other end of the table. My body hummed to life, painfully aware of him watching me.

Once I settled in my seat, I allowed myself to peek at him. His expression was one of bemusement, as if he knew something I didn't. I arched a brow in question.

"I don't bite." His voice drawled, seeping into my every pore. There was no denying his allure, but his soul was ugly and tainted.

Hiding any trace that his words affected me, I cleared my throat. "Maybe not yet." I was treading on dangerous territory; the innuendo of his statement was not lost on me.

His lips curved to the side slightly, insinuating. My hands curled into fists at my sides.

I assumed the conversation was over when he leaned forward, grabbed a piece of toast, and set it on his plate. But then his sharp gaze landed on me.

Roman tilted his head to the side, assessing me. All traces of amusement faded from his face and were replaced by a domineering expression. "Yet."

We sat through the rest of breakfast in silence. Defeating silence that drifted between us uncomfortably with unsaid words that made it hard to focus on anything else. Even the food was tasteless on my tongue.

"Did you bring me inside last night?" I asked in a rush,

eager to break the silence. "Undress me?" My face warmed, remembering I woke up in a nightgown with nothing underneath.

If Roman was surprised by my question, he didn't show it. Instead, he continued chewing on his food while giving me a once-over.

I kept eye contact with him, trying not to squirm under his scrutiny as I waited for his answer.

Once he finished swallowing, he dabbed at his mouth with a napkin and then set it down beside him.

He had a feral charm swarming in those impenetrable obsidian eyes when he answered my question with another. "Would you be satisfied with any answer I give you?"

The way he spoke to me raised my body temperature in aggravation, but I contemplated his question.

He was right; every answer would be worse than the last. I huffed as Roman sat in his chair as if he had all the time in the world for me to answer.

Deep in my gut, I knew the answer. I knew it from the moment I woke up to this nightmare. It was Roman who put me to bed, who undressed me, and saw my most intimate parts. The calmness he presented was predatory. *Of course*, he'd never allow anyone else to see me.

Hoping he could see my distaste, I glared at him. And when he plucked invisible lint off his shirt, I knew the bastard knew I made the correct assumption.

Adding salt to the wound, Roman spoke again, "We're leaving for the courthouse in thirty minutes."

Instantly, my mind scrambled for a way to get out of

this as I gaped at him. I knew it was coming but not this soon.

"I'm not marrying you." There was no purpose for him and me to marry if he already owned me according to the contract. Even thinking about it made me want to snap and gouge his eyes out.

Roman stood from his chair, taking long measured strides in all his glory, until he stood before me.

My breathing slowed and halted when one long finger ran from the top of my cheek to under my chin, tilting my head up. "If I have to drag you to the courthouse today—mark my words, *anima mia*—I will." His voice came out soft, making his threat sound almost pleasant, but I knew better.

I jerked my chin from his grasp and scowled at him. "If you think my compliance will come easily, you're sorely mistaken. Even worse, if you think I care about a father who *pawned* me off to receive his valuables."

There wasn't an ounce of surprise present on his features at my confession.

"I love a challenge." He leaned down, resting his hands on either side of my chair, caging me in. "Don't make this harder than it needs to be. You'll soon find out that you're mine in every way." His hand flexed before gripping my hair tightly as he brought my face up to his.

I clawed at his hand with my nails, hoping I drew blood, but it only made him pull harder. "And let me make it clear. I don't share what's mine."

CHAPTER 7
AURORA

"Where the fuck have you been?" Enzo's voice blared through the phone, causing me to cringe.

"Having the time of my life, obviously." I had enough on my mind and didn't need to add Enzo's attitude to the list.

He didn't comment on my sarcasm. "Last night, I reviewed the contract and the only thing we have going for us is our safety. If the Mancini family sheds blood of the Bianchi family, the contract is broken."

This wasn't the news I hoped for. If that were true, then the contract would stand. Roman wouldn't jeopardize his position in having me.

"I've been up all night badgering our father to fix this while trying to figure out a way for you to get out of this myself and it's bad, Aurora." My stomach dropped as Enzo continued, "If you do anything to jeopardize this unlawful agreement, blood will be shed." Meaning the people I cared most about would suffer.

After a moment of silence, I spoke with distaste. "I leave for the courthouse soon."

My heart pounded furiously as I pondered over the fact that I would be sharing vows with someone I wanted to stick a knife into.

"As a Bianchi, I can't attend," he sighed. "Don't do anything that would add fuel to the fire. They'd rather kill you than be disrespected in any way." A trickle of cold fear slid down my neck. If I defied Roman, who knew what else he'd do to me.

"I won't make this easy for him and I sure as hell don't care if our father is poor for the rest of his miserable life either. I'll talk to you later, Enzo." I hung up before he could respond and rang Irina.

"Hey, wh—"

I cut her off and got straight to the point; time was of the essence. "I'm taking a temporary leave of absence from work. Can you hold it down by yourself?"

"What are you talking about?" she asked incredulously.

I squeezed my eyes shut. "I'll explain later."

"I haven't heard from you since you *landed* in Italy." Her sigh was audible. "What's happening?"

"I'm in a bad situation," I whispered. "I'm handling it though. Trust me, okay?"

There was a momentary pause. "Please be safe. I mean it."

"Always. Love you, Rina," I said, emotion thick in my throat.

"Love you. Call me when you can."

I took a few deep breaths to gather my thoughts. If I played my cards right, I could save myself, even if that meant I had to tie myself to the devil for a short while.

The corridor was vacant as I waited for Roman to finish his call, the muffled sounds of his voice coming from the door opposite me.

After my conversation with Irina, Gianna dropped off three boxes in my room. The first box contained a white cocktail dress, the second a pair of white heels, and the third a jewelry box encasing diamond earrings, necklace, and bracelet.

The contents were luxurious and though I hadn't expected anything from Roman, I knew he did it to keep up appearances. He wouldn't want anyone to think his bride was less than *fashionable*.

"You look... appropriate."

I turned to find my future husband leaning against a wall with his long legs crossed at the ankles, hands deep in his pockets.

He was dressed in black from head to toe. The fabric clung to him, emphasizing his muscular arms and large thighs. The top buttons of his shirt were undone, reminding me of our meeting in the basement.

How long had he been standing there?

"You really know how to make a girl fall for you," I pinched out with a tight smile.

The way his gaze trailed down my body leisurely—as

if he didn't care if I was aware of it—made my stomach clench from the repulsing warmth spreading everywhere his eyes landed. "Maybe not with my words." His voice came out thick, wrapping around me in a heated embrace.

I was uncomfortably aware of how my body reacted to him and I *hated* it. I clasped my phone tighter, allowing the cool metal to bite into my skin.

"Words nor actions," I ridiculed. "The only way someone could bear the likes of you is by force. Unfortunately, you chose me to be that someone."

Roman slowly strode toward me, eating up the space between us in seconds.

Hovering above me, he tilted my chin with his forefinger, catching my eyes with his sinful ones. "This smart mouth of yours,"—he emphasized by running the pad of his thumb across my lips—"has consequences and I've never been shy of dishing out punishment."

Unexpected heat pooled between my legs at his lidded gaze. It was a complete contrast to the way my body coiled tightly from his sadism. "Is that a threat?"

"No, Aurora. It's a promise."

His callous demeanor pricked my skin, igniting a fiery temper within me.

I could either stay compliant, as Enzo had reminded me, or stand my ground.

To be an attorney was to be courageous, so I picked the latter. "I've agreed to everything that's happened to me until now, but you won't silence me. I *will* speak freely, and whether that bruises your ego is not my concern."

I didn't wait for his response as I turned and yanked open the front door, leaving him standing there.

When I stepped outside, I closed my eyes to rein in the many emotions coursing through me. *I wished my mamma was here.*

Everything hurt.

The courthouse was occupied by a handful of couples when we walked in. They all beamed with happiness as though it was the best day of their lives, but they had no idea that it was the worst day of mine.

We settled onto a loveseat while waiting for our turn.

I was too angry to ask Roman about our marriage license, but I knew he had settled everything before today. He was meticulous and calculated, a complete control freak.

"How long have you two lovebirds been together?" I dragged my gaze up to find a woman with short blonde hair, smiling at us. Her husband had his hand on her thigh, mirroring her joyful expression.

I smiled nervously, trying to conjure up an answer that didn't sound like I wanted to murder the man next to me, but came up blank.

Roman must've sensed me stiffen from my indecision beside him because he gave me a sly glance and answered, "Ten years."

His reply caught me off guard and whether it showed on my face, I wasn't sure. We hadn't been together for ten years. We had *met* for the first time that many years ago.

Why couldn't he have chosen a number less significant than ten?

Removing my gaze from him, I turned to the couple once again, whose bright smiles turned forced as if they regretted asking in the first place.

"Yes," I said with a pinched smile. "The day I met him changed me forever." I wasn't lying, but it also had little to do with Roman and more to do with the fact that I had killed someone for the first time, staining my hands red with death.

Shortly after that awkward interaction, our names were called.

We made our way through the double doors, where an officiant stood at the head of the alter and on his right stood a man sporting a black leather jacket.

"Big day," the officiant cheered brightly as we stood before him.

"I would say," the man in leather chimed in. "I'm bearing witness to this vulture marrying a beautiful woman."

Roman's jaw tightened. "Unless you want to bear witness to me severing your tongue too, then I suggest you bite it."

It was apparent these two had a close friendship because if it were anyone else who had talked to Roman that way, they would've thought twice before insulting him.

"Aurora, it's finally nice to meet you." He smiled lazily, ignoring the murderous glare Roman was giving him. "I'm Luca."

Luca was handsome. Caramel-brown eyes, sandy-brown hair, and rough angles that somehow didn't dilute his charisma.

I shook his outstretched hand. "I can't say the same," I said, eyeing the two men. "Though I'm sure you can understand why."

"Others are waiting. Get started," Roman snapped at the officiant, who looked like he'd rather be elsewhere.

Inhale. Exhale. Inhale. Exhale.

In a few short moments, I would be tied down to someone who was out to wreak havoc on my life and cause it to crumble into pieces until it turned into nothing but a pile of dust.

Luca stared at me with a strange expression that I couldn't decipher. It was peculiar, as if he knew me through and through.

The officiant gestured at Roman and me to face each other, which I did with distaste.

After the introduction that we were entering a legal marriage, it was time for the legal vows.

"Do you, Roman Mancini, take Aurora Bianchi to be your lawfully wedded wife to have and to hold from this day forward, for better, for worse, for richer, for poorer, in sickness and in health, to be faithful to her, to love, honor, cherish, and respect as long as you both shall live?"

This was by far the most awkward wedding ceremony I had ever witnessed, and it was *my* ceremony. For fucks sake, we weren't even holding hands.

To top it off, the bastard must've thought I was an uncultured swine because this ceremony was more American than Italian.

Roman had a way of appearing graceful and sinful simultaneously. He stood before me with ease and crisp attentiveness. His soul-snatching eyes were brighter than usual, a contrast to his hardened expression.

This was the longest we had ever stared at one another and all I felt was this hollowness in my chest.

"I do." Two simple words, yet they held the weight of a thousand anchors, and I was on the receiving end of it.

"Do you, Aurora Bianchi, take Roman Mancini to be your lawfully wedded husband to have and to hold from this day forward, for better, for worse, for richer, for poorer, in sickness and in health, to be faithful to him, to love, honor, cherish, and respect as long as you both shall live?"

No. No. No.

My throat closed, forbidding me from saying those two words.

"Anima mia."

There was that awful nickname again, sounding as threatening as the last time he had said it.

"I do," I said with as much excitement as I could muster; none.

"Roman Mancini, as you place the ring on Aurora Bianchi's finger, please repeat after me: This ring I give in token and pledge, as a sign of my love and devotion. With this ring, I thee wed."

My eyes narrowed, realizing I wasn't given a ring to put on Roman and for a reason I knew had everything to do with his reeking sense of superiority.

He must have sensed the moment I wanted to snatch my hand away from his because he clasped it tighter, crushing the bones beneath.

Bracing my strength, I blinked the pain away and clenched my teeth together as he spoke his vows.

"This ring I give in token and pledge, as a sign of my love and devotion. With this ring, I thee wed." He placed a diamond ring on my finger, the rock shining brighter than my future.

"Congratulations! I now pronounce you husband and wife. You may kiss the bride!"

The world stilled as I heard those words.

Roman stepped forward until we were merely an inch apart.

Everything moved in slow motion as he stared down at me, his palm cupping the left side of my face, calloused and warm. Everything that conspired between us was suddenly forgotten with that one gentle touch.

He glided his thumb across my bottom lip, parting my mouth slightly. My eyes closed involuntarily when he leaned in.

I held my breath as my heart pounded, threatening to leap out of my chest.

Then, I felt the warmth of his breath against my mouth before his lips brushed featherlight against my own. Like lethal attraction, I leaned in to seal the kiss, but he pulled back abruptly.

Startled, I opened my eyes to find him staring down at me. His heady eyes were shades darker than before, a fraction of lust reflecting in them.

Embarrassment flushed along my body from my carelessness. My cheeks grew hot as I stepped back from his agonizing presence and rushed down the altar.

CHAPTER 8
AURORA

It had been three hours since I fled the altar—three hours since I humiliated myself.

I put the heel of my palm to my forehead, willing my pulse to take on a healthy beat.

Even now, I could feel the subtle touch of his lips against mine in contrast with the rough caress of his palm lingering on my face.

My stomach twisted, disgusted with myself for leaning in and thinking about a moment with someone who wanted to hurt me in every way imaginable.

I would not wait to find out those ways, either.

Grabbing my phone and wallet, I sent a text to Enzo to meet me in an hour.

The clock read a quarter to eight when I closed the bedroom door. It wouldn't be easy to go unnoticed, but I would go down trying.

I needed a solution to my situation, and I would not

bear a second more in this house, *not* with the one who occupied it.

The house was utterly quiet as I descended the stairs. When I reached the ground level, I couldn't help but gravitate toward the sound of a fireplace crackling.

The sitting room was dark, the only light coming from the fireplace that Roman sat before on a couch. His head was laid back, eyes closed, and a glass filled with amber liquid balanced atop the armrest.

His expression was elusive yet somber—as if he were fighting his inner demons.

Temptation was a step away, knowing he could draw me in with his wicked shadow, but I pulled away from the trance.

Slowly, I backed away, making sure I was as quiet as when I had entered.

"You have a habit of staring at me when you think I'm unaware. Why?"

His voice stopped me in my tracks, sending electric currents up my arms.

I fisted my hand against my forehead for being such an idiot. *Had I never heard the phrase 'curiosity killed the cat'?* I should have left instead of wandering.

I came out of the dark and into Roman's view.

His eyes remained closed, allowing me to take in his now blank expression.

"You can tell a lot about a person when they're alone." He remained impassive. "When they're in their genuine form."

Roman couldn't help who he was—ruthless and unforgiving.

Alas, he opened his eyes, his intense gaze settling upon me. "And what can you tell?"

That was a question I didn't have a pinpoint answer to. Yet my lips moved of their own accord. "That maybe you're not as horrible as you let on." I swallowed thickly.

The sound of the fireplace crackling increased in volume as time stretched between us.

Roman remained unmoving and quiet, assessing me. I, too, remained in place, holding his watchful gaze.

There was nothing to fear at this moment. My life had taken a turn for the worst, and I accepted that it would continue to do so until I found a solution. But for now, I would not show any weakness.

With a tick of his jaw, he suddenly shot up from his seat, striding to me in two steps.

I didn't falter from my position, even when my pulse jumped from his sudden movement.

"Stop looking at me like that." His anger simmered, palpable enough to cause a storm.

I fed into his anger with my own. "*Like what?*"

"Like you believe what you said to be true," he muttered between gritted teeth, his voice sounding almost painful for him to speak.

At a loss for words, I opened and then closed my mouth.

I suddenly became overly aware of my surroundings and the person in front of me. *What was I doing?* I needed to remove myself from his presence and *fast*.

Sidestepping him, I moved toward the corridor when he stopped me with a hand on my forearm.

"Aurora." My name was a warning on his tongue, a fire

set ablaze, coursing through my veins, and intensifying the warmth coming from the fireplace.

I was treading on a path to hell, but I found myself welcoming the devil in front of me.

My eyelids fluttered before I turned and faced him with an arched brow.

Roman tsked and pulled me to him, my body crushing against his solid one.

His heavy hand settled against the small of my back as the other fisted my ponytail and tugged, forcing me to gaze up at him. "It seems that I haven't made myself clear if you're making incorrect assumptions about me," he growled.

When I remained quiet, unflinching against his hold, he tugged my hair harder, and the pain caused me to whimper slightly.

Self-loathing permeated within me when he bent his head and trailed wet kisses up the column of my neck, marking me with his tongue.

He continued his path up to my ear, where he grazed it with his teeth and whispered, "I'm worse than horrible, *anima mia.*"

His mouth on me erupted unwanted goosebumps along my feverish flesh as I breathed through my nose, unwilling to react to the sudden overwhelming sensations jolting through me.

Roman stopped abruptly, peering at me with a scowl etched across his features before he shoved me away from him.

I braced myself on the arm of the couch from the force

of his push as a chill settled in my bones, replacing the heat that had radiated from him.

He balled his hands into fists before stretching them. The livid expression on his face compelled me in place, fearful of his next move. Then he turned on his heel and left the room.

Leaving me with a chill that not even the warmth of the fireplace could thaw.

CHAPTER 9
ROMAN

Aurora Bianchi was a maddening woman.

After leaving her standing in the sitting room, I retreated to the basement to blow off steam.

It didn't matter how much energy I dispensed on the punching bag; my anger was palpable. My fingers vibrated with the urge to wring her neck until her lifeless body lay in my arms.

All I wanted to do was wipe out the Bianchi family and I could, but I wanted to stretch their suffering.

I had no intention of releasing Aurora, nor did I have the intention of giving her father back his wealth. They were submissive to me until I grew tired of them.

This scheme had been in the works for a decade. I took everything from them, knowing death would be too easy.

Aurora had my cousin's blood on her hands, and I would defile her through and through because of it.

It was clear her father did not care for her as he had

offered his daughter to me countless times in exchange for his fortune.

The only reason the Bianchi family had not fallen completely apart was because Enzo had stepped up and started his own line of business in the technology industry. It was a clean route—not enough to gain what they once had, but enough to stay afloat. He was also the only one who seemed to have lost his mind, knowing he was helpless in saving his sister.

Although, I had to admit, a part of me took her for my own selfish reasons.

From the moment I ran into a young and frightened Aurora in that dark corridor all those years ago, I was captivated by her.

Though my unexplainable fascination would end the moment I snuffed the life out of her.

Sweat ran down my face and into my eyes as I pounded my fists against the stiff leather, my frustration building.

The incessant vibration of my phone continued, stopping me from my movements to answer it. "What?" I snapped.

"*Don*, I have your wife"

My fingers curled around my phone in a deathly grip. "What do you mean you *have* her?"

"We caught her trying to leave the premise." There was a brief pause before Ricardo continued, "She's currently cursing out the guard while banging against the gates."

This woman had more bravery than I expected, but she would soon realize it was useless against me.

I gritted my teeth to suppress my anger. "Bring her inside. *Now*."

I hung up and threw my phone against the wall, where it bounced and cracked to pieces on the floor.

My head pounded with aggravation.

It didn't matter that I hated Aurora, she was my wife and if she still didn't understand that there were consequences to her actions, then I would engrave that in her mind until it was *very fucking clear*.

I heard furious footfalls before an angry Aurora stood before me.

A ghost of a smile threatened to slip as I took in her appearance. I could practically see smoke coming out of her ears.

"Fuck you!" she yelled.

We were in the sitting room, once again. This time, I was leaning against the bookshelf with my arms folded across my chest, watching her shake from rage.

"With time, perhaps," I drawled. Satisfaction and surprise seeped into me when she slapped me, hard.

I welcomed the slight sting that clung to my cheek from her weak assault before rubbing my jaw. I chuckled deeply. "Did you enjoy that?" I asked, pushing off the bookshelf. "That split second of superiority?" I walked toward her, a sardonic smile playing on my lips. Each step I took forward, she took back until she was flat against the wall.

There was no denying her attractiveness; she was a

sight for sore eyes. Curly blonde hair cascaded over her shoulders, her smooth skin glowed in the dimly lit room, and those doe eyes that stared at me with trepidation.

I wanted to bend and mold her to my will—corrupt her—and I *would*.

Her breathing shallowed as I caged her in, bracing my hands on either side of her face. I bent my head low and caught her eyes. They were the purest shade of green I'd ever seen and right now, anger coiled within them. I asked again, "Did you?"

"*Yes.*"

The nerve of this woman. It made me want to snuff out that fire within her and claim her right here.

"Good. Now, it's my turn," I said gruffly before crashing my lips against hers.

The kiss wasn't gentle or slow. I wanted to punish her for many things—most of all for having the sweetest lips I had ever tasted. They were intoxicating.

Her hands pushed against my chest, digging her nails into my flesh, but that didn't deter me from taking what I wanted.

Licking the seam of her lips, I gripped her hip roughly, causing her to gasp and giving me the perfect opportunity to slip my tongue into her mouth.

I tangled my free hand in her hair, keeping her lips connected with mine.

Our tongues danced for dominance, pouring our hatred into this heated kiss.

Then I felt her resistance fade as her mouth moved fiercely with mine before she wrapped her arms around my neck, pulling me close and deepening the kiss.

A groan escaped me as I picked her up, wrapping her legs around my waist. Chest to chest, I felt her heartbeat clash against mine.

Her hand settled in my hair, giving it a sharp tug. My lips curled in amusement before I bit her bottom lip, hard, piercing it with my teeth.

Aurora whimpered, the sound shooting straight to my groin. The metallic taste of blood was strong on my tongue as she scrambled to escape my hold.

With a growl, I let her go.

"You're an animal," she heaved with disgust. Her lips were swollen, stained red from where I bit her.

It took everything in me not to kiss her again when she shook beautifully from rage.

I narrowed my eyes at her. "The next time you try to leave this house without my knowledge, you'll do well to remember that while you're mine, you don't have a say in what you do."

Our breathing had turned ragged as we stared at one another, neither one of us backing down from the brutal tensions radiating between us.

"And I'm telling *you* that I'm not yours."

"That ring on your finger proves otherwise."

With a huff, her fingers circled her wedding ring, but before she could pull it off, I yanked her to me. "I wouldn't do that." It was a warning, one I hoped she was smart enough to understand.

She stepped closer. "Then where's yours?" she asked, searching my eyes as if she'd find her answer in them. "I won't be made to appear as a fool in front of others—regardless of why I'm wed to you."

It was hard not to stare at every inch of her face when she was this close. Prominent cheekbones, full lips that were red from our savage kiss, and a button nose that flared out when she was angry—like now. Her features were angelic, a disguise to hide who she really was.

The truth was that she didn't need to worry about whether I wore a ring or not. Despite what she had done, she was my wife now and I hated disloyalty.

"I own you, not the other way around." The words tasted almost bitter as I said them. "It'll be easier for you to accept your circumstances."

Her head shook slightly, the movement almost unnoticeable. "I'll never stop fighting you."

Oh, I hoped not.

"Leave me be, Aurora, and go to your room." My tone carried a dangerous edge, making it known that the conversation was over.

"I'm not a child that you can order around."

My skin drew taut as anger rippled in my veins from her overwhelming presence. "Then stop acting like one!"

I was breathing hard and from completely different reasons than I had moments ago.

The air shifted into something colder, pulling me out of the seductive trance.

Kissing her was the most pleasurable mistake I'd ever made.

She flinched at my tone, stepping around me to leave the room.

I knew she was leaving of her own accord to get away from me and not from my command.

My back was to her when I called her name. I didn't

have to turn around to know she had stopped in her tracks, her gaze boring into the back of my head, waiting to hear what I had to say.

My voice bounced off the walls in a deathly whisper as I said, "Don't attempt to remove your ring again."

A beat of silence passed before the clank of metal sounded on the floor, her steps fading farther away.

CHAPTER 10
AURORA

My lip pulsed from where Roman bit me.

The taste of blood was heavy on my tongue, and I tried not to gag from the metallic tang.

I ran up the stairs to my bedroom and shut the door.

When I entered the bathroom, I dodged the mirror and quickly rinsed my mouth with closed eyes, avoiding the red that surely swirled down the drain.

I touched my mouth with the tips of my fingers, ensuring it was dry, before bringing my gaze up to the mirror.

My lip was swollen and bruised from his assault, marking me his.

This would heal in a few days, but it would be a reminder of him every time I sensed the cut.

It repulsed me and fueled my anger to continue disobeying him.

He could dish out all the punishments he wanted, but

I wouldn't stop rebelling against him, and I hated that for a brief second, I allowed myself to melt into him, into the chaotic kiss.

My phone vibrated against the countertop, displaying Enzo's name. I answered and brought it to my ear.

"It would have been nice if you had told me you weren't coming before I waited for you for an hour," my brother sighed.

It would have been nice if my lip wasn't split, either.

"I forgot I was a prisoner. Remind me never to take you on as a client again."

Sarcasm was my way of coping with every single problem in my life when I probably should invest in a therapist instead.

"Remind *me* never to trust our father again," he mimicked. "The man has been insufferable. I can't stand being in the same room with him when all he does is mope about everything he has lost." I heard the frustration straining his voice as he continued. "Forgive me if my words offend you, but if he cares more about gaining back his fortune over his daughter, I wonder how little he cares for me, if any at all."

His words went straight through me. I had already known this, but I sympathized with Enzo. He had always been my father's favorite, even more after the passing of our mother.

"He will always hold you on a pedestal, Enzo. His feelings toward me do not affect how he feels about you."

"Then why did he *lie* to me? If what you say is true, why did he put someone I care about in harm's way?" His voice rumbled with anger. "I will *never* forgive him for what he did."

His words seeped into me, scattering down to my coiling stomach. I hadn't realized how much Enzo cared for me, even if he couldn't protect me from our father. That much was evident when he kept tabs on me while I was in New York without my knowledge. He must've wanted to keep his distance in case someone got ahold of my coordinates.

"Those are questions that I can't answer for you. It doesn't matter anyway; what's done is done," I sighed. "We can only move forward and figure out how to get me out of here, *alive.*"

"I swore I would get you out, did I not?" he asked, reassuring himself more than me from the desperation leaking from his tone. "But you need to understand, we lost our crew after Roman stole everything from us. We don't have the power to go against him right now."

The start of a migraine feathered the front of my forehead. That was not what I wanted to hear. "You should've been more cautious."

"They caught us off guard. We were lucky they didn't obliterate us the moment you killed their kin."

"He was strategic with his execution," I said, inhaling sharply. "He wants us all to suffer before he goes in for the kill."

"I accepted death long ago, but if it's the last thing I do before I die, I'll get you out of this country that has never shown you mercy."

The sureness of his words went straight to my heart, igniting my will to continue surviving this nightmare.

"We rekindled after all these years and you're welcoming death so soon? Our sibling dynamic must have been more messed up than I thought," I joked, wiping the tear that slipped from the corner of my eye.

Enzo's throaty laughter boomed through the phone, carefree and genuine. "We'll talk soon, *sorella mia*."

"Thank you for not giving up on me."

Unable to speak a moment longer, I hung up.

Enzo was as much of a victim as me. The only difference was, he was manipulated by our father while I was abused.

"Mrs. Mancini, you must come down for dinner," Gianna said through the door. "Your husband has made it clear that locking yourself in your room for another day will not be tolerated."

My palms pressed against the door harder, even though it was locked. "Tell him to rot in hell."

The last few days had gone by painfully slow, though it was my fault. I refused to leave my room. I wanted to avoid Roman at all costs, but it seemed that he was done with my act of silence.

"Either you come out willingly or forcefully. Choose wisely, Mrs. Mancini."

The sounds of her steps drew farther away from the door, causing me to release a frustrated groan. I would rather go with some type of willingness than be forced.

My hand was around the doorknob when the sound of

my phone rang through the air. I reached into my pocket, pulling it out.

A wide smile spread across my face as I answered it. "You have no idea how badly I've missed you."

Irina's chuckle was a sweet caress to my ears. "I would have called sooner if my partner hadn't left me alone to deal with our clients."

Okay, I deserved that. "I'm sorry."

"I don't want an apology, Aurora. I want you to tell me the truth and don't even *try* to lie because I know you better than you know yourself."

The chance of Irina coming to Italy was very high if I didn't explain everything and that was not an option.

"Don't freak out, okay?" I waited for her to respond, but the silence was deafening. Screwing my eyes shut, I blurted out, "I'm married."

The screaming erupted immediately, and I had to remove the phone from my ear to avoid developing a hearing disability. When her voice was at a safer volume, I brought it to my ear again.

"I don't know which is worse, that you didn't tell me you were getting married or that in our last conversation, you said you were in a bad situation. Is this the *bad* situation, Rora?" she asked, panting from speed talking.

"Yes?" I squeaked out.

"That's it. I'm closing down business until further notice and coming."

My mind scrambled to come up with anything that would deter her from coming here. "You can't do that. Our clients need us. *One* of us," I corrected.

"Tell me how this happened. Now," she scolded in

that tone of voice that told me she was two seconds away from strangling me through the phone.

"I'm married to *him*." I didn't need to say Roman's name for her to understand. "I don't have much time to tell you the details, but my father conspired against me and for lack of better words, sold me to his enemy in exchange for his wealth."

"I don't know what to say." For a few moments, she was silent before she spoke again. "Why didn't you tell me sooner? We're attorneys! I could've gotten you out of this."

The bubble of laughter shook my chest, knowing she would say something like that. "You're choosing to be oblivious, Rina. We both know death would be knocking at our door if we acted."

"I need to see you with my own two eyes, and I don't care if I need to commit my own illegal acts to do so."

The determination in her voice was set in stone. "That's fine," I lied. I wasn't allowed to leave the premises and I doubted I was allowed to have visitors. "Wait until I tell you to, okay?"

Her silence showed me that she had not understood my request. *"Okay?"* I repeated more sternly.

"Yes, okay, *fine*, whatever you say," she said exasperatedly, clearly unsatisfied.

"Good. I'll call you when I can."

Slipping my phone into my back pocket, I opened the door and stepped out of the bedroom.

My stomach twisted into knots as I made my way down the stairs.

Like a phantom bite, a faint sting still lingered on my

lip, aching along with the sensation of how *his* soft mouth molded against mine.

Avoiding Roman, I entered the dining room, feeling his eyes touch every inch of me.

Luckily, the only other chair was set at the end of the table, opposite him and not next to him.

I settled in my seat, taking in the meal before me— Margherita pizza.

I was taken aback, not because I didn't love this dish, but because it wasn't something I expected Roman to eat. I assumed he was a complex man in every aspect of his life.

"Is there something wrong with your food?"

His voice traveled the distance between us, reminding me of his intolerable presence. Not that it went unnoticed.

Grinding my teeth together, I looked up. "Not as much as the company."

He shook his head, eyes alight with mischief before picking up a slice of his pizza.

My stomach grumbled as the aromas of the oily goodness invaded my nose.

Starving wouldn't do me any good. I needed the strength to fight back if it came to that.

Slowly, I pulled a slice from the pie before bringing it to my mouth. The flavors of garlic and basil burst on my tongue from the first bite.

It was *delicious*.

We chewed our food in silence, sneaking glances at one another from across the table, the air buzzing from thick tension.

Roman cleared his throat and leaned back in his chair

with one hand resting atop the armrest. "Your lip has healed."

My stomach clenched. He must have been watching me closely if he had noticed that.

I wiped my mouth with my napkin. "It has and it'll be the last time you do anything like that again." That and the kiss.

"It won't be the last time, *anima mia.*" His eyes pierced into me, darkening a fraction more. "I like to think each mark I leave upon you will be a constant reminder of me."

Bastard of a man.

He didn't need to mark me as a reminder of his corrupted presence. He only needed to *exist.*

"It doesn't surprise me that you're a narcissist."

Pushing his buttons was probably not the most logical thing to do, but it came naturally when he vexed me beyond belief.

If my response amused him, I couldn't tell with the way his jaw ticked. "Perhaps I'll bite your tongue next."

That subtle threat shouldn't have evoked the warmth rushing to my core, but it had, and I hated that my body betrayed my heart.

Realizing this conversation could lead to his teeth sinking down on yet another part of me, I changed the subject. "Am I allowed visitors?"

Roman raised his brows at me, looking at me with feigned curiosity. "It would," he enunciated. "Save me the trouble of tracking down your little friend."

The weight of his words covered me in a sheath of ice. "You tapped into my phone?"

"Don't sound surprised." He pulled invisible lint off the sleeve of his dress shirt. "Your phone calls were entertaining, to say the least."

Calls. As in plural. That meant, he'd heard every single conversation between Enzo and me. He knew that we had been trying to find a solution for me to escape.

Cold sweat ran down my back. I didn't know what was more terrifying, Roman's calmness or being caught.

"You do understand that I'm not keen on people knowing my business, yes?"

I bit the inside of my cheek, hoping he wasn't suggesting the worst thing imaginable.

"Therefore, you'll have to forgive me for what I do to your friend." He asked for forgiveness, but his tone didn't convey a hint of sincerity.

The urge to cry and plea on my knees for Irina's life was palpable. My mind raced with trepidation as my breathing shallowed. "Please," I whispered. "*Don't* hurt her."

He tilted his head to one side, assessing me.

"*Please.*"

"How far are you willing to go for her safety?"

"I'll do anything." My pride could take a backseat because when my best friend's life was on the line, I wasn't foolish enough to cross him.

He hummed his approval, causing an internal rage to simmer inside of me. "Looks like you'll satisfy me after all."

CHAPTER II
ROMAN

It had been weeks since Aurora offered herself up on a silver platter to spare her friend's life and while I had no intention of following through with my idle threat, I wanted her at my mercy.

I'd seen very little of her since then though, due to the intensity of my work. It wasn't surprising, considering I ran a criminal enterprise of money laundering and drug trafficking, among other things.

The only times I saw Aurora were during meals and they were horrendous, filled with silence and vibrating anger.

It didn't matter if I saw her, anyway. Knowing she was under the same roof as me was agitating. I felt her *everywhere*.

She was a siren, beckoning me with her presence, making me want to claim her lips again—her body and mind.

That kiss had messed with my head. The way her lips

molded against mine, the way she felt against me, smooth and responsive. That moment replayed in my head repeatedly.

"Have you consummated the marriage?" Uncle Stefano asked, eyeing me precariously.

His tone of voice indicated that I was less than capable. "It's hard to do that when my wife hates me as much as I do her."

He rubbed his jaw in thought. "You're telling me you haven't *charmed* your way in yet?"

Too many questions made my body break out in hives and that included from family as well. It was prying and irritating. "I'm telling you to trust me."

My uncle raised me after my parents passed away when I was a teenager. He took care of me and taught me everything I needed to know. And when his only son—my underboss—was killed, I owed it to him to seek out revenge.

"I've been trusting you for the past decade. There are other ways to speed up the process," he suggested. "*Other* tactics."

"I will not be forcing myself on her, *Zio*," I replied. "Besides, I'll have her begging for mercy sooner rather than later." Big emerald eyes clouded my vision. "I've already established a middle ground with her." That started with my tongue down her throat.

"Don't play with your food, Roman. Swallow it or spit it out," he scolded. "I'll head out, but I expect progress reports."

I nodded my head in acknowledgment, suddenly needing to release the tension that weighed down on me.

When my uncle left, I texted Luca, letting him know I was on my way.

The Underground Club was exclusive to high-society families.

After passing through the large gates, I dropped my car off with the valet.

The outside of the building had a vintage aura to it. Alluring to the eye, with black and gold linings.

I punched in the code and entered.

Black marble floors with high ceilings were decorated with intricate art and chandeliers.

"Mr. Mancini, what a pleasure." Giuseppe—the host—greeted me in surprise.

"Giuseppe," I regarded him with an appreciative nod. It had been a while since I came to the club. I hadn't needed to until now.

I made my way across the grand room and down the basement.

The Underground Club had many amenities to entertain guests, but its highlight were the occasional events. They were extreme and over the top.

Luca was already in the boxing ring, wrapping his hands in tape when I set my bag down and did the same.

"To what do I owe the pleasure?" Luca smirked at me, knowing fully why I was here.

I stepped into the ring and circled him, causing him to turn with me. "If I wanted to talk, I would've gone to a therapist."

Before he could respond, my fist landed against his jaw.

A deep laugh rumbled from him. *Sick bastard.* "Oof, I guess marriage really isn't for everyone."

The muscle in my jaw ticked, ready to land another hit.

Luca was quick on his feet this time. He ducked, dodging my aim before his arms wrapped around my waist. He slammed me on my back, the pain diluting my anger.

I recovered fast, using the outside of my leg to pull him down before I laid my forearm against his throat.

He smiled at me mischievously. My anger resurfaced like an ugly demon waiting to pounce. I applied more pressure on his throat, gritting my teeth.

"You're lucky you're my friend," he sputtered. "I'm going easy on you because it seems that your ego has taken a hit—undoubtedly from a certain someone." I breathed hard, knowing he had given me a free pass to release my anger. "And as your friend, I'm telling you that you won't survive her."

"What the fuck does that mean?" I spat out.

"It means, I only needed to meet your pretty little wife once to know you're in for it."

I'd think he was trying to be funny if it wasn't for the seriousness with which he said that.

Despite his absurd statement, I wanted to bash his face in for calling my wife pretty. Instead, I released my hold on him and got to my feet. I didn't want my actions to justify his theory.

"Don't sweat it. You could always file for divorce." He winked, which earned him a snarl from me.

It wasn't that Luca was ignorant to my plans—no, he thought my heart would miraculously soften up to Aurora. As if she wasn't the one who murdered my kin.

Leave it to Luca to be optimistic.

We went a few more rounds, landing brutal punches on one another.

By the time we finished, we were left with cuts and bruises. It wasn't the first time and wouldn't be the last. I welcomed the pain and luckily, Luca didn't mind it either.

The house was quiet when I arrived home, which was unsurprising. It was nearly three in the morning.

I headed toward the kitchen to grab a glass of water before tending to my wounds but stopped halfway in when I saw someone standing by the sink.

Their black curls were vibrant against the soft glow of the island light. I stared, knowing exactly who it was. She had haunted my dreams for a decade now.

Aurora was unmoving, holding a glass of water in her hand. She appeared distant, as if in deep thought.

I realized then that even though I *tried* to ignore her these past few weeks, I didn't like her doing the same.

"Penny for your thoughts?"

"*Shit.*" She jumped back, her hand resting against her chest as she faced me.

Fuck me. What was she wearing? If that was her definition of sleepwear...

I swept my gaze from her red-painted toes all the way to her face, where a blush crept slowly across her cheeks. She wore a black silk set that unfurled a strong tenor of want in the pit of my stomach. It was the only thing I could focus on as heat rushed to my cock.

Aurora cleared her throat, causing me to stop eye fucking her. "Was there something you needed?" she asked.

My lips twitched in amusement. *What a loaded question.*

I walked the short distance to her, stopping just out of reach. "There are many things I need, but right now, a glass of water will suffice," I said before grabbing the glass in her hand.

The whisper of contact left my skin buzzing. I clenched my teeth, restraining myself from doing something stupid—like kissing her again.

The air thickened, overheating and suffocating. It grew taut between us, ready to snap in two.

Her eyes widened a fraction when I turned the glass and brought it to the exact spot her lips had been and drank deeply until it was empty.

Her nipples strained against her top, bringing my attention to them and I knew, *I knew,* if I slipped my fingers between her legs, I'd find her wet.

Her arms crossed against her flushed chest. "You're bleeding."

"And you've changed your hair."

"Gianna did it. I didn't see the point in keeping up a false appearance when it rendered useless." An austere expression shadowed her features. "Besides, a lot can change in two weeks."

It had. For one, I took her life into my hands and put her smack dab into the middle of mine.

"What else has changed?" I challenged, taking a step toward her. Aurora squirmed under my scrutiny but held her ground. *Good girl.*

"What else..." *Another step.* "Has changed, Aurora?" I stood close enough to notice her pulse fluttering against her throat.

Dark satisfaction filled my chest, knowing I had as much of an effect on her as she had on me.

Her gaze trailed my face and she flinched, turning away. "You should tend to those cuts, or they'll get infected." Either she was thoroughly disgusted, or she was playing coy.

I didn't press further on the matter, solely because my mind was racing at the ridiculous notion that she cared.

"I could wake up Gianna for you." I might've believed her concern if I didn't know what she was capable of.

Laughter exploded from within me, so loud and candid that confusion edged around her eyes.

My hand shot out, circling her throat.

She was caught off guard, her pulse thumping heavily against my hand. I bent my head, eye level with her. "I don't fucking *want, need,* or *like* you to do anything for me."

For the first time since we'd met, Aurora had never looked at me the way she was now. Her soft features had hardened into stone, eyes blazing from fury as she breathed hard through her flared nose.

She stepped forward, causing my grip to tighten around her throat. "Then what the hell am I doing here?" she asked as her gaze narrowed in on me. My own breathing had picked up speed. "To punish me, right?"

Her voice rose in volume. "If that's it, I can tell you *right* now you're doing a pitiful job."

My fixation dropped from her eyes and settled on her plush bottom lip, that was now healed from the bite I had inflicted.

Blood rushed to my head, her intoxicating scent heightening my heated skin.

"Get on your fucking knees, Aurora."

CHAPTER 12
AURORA

Luckily, the blood had crusted against Roman's cheek, making it easier for me to endure his physical appearance.

He tilted his head, raising his brow in provocation. "You said you'd do anything, yes?"

My heart sank as our last conversation replayed in my head, reminding me that my best friend's life was at stake.

"Show me you're not all talk and get on your knees."

His gruff voice made me clench my hands into fists at my sides, nails digging into my palms to refrain myself from gouging his eyes out.

With a click of my tongue, I held his gaze and slowly lowered myself to the ground.

"Untie my sweats."

His gray sweatpants did nothing to hide the bulge between his legs.

My pulse thumped against my throat as heat crawled up my body until it reached my face.

Again, my body betrayed me from how I truly felt.

"What—"

"Untie it, Aurora. Then put that smart fucking mouth of yours to good use."

This would lead to something I wasn't sure I was ready for.

Yet my dampened underwear proved otherwise.

Maybe I'd bite it off and put him at *my* mercy.

Before I could reach the strings, he roughly pulled my hair back with his hand. "I fucking *dare* you," he seethed.

The malicious gleam in my eyes must have shown my intentions.

I shrugged his hand off with a shake of my head, shooting angry daggers at him with my eyes.

If he uttered another command, I would lose it, so I took matters into my own hands.

Untying the front of his sweats, I pulled them down, his erection springing free and dripping with pre-cum.

Ignoring the urge to pull back from the sheer size of him—knowing it would feed into his ego—I wrapped my fingers around his thick length as best I could and closed my lips around the tip.

Roman moaned deeply, watching me through his hooded eyes as I gently sucked around the soft skin of his hard cock.

The sounds of his pleasure vibrated along my skin, all the way down to the wetness pooling between my legs.

I clenched my thighs as a fresh wave of hatred bloomed in me—not only for him but for myself.

Leisurely running my tongue along his length in long,

smooth strokes, I dragged my teeth against the underside of his shaft, earning me a hiss from him.

I lifted a brow at him, showing him how satisfied I was by the sound of his displeasure.

He narrowed his eyes at me before fisting my hair harder, pulling strands free and thrusting into my mouth with a viciousness that made me gag from the intrusion.

He didn't wait for me to adjust to his size as he continued ramming his hips forward in quick and short thrusts. "Fucking your mouth is only the beginning."

Tears welled in my eyes every time he hit the back of my throat, choking around him.

Wanting this to be over along with the aching pulse of my clit, I wrapped my fingers around the rest of his veiny cock, feeling him grow heavy on my tongue.

"Remember when you idly threatened me if I continued commanding you left and right?" he grunted, shoving himself inside me without pause. "Yet here you are, baby, taking my cock like a good obedient girl."

Without meaning to, I moaned around his shaft as the slickness between my legs grew from his praise.

Roman cursed, tilting his head back as he thickened in size.

Tears streamed down my face as I worked him harder in my mouth, enjoying the vulnerable position he was in and knowing *I* was the one causing his undoing.

He withdrew to the tip, allowing me to inhale a lungful of air before entering me again, this time slowly.

"I think you're enjoying this as much as I am."

Inch by inch, he pushed inside my mouth, watching me while doing so.

His eyes were dilated, dark, and savage.

Saliva drooled down the sides of my mouth as he picked up speed, pumping his hips viciously.

His cock twitched and I knew he was seconds away from coming.

I pushed against his thighs to free myself but his grip on my hair held firm. "I want to watch you swallow every single drop."

My eyes bulged as the first spurt of his come slid down the back of my throat. He thrust twice more before stilling. "*Fuck*, Aurora." A feral-like sound ripped from his throat as he expelled himself into my mouth, forcing me to swallow the warm, thick liquid.

When Roman jerked himself out of my mouth, I flexed my jaw to fix the strain on my muscles.

With a wipe of my lips, I stood from the hard floor while he tucked himself back in his sweats.

Flustered from the aroused state I found myself in, I walked away from him till I was in the confinement of my room.

That night, sleep didn't come to me as I tossed and turned from desire till the muffled sounds of voices came through to my bedroom.

Swinging my legs off the bed, I walked to the door and pressed my ear to it.

After my failed attempt to hear, I unlocked the door and slipped out of the room.

"Where is she?"

My heart thudded against my chest, stopping me from taking another step.

"I swear to God, if you laid a hand on her."

Recognition dawned on me, placing that voice to a name. *Raphael.*

A million questions ran through my mind, the most prominent being, *what was he doing here?*

"She's not yours to be concerned with."

Roman's voice drifted up the stairs to me, causing the warm summer night to chill below zero within seconds.

My feet moved at their own accord. I didn't have the answers to my questions, but I would not wait around to see the result of their conversation.

"Raphael," I called, panicking as I reached the final steps and lunged at him.

"Aurora." He patted me everywhere with his hands. "Are you okay?" He pulled me back, allowing me to see his distraught features.

I nodded as my heart swelled from seeing a familiar face. "How did you know I was here?"

"I'll explain everything later." His hand circled my wrist, pulling me toward the front door, but all I could focus on was the deadly aura coming from Roman, who stood five feet away from us.

My mind was torn into pieces, unable to process what was happening.

All I knew was, leaving with Raphael was not an option unless I wanted to jeopardize not only his life but Irina's. He'd already risked his own by coming here and I was petrified of what would happen to him.

"Raphael, let go of me." I pulled my arm, trying to free myself from his hold.

"No. We're leaving."

Inhale. Exhale. Inhale.

"*Stop.*"

"I'm not leaving you here!"

"Enough!" Roman's voice boomed through the foyer, his blistering gaze settling on Raphael. "You have a second to get your hands off her."

Raphael let go of my arm with distaste, stepping in front of me in a protective stance. "Should we bring forth how truly disgusting you are?"

My breathing shallowed at his words, noting the underlying meaning in his tone.

"By all means." Roman waved a hand in the air, a challenging expression on his face. "It'll only hurt you, *brother.*" A brutal grin slowly carved its way on his mouth, and I knew at that moment, things would take a turn for the worse.

My throat thickened as my body fought between hot and cold, taking in his words. I felt everything at once, too much of it.

"Br- Brother?"

Raphael turned back to me, pinching his lips together, as though fearful of what would slip out.

"What is he talking about, Raph?"

He flinched at my desperate tone, eyes wide and full of anguish.

The furrow between my brows deepened at his silence. I turned to the man opposite us, ears pulsing from the thumping beat of my heart.

With a hard swallow, I spoke sternly despite the anxiety rippling through me. "Tell me."

Roman was void of emotion while he stared at me with a coldness in his eyes.

Raphael finally found his voice and spoke with weariness edged in his tone. "Let me explain."

"*No*. No, I want to hear it from him," I rushed out, nodding my head toward Roman, whose gaze traveled the length of my face before settling onto my eyes.

"We're brothers."

A heavy weight settled onto my shoulders, threatening to crush me to the floor as time stood still. Someone was saying my name, but the roaring beat of my heart drowned it out.

We're brothers.

A painful sob escaped me, causing me to press my fingers against my mouth to silence it.

"Come on, Aurora," Roman said, slicing through the blurred state I was in. "Did you think I wouldn't keep tabs on you?" His words were clear and the meaning behind them even clearer. Raphael coming into my life wasn't coincidental.

Something disturbing passed through me, leaving me bare. I felt used, like the skin on my bones was tampered with.

My voice shook with rage, and I hated that I couldn't tame the tears burning a path down my cheeks. "You're *exactly* who you said you were. You're *worse* than horrible."

He raked a hand through his hair, pinning me in place with his daunting eyes. "That's right. *This* is who I am," he confirmed maliciously. "Whether you like it or not."

My vision blurred as I turned to Raphael. "It was all a lie," I murmured, my voice breaking. I rubbed my palm in a back-and-forth motion against the nagging pain in my chest. "Our relationship was a lie. You were my first in every way and... and—" I stopped abruptly, feeling faint as a renewed realization of the situation seeped into me.

Roman had sent his brother to spy on me. His brother, who I had given years of my life to. A relationship built on lies.

Blinking away the haziness, I saw both Roman and Raphael step toward me.

"Don't come near me." My hands shook in surrender. "Either of you," I whispered in defeat.

"Aurora, *please*. It's not like that," Raphael choked, pulling at his hair. "Yes, I was given a task, but I fell in love with you and when I did, I stopped giving him information. I'm *still* in love with you, *dammit!*"

His words brushed past me like the subtle touch of a breeze. It came and went like the last bit of love I'd held for him.

Without a glance in either of their direction, I turned my back and walked away.

CHAPTER 13

ROMAN

You're exactly who you said you were. You're worse than horrible.

Every time I closed my eyes, I saw Aurora's tear-stricken face from that night, like I had truly disappointed her despite her knowing *exactly* who I was and what I was capable of.

At least now she would believe me.

Yet, hurting her with that information hadn't brought me a semblance of satisfaction as I had expected. Instead, it felt like a loss when it was supposed to be a victory.

That night, a foreign sensation had clawed its way up my spine when she walked away, and the feeling hadn't gone away since.

Maybe that's why I informed Gianna to tell Aurora that her friend from New York could visit.

I ran a hand down my face. It was infuriating enough that my wife occupied not only my house but my mind and now I was experiencing an emotion I never had before because of her. *Guilt.*

"Tell me something good, Roman," Uncle Stefano requested, pulling me away from my unwelcome thoughts.

"I stayed at the penthouse this month to ensure ship-ments were going through smoothly. I wanted to assess the crew, too. They're competent, but I don't trust them. No feds circulating the premises, though. For now."

In response, I received a glare and arched brow from the bearded man sitting across from me. "That's not what I'm asking, and you know it. What of the girl?"

I ran my tongue across my teeth in distaste. "She now knows that I'd been keeping tabs on her before the contract."

"Hm. You don't seem happy about that."

Simmering rage rushed into my bloodstream without warrant. "I should've never sent Raphael to New York. I can't trust him." Because he fell in love with Aurora, and it unsettled me that I had the urge to snap my brother's neck in half.

"I never did ask you about that," Uncle Stefano muttered to himself, wrinkle lines etched onto his forehead.

"Excuse me?"

"The intel you gathered during your *stalker* phase. I never asked," he repeated.

"Superficial information that couldn't be used to my advantage," I rasped, recalling the simple facts I knew about Aurora. How she drank her coffee iced, never black, or when she was engrossed in her work, she forget to eat. I had made Raphael run through every single one of their interactions, no matter how insignificant. "That girl is under wraps, but I plan on unfolding every single layer till she's nothing but scraps."

"Don't disappoint me further. Consummate the marriage. That girl is here to breed and serve, nothing more." He eyed me with skepticism before standing to his full height. "I'll see you tomorrow night."

And with that, he left my office without another word.

How my uncle knew Aurora and I hadn't completed our marital duty yet was lost on me, but I knew why he was eager.

He thought that once Aurora was underneath me, it would lock her fully in as a Mancini with no way out.

You were my first in every way.

Aurora's words replayed in my head. She had experienced all her firsts with Raphael. Her virginity was given to a Mancini, but it wasn't me and that fact coiled my muscles tightly.

No wonder she knew how to work me in her perfect mouth on that kitchen floor many nights ago. I could still feel her wrapped around me, making me come the hardest I ever had.

With a shake of my head, I glanced at the clock on my desk, noting it was almost ten in the morning. I sighed as time ticked away, getting closer to the masquerade event taking place tomorrow night at the Underground Club.

I arrived back from a business trip a few hours ago and came straight to my office. I wasn't ready to go home yet.

Grabbing the black gift box from underneath my desk, I opened the lid, staring at the contents.

It encased Aurora's attire for tomorrow night and I hoped she wouldn't defy me despite our last interaction.

It would be our first public appearance together and not attending wasn't an option.

In less than forty-eight hours, I *would* see her.

I'd see that long black hair, that silky skin that begged me to reach out and have a taste as I'd done with her soft lips.

I cursed myself for being attracted to her. It was a disease, one that I'd be rid of as soon as I was rid of the Bianchis.

I picked up my phone and called Gianna.

"Sir," she answered. Her tone of voice was motherly despite her calling me sir.

As someone who lost both parents at a young age, Gianna quickly filled that spot in the areas that mattered. She cared after me since I could remember and despite the bad decisions I made as I grew older and into this role, she never perceived me differently. She was loyal, but I knew if she ever wanted to walk away from all of it, I'd let her.

"Where's Gianna and what have you done with her?"

"*Altri sono in giro.*" Her voice came out in a whispered muffle.

Now, I understood why she called me sir. She was around the staff. "What has she been up to today?"

"Your wife went out with her friend an hour ago. Of course, Ricardo goes everywhere they go." I had made sure my security team was set in place while I was gone, and it seemed that Aurora hadn't made a fuss over it. "They should be back in the afternoon."

"Good. I'll be home tonight."

When I hung up the phone, a call flashed across my screen.

Here we fucking go.

We'd been sitting in this café for far too long, without a single word exchanged.

Green eyes stared at me with fury, a shade darker than his sister's. His were more *deadly*.

"When I was generous enough to accept your request to meet, I didn't expect to sit here in silence," I said. "I'd suggest using what little is left of your time wisely."

No reaction, save for the narrowing of his eyes.

"You came here alone, which means your father doesn't know about this little meeting."

He tapped his fingers on the wooden table between us. "What do you want with my sister?" Enzo asked.

I couldn't help the sinister laugh that escaped me. Not because I was surprised by his concern for Aurora, but because that was a question with *many* answers.

What *did* I want from Aurora? I knew I wanted her.

"Are you searching for an appropriate answer or—"

"Don't fucking play games with me."

"Then understand I'm in no mood for games either. What I want with your sister isn't your *damn* business."

"She'll always be my business whether you like it or not. I won't stop until she's out of your depraved hands."

He was brave and tenacious, which was respectable. But it was futile against me.

"What can I offer you to let her go?"

Another laugh escaped me. "You can't offer me what you don't have."

"Then let me take her place."

"As I said, you can't offer me what you don't have." And because I knew it would get under his skin, I added, "Unless, it's your sister's pussy." I tilted my head in feigned shock. "Although, I didn't need you to offer me that." *I'd take it anyway.*

As expected, Enzo shot up from his seat, his hand grabbing my collar and pulling me to him. "Shut your fucking mouth."

"I appreciate your futile efforts." I smirked as I grabbed his arm and tugged him off me. "Key word, *efforts.*" I stood, dusting off the spot where he touched my suit. "Have a nice day, Enzo."

No one could replace Aurora. She was mine to do with as I pleased.

When I turned to leave, his voice stopped me in my tracks.

"Wealthy or not, if you hurt her, I *will* kill you."

CHAPTER 14
AURORA

Some people think the worst part about betrayal is when it happens by someone you trusted—but it's not.

The worst part about betrayal is losing yourself completely, trying to understand how you let it happen.

Every morning was the same; I'd wake up and overanalyze every interaction I ever had with Raphael.

I couldn't accept that he and Roman were brothers. I couldn't accept that Raphael had *spied* on me for his brother.

He'd tried contacting me several times, but I loathed him for what he did. It didn't matter that he fell in love with me because what he did was unforgivable.

I gave myself to him wholly and it wasn't genuine. I felt dirty, as if there was a transparent layer of grime I couldn't get rid of, no matter how hard I scrubbed myself raw.

What hurt the most wasn't that Raphael pursued me

to fulfill his duty. What hurt the most was for a decade, I was hiding from someone who had me under surveillance the whole time.

I had never accomplished my goal of being free.

And how was it that the one person I hated, managed to ignite unexplainable emotions I had never experienced before from a single kiss? *Ever.*

It had been over a month since Roman and I kissed, and his touch lingered on my lips as if it happened yesterday.

I wish it had vanished like a puff of smoke in that foyer.

However, I'd woken up the following morning after that disastrous night with Roman nowhere in sight.

He hadn't been home since, and I had been told he was out of town for business.

It stung knowing he could move on from what happened, but his world hadn't fallen apart in a matter of minutes as mine had.

After all, he was the one who dished out my pain on a silver platter.

"What do you have planned for me today?" Irina's voice broke through my depressing thoughts. "I deserve an amazing last day."

When Gianna informed me that I was allowed to have Irina over, I hesitated. It didn't make sense to me when Roman threatened her life.

I didn't act on my visitation rights for the first few days, but then I received a single text from Roman.

No harm will come to your friend. You have my word.

Even then, I was skeptical, but Roman had never lied to me once. He was an awful person, but he was honest.

So, I invited my best friend.

I had caught her up on everything that spiraled since I landed in Italy, and she went feral.

She left Raphael messages and voicemails calling him every curse word in Russian, but she knew she couldn't risk being reckless when it came to Roman.

I turned to face her, where she laid next to me. She did the same, her almond-shaped blue eyes watching me with concern.

"Don't hate me, but I was hoping we could wing it and see where the day takes us."

If it weren't for Irina, our business back in New York would have crumbled to the ground. I had virtual meetings with our clients while Irina stepped in when needed, for face-to-face meetings.

"I'm glad you said that. Being spontaneous will keep us young."

"Where'd you learn that?"

Her smile was wide when I regarded her oddly. "From myself."

Irina and I had been tourists this afternoon, wandering around Italy as if it was my first time in the country.

Italy was beautiful, rich in culture and architecture. It

didn't matter whether I grew up here. It was hard not to gape in awe at everything that came into view.

"What's happening there?" My blonde friend stopped in her tracks on the cobblestone, peering up at a large white building to our right.

There was a majestic spark to it. It was bold, standing alone, and making a statement. The intricate details ran along every inch of the building, designed with gold lines, swirls, and unique shapes of all different sizes.

To the side, there was a long line of people waiting to get in. Everyone was dressed in either tuxedos or evening gowns.

"I think it's a private event." I could feel my arms growing numb from carrying all my shopping bags.

I should've let Ricardo take them. I knew he was following us, lurking somewhere even when I told him not to.

I thought once Roman was out of the house, his *dogs* would follow him.

"Let's check it out." Before I could protest, she grabbed my arm, leading us to the building.

"We won't even be able to get in!"

She shot me a grin. "You're a Mancini. Of course, you can."

A sense of dread coiled in my stomach. My adventures today had dulled thoughts of Roman until now.

"Irina, we can't cut in line!" She was always the rebellious one in our friendship and if I was being honest, it was thrilling when she'd include me in her mischievous games.

"Sure, we can." Her long legs strode toward the hostess, who eyed us skeptically as if she knew we would cause her trouble.

"Can I help you?" she asked, cocking a dark eyebrow. I didn't miss her patronizing tone and neither did Irina because I felt her tense beside me. If I didn't say something, she would, and it'd be much worse.

I squared my shoulders, standing taller. "We're here to attend the event. My name is Aurora. Aurora *Mancini*." My smirk was visible as the hostess' eyes grew wide.

She composed herself, searching the list in front of her before glancing up at me again. "Do you have identification on you to prove that?"

I stood dumbfounded, not expecting her to ask that question. I didn't have anything that would prove what I said to be true. I wasn't even wearing my ring.

"You're holding up the line, Alicia. What seems to be the problem here?"

The voice came from behind her, masculine and stern. A chill settled in me at the deep impatient tone.

Alicia turned and her face went crimson red. "Sir, these ladies want to enter, but they're not on the list. One of them is even claiming to be a Mancini," she mocked, narrowing her eyes at me.

The man came into view, and I wanted to shrink into myself. *Luca.*

God, I wanted the world to swallow me whole.

He was freshly shaven, his sandy-brown hair pushed back, and polished from head to toe, wearing his signature leather jacket. His hands were deep in his pockets, his caramel-brown eyes sparkling with amusement.

"We were leaving, actually." I laughed, folding my lips in a pinched smile.

Irina peered over my shoulder. "No, we weren't..." Her voice drifted into the summer breeze when she saw the fine-sculpted male before her.

"Irina," I hissed. *Traitor.* She ignored me, staring straight at Luca with mischief dancing in her eyes. She was an idiot challenging a man like him. Then again, wasn't I doing the same with Roman?

Turning to Luca again, I found him holding Irina's gaze. His head tilted, eyeing her openly with a slight smirk playing on his lips. "Let them in, Alicia."

Okay, weird.

"Yes, sir."

My troublesome friend snickered behind me before she slipped her hand in mine, pulling me along.

Stepping inside the building, I immediately knew this was an art gallery.

Guests mingled, drinking their champagne. The ambiance was sensual, dimly lit with soft overhead lights cast over the art.

We walked around the museum, admiring the exquisite art. It was different from what most would expect. This art was exotic and erotic.

We stopped at the last piece, a painting named *Arte Della Lussuria*—Art of Lust.

The painting was distorted, allowing each person to have their own perception of it. Colors clashed with dimensions.

I perceived it as a blurry-shaded man and woman enveloped in one another, high on pleasure.

"Anyone could create this. What's so artistic about two people *ravishing* one another?" Irina always spoke what was on her mind, no matter how crude or unwanted.

"What unfortunate thinking, *piccola ribelle*." Luca appeared out of nowhere, gazing down at my blonde friend as she continued staring at the painting, ignoring him.

I held back a laugh because if there was anything Irina hated, it was when people—men—commented on her opinions.

The irony of it was *little rebel* was quite fitting for her personality and apparently, I wasn't the only one who thought so.

The awkward tension grew until Irina replied, her eyes clinging to the erotic art. "You're part of the male population; of course, you'd think that way. And I don't speak Italian, *mudak*."

Over the years, I had learned enough Russian by being around my best friend to know she had called him an asshole.

My cheeks grew warm from silent laughter. A Russian and Italian arguing? I needed to flee the premises immediately.

Luca bent his head, whispering something in Irina's ear before stalking off, leaving her flustered.

As color crept along her cheeks, I almost dared not ask what he said. *Almost.*

I grabbed her elbow. "What did he say?"

She ran her tongue along her teeth, irately. "*Nothing.* Now, let's go. This place wasn't as great as I thought."

"Mhm." I followed her lead as we left the building.

I had made my way up to the balcony, looking out at the slanting rays of the setting sun.

It was almost time for Irina to return to New York and I didn't want her to go.

The sliding doors drew open and close before Irina came beside me. "Here," she said, holding out a cup of tea for me.

I took it, letting the warmth of the cup soothe me.

She fidgeted beside me, inhaling and exhaling. I rolled my eyes, knowing she was holding back whatever it was she wanted to say.

My Russian friend never missed an opportunity to open her mouth, not even when it came to me.

She was as dear to me as I was to her, but we never strayed from being open with one another.

"Would you quit that?" I gestured to her with a wave of my hand. "And spit it out," I said, realizing too late my voice came out harsher than I expected it to.

She hesitated, tucking a strand of blonde hair behind her ear before speaking with caution. "Are you going to avoid my question forever?"

"Which is?" I knew what it was, but I didn't know how to answer it.

"*Aurora.*" With the way she dragged my name, I knew she was calling out my act of ignorance. "What's your plan? You can't be a slave to him until he decides to end your misery and kill you."

Leave it to Irina to be excruciatingly blunt, although

that same question was tucked in the back of my mind, gnawing at me. Every. Single. Day.

Her question floated between us as I untangled my unrelenting thoughts.

"I can't just walk out of here." I threw a hand up. "It doesn't matter whether he's here or not. The man has eyes and ears *everywhere*." I swallowed thickly. "It's not the right time."

Turning away from her, I made my way back inside because suddenly, being outside felt just as suffocating.

My hand was on the sliding doors when Irina's voice halted me from taking a step further. "What is Enzo doing while you're holed up here?"

Recalling the last conversation I had on the phone with my brother, I sighed. "He's trying to get me out of here, but it's been difficult when they had their money and people taken from them. Our father hasn't been useful, but no surprise there, even though he still doesn't possess his assets like he was promised."

"That scummy old man has been out for you since your early teens."

"No surprise there either." I slid the door open, slamming it shut behind me. I was angry, not at Irina but at my circumstances.

The moment I walked through the house, navigating my way to my bedroom, I felt it.

The change in atmosphere. Like an electric current flowing all around me, pulling me in.

Roman was here.

An unwanted butterfly took flight deep in my stomach, knowing he was near.

I made it to my door when my foot caught on something.

What the hell?

Haunching down, I found a large black rectangular box with a silver bow on it.

I picked it up and entered my room, examining the box suspiciously before setting it atop my bed.

Giving into curiosity, I untied the bow and opened the lid. There was a note on top of the contents inside. Plucking it out, I read the neat handwriting.

Inside, you'll find what you need for tomorrow. Be ready at 6 p.m.

Gianna had mentioned to me this morning that there was a huge event taking place tomorrow evening and I had a suspicion that this gift was related to that.

Pulling the tissue paper away, I gasped at the vibrant color of the fabric.

I held the gown in front of me.

It was beautiful, but I couldn't wear it.

If I wore it, that meant I obeyed his command, *again.*

Gifts from the devil always came with a price, one that I wasn't willing to pay.

Grabbing the scissors from my bedside drawer, I began creating my masterpiece.

I was done being compliant and helpless.

Roman might've bound us together through tainted ties, but it didn't mean I'd go down easily.

CHAPTER 15
ROMAN

I t was six in the evening, and my intolerable wife was nowhere to be seen.

Gianna rushed down the stairs with weary eyes, coming to a stop in front of me and huffed. "*Donna testarda.*"

I opened my mouth to question her about what she meant when the sounds of rustling diverted my attention to the top of the stairs.

Fuck me.

My breath caught in my throat as Aurora descended the stairs, holding my gaze with every passing step.

Now I understood why Gianna had called her a stubborn woman. She had tailored the gown, leaving scraps of the dress barely covering her.

The burgundy gown trailed long with two slits running up each leg to her hips. The bodice was tubular, lifting her perky breasts.

My skin ran hot as my pulse beat at a rapid pace.

Aurora turned slightly, giving me a view of her naked back and the two dimples decorating the small of it.

My head bent low as I gave into a smile. Beautiful *defiant* siren.

Then irritation rippled through me, thinking of all the men who probably wanted to do the same things I did.

There was no time for her to change and even if I asked, she'd fight me on it to the last second.

When I peered up at her, she was standing before me, with her chin tilted high. Anger simmered in her emerald-green eyes, that were emphasized by the embellished mask.

Reigning in my own temper, I tipped my head up, staring at her through lidded eyes before closing the distance between us.

I expected her to cower, but the only trace of hesitation was the parting of her red lips.

My hand moved of its own accord, feeling her shiver beneath my touch as I pushed a lock of hair behind her ear.

Her chest rose and fell fast as her eyes searched back and forth between mine before diverting her attention with a slight head turn.

I followed her gaze, catching her eyes once more, trailing my finger down her left arm and feeling her skin rise.

When I caught her hand in between my own, I brought it between us.

With my free hand, I pulled out the platinum ring from my breast pocket—that she had the nerve to take off when I'd told her not to—and put it on her fucking finger where it belonged.

Despite my soft caress, my voice rang lethal as I spoke, "If another man is stupid enough to touch what's mine tonight, I won't be responsible for what happens to him."

Fury clouded her expression—an emotion I was familiar with—as I pulled back.

Seconds passed and she didn't say a word. Not one word.

The masquerade ball was in full swing by the time we arrived. The theme was black tie, and the décor was exquisite.

Splashes of black and gold spread across the venue. Shimmering chandeliers hung low, illuminating the guests dressed in gowns and tuxedos.

"If it isn't the beloved newlyweds." Luca approached us, smiling down at Aurora, his gaze lingering too long on her for my liking.

"Thank you for the other night," Aurora said casually, as if I wasn't standing right next to her. I pinned Luca with a murderous glare.

He turned to me, grinning. "It was my pleasure."

With a tilt of my head, I stepped forward, ready to smash his head onto the marble floor.

He chuckled, putting his hands up. "Relax. Aurora and her friend stopped by my building." His eyes roamed behind us, a mixture of hope and rage looming in them. "Speaking of friend, she's not here, is she?"

"Unfortunately, she couldn't attend. Her flight back to New York was last night."

Their casual conversation made me want to smash his head in after all.

Luca nodded once, turning on his heel. "Enjoy the party."

Before I could question Aurora about their interaction, Uncle Stefano appeared.

The impulse to hide my wife from his line of sight was surprising.

"Roman, are you going to introduce us?" he asked, eyeing Aurora as if she was the filth on the sole of his boot.

Clamping my bottom lip between my teeth, I tsked. "Aurora, this is my Uncle Stefano."

She plastered on a fake smile, looking every bit uncomfortable when my uncle held out his hand.

She hesitantly clasped it with hers, face tightening when he didn't let go.

"While you may feel of importance attending this gala, you'd be wise to remember your place as nothing but a piece of our property."

The veins on my uncle's hand protruded as he tightened his hold, causing her to hiss.

My hand shot out, fisting his sleeve, and forcing his hand off her.

No one was allowed to have her pain and misery except for me.

Dismay crossed his features as he glared at me before stalking off.

Aurora stared at the back of my uncle's frame with a

blank expression, and I didn't like that I couldn't read her at this moment.

The taut tension suffocated me as she turned and walked away without a glance in my direction.

This woman knew how to strike a nerve.

It shouldn't have aggravated me at all that she was giving me the silent treatment, but it *did*.

This fascination I had for her was incessant. I wanted her in the palm of my hands, baring herself to me and when I had my fill, I'd get rid of her. *I would*.

The party droned on, and I hadn't spoken to Aurora since she started munching on delicacies.

"How many shipments are going through next month?"

The events held at the Underground Club were more for networking purposes than enjoyment.

While Nicolai continued blabbing about the market and how it was the perfect time to invest, he didn't have my attention.

My gaze was fixated on the alluring creature across the room, and I found myself constantly searching for her even when I didn't mean to.

When Aurora's head tipped back in laughter, my eyes narrowed on the man across from her at the bar.

"Roman," Nicolai drawled, failing to get my attention. I assumed he followed my line of sight because he asked, "That's your wife, right? Oy, she's stunning."

My jaw tightened at his words. Nicolai was one of the youngest in my crew. The night I had found him—frail and scared—I was drawn to him. Something in me told me he needed saving, so I had. At twenty-one, he had been more useful to me than most of my men. He was family—a brother.

I knew he meant no harm with his comment, but it still aggravated me. "Nico?"

"Yeah?"

"Shut the fuck up," I said, leaving him behind as I strode toward my target.

Aurora must've sensed me near because her smile faltered as she turned her head in my direction.

She'd never smiled at me, and that fact alone made my blood boil. I didn't care if she hated me or if I didn't deserve it. I wanted it anyway.

"Leave us." My command was directed to the foolish boy while my gaze bore into the side of my wife's head.

A moment later, I took his spot, standing before her. "Indulge me for a moment. Do you enjoy pissing me off, or has the ache between your legs become too much to bear?"

Her eyes narrowed at my crudeness while her lips thinned, refusing to utter a word to me as her nose flared. I knew exactly what that meant.

I leaned in and whispered, "The answer to question one, yes, it does. And two, I'm right here, baby."

A scowl etched across her features as she took a swig of her drink before slamming it on the bar's island.

Gathering her dress, she turned away from me, ready to stalk off.

Before my mind caught up to what I was doing, I grabbed her by the elbow and pulled her onto the dance floor.

Her body crushed against mine like the missing piece of a puzzle.

Dipping my head, I brought my lips down to her ear. "Make no mistake, *anima mia*. The next time I hear your sweet voice, it'll be my name on your tongue."

When a haunting melody erupted through the speakers, I pushed her away, holding onto her hand before she twirled into my arms again. Her back was warm against my chest as we swayed to the rippling sounds of a violin.

Her eyes were closed when I turned her to face me again, her expression mirroring pure bliss as if she were elsewhere.

Feeling her take control of our movements, I let her go and stood back as she danced to the tune of the music. Twirling and twisting, catching the eyes of everyone around.

The dance floor emptied till she was the only one left.

A smile broke out on her face as she swayed to the music, and I found myself capturing it and engraving it in my memory.

The somber beat picked up, as did her feet. Her arms moved above her head as she spun, faster and faster.

The burgundy gown swirled around her enchantingly as her pinned hair loosened its hold, cascading around her in waves.

A steady ache grew between my ribs the more I watched her and my need to claim her in some way, potent.

The beat slowed and ended with her arms spread wide. Her back arched as her smile widened.

An applause broke around the room, startling her and her eyes snapped open. She straightened herself as embarrassment colored her cheeks at the unexpected attention.

Her gaze searched the room before it fell on me and the panic lining her widened eyes had me crossing the dance floor to reach her.

I grabbed her hand, feeling her struggle against me. My grip tightened, walking in the direction of the stairs.

A soft laugh escaped me. Even now, she was too stubborn to speak—to tell me to stop.

Aurora shuffled behind me as she tried to keep up with my long strides.

I took the stairs two at a time before walking down the long hall and opening the door to the library.

Once the door shut, I wasted no time pushing her against it. Her eyes widened a fraction as I held her hands above her head and sealed our lips together, kissing her long and hard.

My tongue swept across the seam of her lips, demanding entry. To my surprise, her tongue darted out, gliding against my own. A hum of approval vibrated between us as heat rushed to my hardening cock, straining painfully against my pants.

Breaking apart, my eyes searched her lust-filled ones, gauging her reaction. With her red lipstick now smeared and her loose curls, she appeared wanton, ready to be tamed.

I grabbed the back of her thighs, lifting her up before wrapping her slender legs around my waist.

Her head tipped up against the door, giving me access to her delicate neck. I sucked on the soft flesh, moving down to the tops of her perky breasts, biting, nipping, and kissing.

She was maddeningly perfect.

A moan escaped her when I ground my hips against her, feeling the heat between her thighs.

"Look at me." She did and I kissed her, again. Once. Twice. "I want to taste you, baby."

When she didn't answer, I thrust against her harder, causing her to cry out.

Her nails dug into my shoulders as I continued grinding myself into her perfect body.

My cock pulsed, hot, and heavy and I knew if I didn't stop, I'd come like this. Only she was capable of that.

I let go of her right leg, letting it rest on the floor. Using the tips of my fingers, I caressed the top of her thigh in light strokes.

She bit down on her bottom lip at the sensation of my rough fingers taunting her smooth skin.

Her breathing grew uneven as I inched closer to her cunt, her arousal seeping down her legs.

Aurora's heart could hate me all it wanted, but her body fucking loved me.

She inhaled sharply as I dragged a finger along her slick folds, finding her bare. *Fuck.*

I couldn't help myself as I plunged a finger inside her. The unexpected intrusion made her back arch off the door as her mouth gaped open in a silent cry. "Your tight cunt must have a mind of its own if it's dripping for *me*." Her pussy clenched around my finger, proving my point.

Letting go of her other leg, I dropped down to my knees, pulling her right leg forcibly to rest on my shoulder. I grinned when she gasped at my aggressiveness.

Attraction was a deadly weapon because at this

moment, Aurora was a goddess, and I was her starving servant, ready to feast.

Her brows furrowed with indecision while her eyes filled with lust.

I held her gaze and grabbed her ankle, kissing it softly, making my way up her leg. "Do you like that I'm on my knees for you?"

The rise and fall of her chest grew, desire blooming on her features. She watched me intently, waiting to see what I'd do next, and *that* made my need for her grow.

Pulling the front of her dress to the side, I bared her wet cunt on display.

She panted softly, knowing how close I was to tasting her. "I take that as a yes."

A shiver ran through her as she buckled against the first glide of my tongue. The sound of my own satisfaction vibrated against my throat. She tasted perfect, like I knew she would.

"If it wasn't clear before, when you come on my tongue, I'm *keeping* you." I swirled my tongue around her clit, sucking it into my mouth.

Despite her desire to watch, her eyes screwed shut as she grabbed my hair and started chasing her pleasure, riding my face.

Her moans grew louder and louder, cascading down my spine in electric waves, heightening the need to sink my cock deep inside her.

Her efforts to take control were mute as I kept my pace slow, pumping two fingers inside her, curling them to hit the spot that finally brought my name on her lips. "Roman..."

Her velvety voice raked along my skin as she pleaded for release, but I needed more than that.

"I know, baby. But I need you to beg," I said, thrusting my fingers in and out of her. "Now that I've had a taste of this pussy, I'll keep coming for more."

A groan of frustration masked the erotic sounds slipping from her mouth. She pulled my hair harder, rocking her hips faster.

I tsked playfully before pulling out my fingers. Aurora's eyes opened, glaring at me with fury. Her beauty was incomparable.

Feeling her resistance, I held her leg firm. "Only once."

The air was chillingly warm and thick, closing in on us.

Her and me.

Me and her.

There was a momentary pause before she pulled me in with her foot. *"Please."*

That was all it took for me to take her in my mouth again, plunging my tongue deep inside her.

Her sharp cries echoed around the room as I continued fucking her with my tongue.

"You taste fucking incredible." I grazed my teeth along her throbbing clit, feeling it pulse with need. "You taste like *mine.*" I bit down, causing her moans to bleed into a scream.

Flattening my tongue on her bundle of nerves, I eased her pain with pleasure.

With two fingers, I gathered her arousal on my fingers, her skin soft and dripping.

I brought it to her mouth. "Suck."

She hesitated, but a gleam of want sparked in her eyes.

I didn't wait for her to make a choice, not that she had any to begin with, before smearing her wetness along her lips.

Green orbs stared at me in surprise, growing wide as I dipped my fingers inside her mouth. *"Suck."*

Her hot tongue swirled around my fingers, the sensation shooting straight to my groin. "You obey me so good, don't you, baby?"

Darkness pooled in her eyes before she bit down on my finger, but I knew my praise made her wetter. I could smell her arousal seeping from her pussy.

Removing my fingers from her mouth, I asked, "What do you taste like?" I raised an eyebrow, waiting for her answer. *She knew the answer.*

My grip on her thigh tightened, imprinting her with a bruise.

I lowered my head down to her awaiting cunt, teasing the flesh until she was trembling, her breathing erratic.

When I brought my head back up again, I could feel her wetness dripping down my chin. "What do you taste like? I won't ask again."

Her cheeks were flushed and her eyes hazed over in fervor.

"Go fuck yourself..." Her voice drifted as I glared at her, daring her to make me repeat myself.

Her bottom lip curled between her teeth before she strained out, "Like yours." Her voice came out softly and I almost didn't hear it.

Yours.

"That's right. *Mine*," I agreed, before latching onto her, eating her as if she was my last meal.

She slumped back on the door, losing her balance. Her heel dug into my shoulder as she moved her hips to the rhythm of my tongue.

Feeling her pussy tighten further, I knew she was close. I added a third finger, spreading them inside her. "Come, baby," I said before leisurely sweeping my tongue against her clit.

She shuddered against me as another cry fell from her lips, her orgasm coursing through her.

Drawing out her euphoric high, I continued sucking on her clit.

She had my fingers bound tightly; I couldn't even pump them inside her.

When her breathing evened out, I slid my fingers out of her.

I stood and moved to the side to grab a tissue from the low-set table on our right.

Aurora tracked my movements as I cleaned between her thighs and fixed her dress.

"Let's go," I said, grabbing her hand.

She didn't budge, her eyes staring down at where I was still hard, the evidence clear.

I had done enough damage tonight and it pissed me off knowing she knew the effect she had on me.

"A simple, 'thank you for eating my pussy' would suffice." Her pleasure was mine, yet the words that left my mouth had her storming out of the room.

The event had ended by the time we headed downstairs, and everyone was already in their private rooms for the night.

Something I forgot to mention to Aurora.

"I'm not sharing a bed with you." She crossed her arms in annoyance.

"I can still taste you on my tongue, yet you *don't* want to share a bed." The sarcasm in my voice was evident as I tilted my head at her stupidity.

Her cheeks reddened as she huffed, pacing back and forth at the foot of the bed.

Content in watching her sort through her dilemma, I leaned against the dresser.

That raw ache reappeared, caving its way through my chest. The feeling was terribly unfamiliar, and I pressed myself further into the dresser to get away from it.

All the while, Aurora was oblivious to the turmoil spiraling right in front of her as she continued muttering to herself.

CHAPTER 16
AURORA

"I'm going to shower and try to wash *you* off me," I seethed at him, though I was frustrated with myself.

I can't believe I let him—dammit, I couldn't even say it in my head. And when he told me to taste myself...

Bastard of a man is what he was.

"If that's your solution, by all means, go ahead," Roman mocked, his brutal lips curling at the side.

I slammed the bathroom door shut in his face, which earned me a rough chuckle.

Like the suite, the bathroom was also grand. The white marble floor was cold as I tiptoed toward the large shower that could fit at least ten people.

I stripped and stepped under the shower head, where the water protected me in a heated embrace.

One thing I loved about showers was that whenever I took one, I felt free of all my regrets and inconveniences, and I'd come out feeling like a new person. But not this time.

With my hands plastered on the shower wall, I bowed my head.

Roman had disrupted that and now I couldn't obliterate my feelings into nothing.

I knew I should've never let it get past kissing. It should've *never* even gotten to us kissing. He didn't force me into anything I didn't want to do, so why did I feel used?

It repulsed me that I wanted him, and I hadn't got a clue of the reason why.

It might've been because I felt happy for the first time in ages on that dance floor or the way Roman looked at me as if he didn't hate me for a split second.

That look. It was feral, like if he couldn't have me, he'd burn the whole world to the ground.

And I'd let him do it as long as he burned with it.

I may have let my guard down, but I wasn't stupid to think his heart was anything but a cold, hard stone.

I shut off the water and wrapped myself in a towel.

Clearing the foggy mirror with my hand, I gazed at myself, unrecognizable.

My cheeks were rosy, my eyes a brighter green, and my lips swollen and pink. This face didn't reflect the dread of how I felt about Roman.

With a sigh, I turned away, ready to change, but then it hit me.

I didn't have anything to wear. *Shit.*

Thinking on my feet, I realized my options were limited.

What if I quickly grabbed my phone before he saw anything? Then, I could call the front desk for help.

Irritation bloomed in me like a bitter seed. If we were a normal couple, this wouldn't be an issue.

"To hell with it," I cursed, opening the bathroom door.

Roman jerked his head at the same time I said, "Don't."

He was still leaning against the dresser, in the same position where I had left him before entering the bathroom. Deciding not to ponder on that fact, I carefully watched him. "I will gouge out your eyes if your head so much as moves an inch my way. I came to grab my phone, which is..."

On the *damn* dresser.

Roman's head bent low, attempting to hide his amusement.

I clutched the towel around my body tighter. "Close your eyes." He opened his mouth to most likely protest, but whatever he was about to say was cut off when I said sternly, "*Close.*" And because he did, I couldn't help but savor his obedience. "*You obey me so good,*" I drawled, dishing back the words he had uttered to me moments ago to make sure he understood my immense satisfaction.

His displeasure at my praise was evident as he poked his tongue against the inside of his cheek.

I grabbed my phone and found the number for the front desk before dialing. As it rang, I fixed my gaze on Roman to ensure his eyes remained closed.

He was so close, I could smell all the scents that made him, *him.* Sandalwood, a hint of mint, and fresh.

The line rang and rang before it went dead. *Great, just what I needed.*

Turning my phone off, I slammed it on the dresser. "For a luxury... whatever this place is, it sure has poor customer service."

Roman's head tilted to one side. "What did you need?" he asked innocently, a contrast to what he was.

"*Clothes!*" I shrieked. "It's all your fault, too. If you had told me I would be holed up in here with you, I would have packed appropriately."

He was silent, reaching for the buttons on his dress shirt.

My heart sped up, watching him clasp onto the first button. "Wh- what are you doing?"

"Giving you something to wear." I couldn't help but watch as his fingers undid each button. "Don't worry, baby, look all you want. It's not like I'll know anyway," he added.

"I'm *not* and don't call me that."

He pursed his lips, sensing the lie as he continued baring his chest to me for the first time.

Before he slipped it off entirely, I noted the many tattoos adorning the length of his arms all the way to his broad chest and down his solid stomach.

Roman's physical appearance was otherworldly. Firm muscles stretched when he shrugged the shirt off. Built to perfection, I imagined if he took off his pants, I'd find a pair of toned, thick thighs.

He handed me the shirt and without thought, I took it like an idiot, outing myself. Now he knew for certain that I was staring at his strip tease.

I entered the bathroom again, dropping my towel onto the floor and gingerly slipping the shirt on.

The soft material hung loosely, stopping mid-thigh, and enveloping me in a gentle caress. His scent lingered, invading my senses with all things Roman.

It shouldn't have felt *this* good wearing his shirt.

Shaking my head from the disturbing thought, I brought myself back to reality before opening the door.

The beast of a man occupied half of the bed, wearing only his boxers. *Thick thighs.*

His eyes trailed my body, starting from the tips of my toes and burning a path until they settled on my face. "Are you going to continue fighting me? Come on, it's late."

He sounded tired. *I* was tired. "I'll be okay on the floor," I sighed.

"We can either do this the hard way or the easy way, *anima mia*. Get on the bed."

And because I'd rather do things of my own free will—at least in some sense—I laid on the other side of the bed.

I turned my back to him, making sure I was as far away from him as possible.

I wouldn't be getting any shuteye tonight and it didn't help that Roman's body heat mingled with mine.

The bed dipped along with my stomach, knowing he was facing me.

I forced myself to focus on the moonlight coming through the hexagon-shaped window.

Nighttime was precious. It was during that time when most people were okay with taking risks and allowing themselves to do things they usually wouldn't do during the day. And maybe that's why I indulged the need to turn, only to find Roman wide-eyed, staring at me already.

Resting my head on the back of my hand, I watched him watch me.

His eyes were their own shade of midnight, dark and yet luminous against the glowing moon.

"Where did you learn to dance?" he whispered, as if we were in a bubble and anything beyond that volume would burst it.

The smallest of smiles crossed my mouth before I swallowed thickly. "My mother."

I was never good at talking about the hardships I endured in life and maybe that's why I always laced it with humor. "Don't worry. After she died, my father filled her shoes in *just* fine."

The glow I saw in his eyes seconds ago dimmed as his expression hardened.

He didn't say anything for a while, and I grew comfortable in the bubble we created.

With each passing minute, my body grew restless.

"My mother was my favorite person, too."

I don't know what threw me off more—him talking to me about his mother or the fact that he said 'too' at the end as if this was our commonality.

It was scary to think I shared anything in common with him.

It was even scarier the way my heart soared, as he gave me a piece of himself. He *had* a heart and one that might not be made of cold, hard stone.

"And your uncle?" I asked, recalling earlier in the evening when I had the misfortune of meeting him. He had squeezed my hand in a deathly grip, and I knew he had done it on purpose to hurt me, but I appeared unfazed.

"He's the father of the man you killed," Roman replied, his tone clipped.

The bubble we were in finally burst, as I had expected.

Without another word, I turned my back to him, resenting myself because even though I hated the Mancinis, I hated what I had done even more. I could never wipe my hands clean of the blood on them.

Sleep must have overcome me because the sound of my phone vibrating woke me from a slumber that I hated to admit, was peaceful.

Somehow throughout the night, Roman and I each moved to the middle of the bed, our limbs tangled.

Gently removing myself from his grasp, I grabbed my phone. Within seconds of seeing the number on the screen, my peace was replaced with trepidation.

I tiptoed to the bathroom and shut the door before answering. "Why are you calling me?"

My father's jagged voice came through the line, causing me to wince involuntarily. "I have bad news."

I froze, pinpricks of ice spreading throughout my body, waiting for him to continue speaking.

"Your brother is dead," he exhaled. "Which means the contract is void. You're free, Aurora."

Cold sweat broke out in hives on my skin, the phone slipping through my trembling fingers, and crashing onto the tile floor.

Your brother is dead.

The words echoed in my head, sounding absurd with each passing second. I spoke to him the other day and he was fine.

He said we'd have plenty of time to catch up on lost years as siblings. He said he wouldn't leave me like this. He—he...

The sob that racked through my body was ear-piercing and painful as I dropped to the floor.

The contract was void, but none of it mattered when my brother was dead.

My heart cracked right down the middle, splitting in two, the pain seeping into my blood and numbing me whole.

The door of the bathroom opened. "What's wrong?"

Roman went down on his haunches in front of me, staring at me with a hint of concern swirling in his eyes, the crease between his brows furrowed.

I wept harder because this was it, his eye for an eye, only I didn't pay the price.

He never claimed to be a saint, yet disappointment set in, suffocating me along with the bile in my throat, threatening to rise.

I couldn't breathe.

His touch burned like acid when his heavy hand settled on my shoulder.

"*No!*" I said, shoving his chest.

My rage and frustration were unleashed and I was relentless as I continued shoving him. My efforts to hurt him as he had hurt me weren't enough. My hands balled into fists, punching at his chest before I slapped him across the face.

Confusion and anger flashed across his features. "What the hell is wrong with you, Aurora!"

A fresh set of tears streamed down my face, hot and thick. "Did you get a good laugh in tonight, knowing I was oblivious to what you had done?"

He inched back. "What are you talking about?"

A laugh mixed in with my sobs at his attempt to act naïve. "Enzo's dead because of *you*," I yelled. He opened his mouth to cut me off, but I continued, "Although, I should thank you for the breach of contract. I'd *hate* to be your wife for a second more."

I scrambled off the floor and left him sitting there in the bathroom.

He didn't come after me, not even when I slammed the door to the suite shut.

CHAPTER 17
AURORA

The house was lifeless, even more so without Enzo.

After I left the suite, I grabbed a cab and came to my father's house, slipping through the secret entrance.

I would've been mortified if I was caught wearing nothing but a man's dress shirt, so I changed into what few clothes I had in my bedroom.

Making my way down the long corridor, I stopped at the black wooden door—my father's office.

This would be my first time seeing him after a decade and I felt nothing.

There was a hollowness in my chest that was void of all emotion when it came to my father. He had hurt me too many times in the past for me to feel anything.

Whether my father knew I would be visiting or not wasn't my concern. I needed answers and I needed them *now*.

I knocked once before entering.

My father peered up from his desk, unflinching.

He had aged better than I expected, with salt and pepper hair that reached the nape of his neck and wrinkles that somehow didn't detract from his handsomeness.

Without a doubt, if Enzo was alive, he would have looked exactly like our father at this age.

"I'm not surprised you came," he said, removing his glasses.

I sat on the leather chair on the opposite side of his mahogany desk, facing him. "Good because I'm not leaving without answers."

"Answers... to what?"

His callous demeanor had me biting my tongue, wanting to unleash my wrath on him. *What kind of father didn't want to rain hell on the people who killed his son?*

"The first being, how was Enzo murdered?" I asked with a quirked brow.

He leaned back in his chair and laced his fingers together. "He was found dead with a gunshot wound to the chest."

"Enzo was meticulous. It's hard to believe that he was gunned down."

My father regarded me closely. "He must've been ambushed. We won't know for sure."

We won't know. Oh, but I planned on finding out.

I swallowed, trying to get rid of the tangy taste in my mouth before asking my next question. "And the funeral, when is it?"

"There won't be one. I have my men burying him right now."

Something in me snapped and I let my pent-up rage surface.

I stood and slammed my palms on his desk. "You had *no* right! Enzo was *my* brother, and he deserved a funeral."

My father mirrored my actions, getting in my face. "He was *my* son and last I checked, you haven't been a part of this family for over a *damn* decade! Know your place because it will *never* be with this family."

That hollowness in my chest filled with agony. Physical abuse didn't hurt as much as the words that came out of his mouth and I knew he meant every single syllable.

It was hard to believe that this was the same man who had loved me once upon a time, like a father was supposed to love his daughter.

I blinked away the burning sensation tightening the back of my eyes. I had cried over my father enough already and the last thing I wanted was to satisfy him with more tears.

"Is it because I look like her? *Mamma?*" I laughed bitterly. "It is, isn't it? And you can't *stand* it. I bet you even wish I was dead instead of her."

He sat back down in his chair, eyeing me with cool indifference.

Understood.

"Was there anything else you needed?"

At this moment, I needed him to self-evaluate himself and figure out why he'd become such a horrible father because losing his wife wasn't cutting it. He couldn't blame anyone but himself.

"No, but you do." I pushed off the desk and crossed my arms. "You sold me to the Mancinis to get back everything you lost, and we both know a breached contract still won't make them hand it over. Stop trying to manipulate me and spit out what you have to say."

A hint of a smile played on his lips. "I've underestimated you. Very well," he said. "You're in a unique position that could help me."

"Position?"

He nodded. "You're still Roman's wife and if we play our cards right, we can destroy him for what he's done and take back what is rightly mine."

I sat back down in my chair, digesting what my father was implying.

"Even the most soulless man learns how to love." His eyes drifted away for a moment before settling back on my face. "You will go back to him and earn his trust. How you plan on doing that is up to you. Then, you can spy on him and find crucial information we could use as leverage to help take him down. Or find the files on my assets."

It was a very risky plan and hard to believe Roman would have that type of information lying around, especially in his house.

More importantly, I walked out on him only a few hours ago. He wasn't naïve to think I had forgotten about what he had done so easily.

Yet, I sat quietly, contemplating whether it would be worth gambling my life over.

Roman took my brother from me and after the tender moment we shared last night, how could he have faced me knowing what he had done? That was inhumane, even for him.

I rubbed my sweaty palms against my jeans, my decision made. "This is for Enzo."

My father's smile was wide, his hand waving in the air. "For Enzo."

CHAPTER 18

ROMAN

"Enzo Bianchi is dead. Did you have anything to do with that?"

"And jeopardize prolonging their suffering?" Uncle Stefano divulged, taking a hit from his cigar before blowing out a puff of smoke. "No."

The pounding in my head intensified. For the past week, I'd interrogated my men thoroughly and they weren't too happy about me questioning their loyalty.

I gritted my teeth. "Someone did, and I'm being blamed for it."

He shook his head with a shrug of his shoulders. "Why does it matter? We would have killed each of the Bianchis one by one anyway."

That was the problem. For some reason, it mattered, and it all had to do with the five-foot and seven-inch woman who walked away from me last week.

Admission was never easy, not for me, but that moment in the suite at the Underground Club, we laid bare a piece of ourselves to one another. It was as if we had forgotten who we were for a split second—forgotten that we hated each other. The fine line between physical and emotional attraction had blurred, and I couldn't undo the damage.

"I don't want to be accused of a crime I haven't committed."

Uncle Stefano waved a hand in the air carelessly, "Semantics. It's one less Bianchi to worry about. Let's focus on what the next step is."

"The next step?" I huffed out in exasperation. "You do understand that because I've been falsely blamed, the contract is void." Not that a piece of paper would stop me from taking back what belongs to me.

"She's still your wife."

Whether Aurora knew it or not, our marriage wasn't void.

"And you let her walk away," he sneered. "When you should've shackled her in the basement and kept her prisoner."

The lack of sleep from the past week must have messed with my head because the way my uncle spoke about Aurora sent needle-like sensations down my spine.

I sipped my whiskey, the burn dulling the ache that had suddenly rooted in my gut. "According to Ricardo, she hasn't left Italy."

Aurora had gone to her father's house, which surprised me, considering the relationship they had.

"Oh?" he grumbled. "It seems you still have time to redeem your actions after all. Don't forget that she's responsible for my son's death. *Your cousin.*"

I pinched my lips together to suppress my anger. "I haven't forgotten, *Zio*."

Images of Aurora on that dance floor surfaced to the forefront of my mind. She had looked so serene and angelic that it had me questioning whether she was capable of even hurting a fly.

But beauty was an illusion. It didn't matter if it was in the eye of the beholder.

CHAPTER 19
AURORA

The golden sun slowly set as I drew closer to Roman's manor, and I wished that I didn't have to face him alone.

I had spent the past week at my father's house and even that had been too much. Fortunately, we stayed out of each other's way, and it gave me the time to build up my courage to face the devil.

Before inserting myself back into the devil's presence, I had to buy myself a new phone. If my father was going to keep in touch with me, I couldn't use the one Roman tapped into.

The car pulled up to security, where Pip, my father's driver, exchanged words with the guard before the gates drew open.

I was really doing this, risking my life to bring down a Mafia Don.

Dammit. But even though I was on the verge of passing out from fear, an unwanted sliver of excitement shot through me, knowing I'd see the beautiful bastard. There was no explanation for it other than I must be deranged.

"You need me to come in?" Pip asked, peering at me through the rearview mirror.

I shook my head, not trusting my voice, before getting out of the car.

Walking up to the wrought iron double doors, I raised my fist and knocked. I knew I was being a coward because a perfectly crafted doorbell was within my reach.

Five minutes passed and it didn't help that I was already wallowing in my self-destruction. I was a second away from saying good riddance when the door swung wide open.

A young man stood before me, who appeared to be in his early twenties, with blonde hair, and chocolate-brown eyes.

"Oh, uh, hello."

And then he smiled, broad and boyishly, despite his ironclad suit.

Someone called for him a second later, a voice I didn't recognize. "Nicolai, who is it?"

Roman had company and to think I'd assumed I would feel better if I wasn't alone. I was sorely mistaken.

"Roman's salvation," the young man—whose name was apparently Nicolai—whispered, amusement evident on his soft features as he opened the door wider for me to step through.

Walking over the threshold, I wrapped my fingers around the straps of my bag to stop them from trembling.

I followed Nicolai down the foyer, where he took a left

turn and entered a room I hadn't been in before, but by the looks of it, this was an office.

I stood outside the door, not ready to face my impending doom.

"Who was it, Nico?"

I would recognize that voice anywhere. Roman sounded tired, his voice ragged and low.

Nicolai shifted his gaze toward me with a quirked brow. I inhaled deeply, reining in the emotions surfacing before stepping inside the room.

My eyes found Roman's immediately—like a magnet, he always pulled me to him.

"I see," he clarified, pinning me in place with a deathly stare.

I didn't know what else to say except for, "Can we talk? *Alone.*"

There were at least a dozen other men here, but I didn't pay them any mind even though the air stiffened with male energy.

Patiently waiting under Roman's scrutiny, I thought as though he might turn me down, but he surprised me when he said, "Everyone leave."

It all happened terribly fast.

Someone grabbed me by the arm, pushing me against them as the flash of a knife came into view. *Shit.*

I was stoic and confused as to what the hell I had gotten myself into.

The man pressed the knife against my throat and my eyes widened in shock at the coldness of the blade.

I stared at Roman, waiting to see if this was his order, but he was expressionless, void of emotion.

"I'm tired of this, *Don*. The whore needs to get what she deserves, and you haven't done anything to see to it," the man holding me seethed.

Roman's eyes narrowed, blazing as he glared at the man. "Get your hands off my fucking wife. *Now*."

In seconds, the atmosphere changed. I squeezed my eyes shut when Roman held a gun in my direction and didn't hesitate before firing, the sound ricocheting off the walls, deafening.

I accepted death.

Except I was very much alive as warm liquid splattered the left side of my face. *Oh, no.*

I didn't dare open my eyes because if I did, I knew this wouldn't end in my favor.

"Does anyone else want to attempt hurting my wife in front of me? I have plenty more bullets," Roman snapped, his voice booming as loud as the gunshot. The room was silent. "No? Then get the *fuck* out."

Despite the metallic smell of blood overpowering my senses, the one thing that was on the forefront of my mind was that, for the first time, Roman had called me his wife. And considering the position I was in, that shouldn't have elicited the sensation of butterflies in my stomach.

I heard the shuffling of footsteps fading before the door clicked shut. Then silence.

The hairs on my neck stood to attention and my breathing shallowed.

Even with my eyes closed, I knew he was nearby, his presence all-consuming and suffocating.

"Open your eyes."

By the sound of his voice, I was right. He was a step away.

"Roman, *I can't.*" My voice broke to a whisper. I rarely used his name and I hoped he understood the seriousness of what I said.

The only response I received was his hand circling my throat, his thumb dragging across my skin. I winced at the burning sensation and realized the man Roman shot must've nicked me with the knife as he went down.

"Are you scared, *anima mia?*"

I swallowed against the pressure of his strong fingers. I would *never* admit my fear of blood to him. He'd think I was weak and use it against me. "No."

He could crush my windpipe in one swift movement and the thought of dying at the hands of this man...

"Open your eyes," he repeated, squeezing my throat further to emphasize his demand.

And I did, if only to get closer to leaving this room.

My heart violently crashed against my rib cage when my eyes locked on his—a dark abyss, wild and feral.

Roman's demeanor had changed entirely from when I saw him last. *This* was the man who everyone feared and would rather die at their own hands than be at the receiving end of his wrath.

"*Liar,*" he taunted. "Though I must admit, you're far prettier when you're scared."

I'd never experienced such intense whiplash until I met Roman Mancini and I had a suspicion that it was a feeling I'd get accustomed to.

"I'm *not* scared."

His head bent low, mirroring my height. "Your pulse

skittering against my thumb says otherwise." He applied more pressure. "*Unless* it's for an entirely different reason." One corner of his mouth tipped up, and it was then that I noticed his unkempt beard.

Roman was never one to falter in appearance or control, yet here he was, untamed.

Awareness rippled through me at the unbelievable conclusion I came to.

I was the cause.

A slow smile spread across my face. "It's *skittering* because my hatred for you runs *so* deep, it enrages me."

He inched closer to my face, his cheek sliding along mine. The light touch of his lips against my earlobe caused my eyes to flutter unwillingly.

The exact moment my gaze fell to the floor, where blood was pooled by my feet and a man lay with a bullet wound between his eyes, Roman whispered, "And what is it you think I feel?"

And then darkness.

CHAPTER 20
ROMAN

Aurora passing out was something I hadn't expected, yet here we were.

She felt solid in my arms when I lifted her, one arm underneath her legs and the other around her shoulders, before exiting my conference room.

I called for Nico and a second later, he came, his gaze falling between Aurora and me.

"Tell the guys to clean this shit up and then get out of my house."

He nodded but didn't make any move to leave, his eyes fixated on Aurora. When he glanced at me, I lifted a brow, daring him to say something.

He knew better than to interfere. Yet, I had a soft spot for him that I'd never admit, hence why I didn't strangle him for his behavior.

Pushing past him, I made my way up the stairs to my bedroom, where I could keep a close eye on the siren in my arms.

Putting Aurora under the covers of my bed was an uncomfortable feeling and I hated that it wasn't because she didn't belong, but because what should've been wrong felt *so* right.

I entered my bathroom, grabbing the first aid kit and a damp towel. There was a cut on Aurora's throat and if I hadn't already put a bullet through the fucker who was responsible, I would've tortured him to death.

No one was allowed to inflict pain on her but me.

When I settled onto the bed beside her, I moved swiftly, wiping dried blood off her face.

My body vibrated with restless energy. I couldn't *stand* to see her this way.

I clenched the towel tighter, my knuckles turning white. *For fuck's sake, what was I doing tending to her wound?*

Aurora stirred before jolting upright, scooting higher up on the bed away from me.

I put my hands up in surrender, if only to amuse her. "Relax, I'm taking care of your cut."

Her green eyes widened a fraction before narrowing. "Since when do *you* care for anyone?"

"Since now," I bellowed through clenched teeth. "Shut up and lay back."

She stared at me for a moment, and I could see her reluctance as she struggled to understand what *I* hadn't begun to understand.

Whatever willpower she held onto dissipated before her head settled onto the pillow. Her button nose scrunched up as she watched me, her gaze never leaving my face as I cleaned and bandaged her neck.

"All done." I gathered the supplies before standing.

I turned on my heel to leave but stopped when her soft hand clasped my calloused one, giving it a squeeze. "Thank you."

With pinched lips, I faced her and nodded. It was all I could afford to do. I had already made poor choices when it came to Aurora and the last thing I needed was to appear weak in front of the others.

When her hand didn't leave mine, my pulse skidded.

"Are you going to hurt me?" Her voice was small, a contrast to her usual boisterous self.

"Not tonight."

After a much-needed long shower to relieve some tension on my body, I re-entered the bedroom, where I found my wife asleep.

Crossing the room, I sat on the window seat and leaned forward with my elbows resting on my knees, watching her as I always did. And I *loathed* myself for it.

My hands shook at having her near me and not knowing what to do.

It would be relatively easy to end her life right now while she was unconscious and rid myself of her.

The past week had been hell.

I was conflicted as fuck. Something I rarely experienced and it was Aurora who elicited this phenomenon.

It shouldn't have bothered me as much as it had when she accused me of murdering Enzo and proceeded to leave without hearing what I had to say.

After all, she was a Bianchi, yet every step she took away from me left me questioning every morsel of lies I told myself regarding my feelings for her.

So, I let her go while watching her from a distance.

I stood and walked to the bed, looming over her.

Aurora's guard had fallen if she was sleeping in *my* bed when she knew danger was all around her.

She looked at ease, and I couldn't help myself as I caressed her soft cheek with my tainted fingers.

Her skin was warm, and I *itched* to touch more of her.

I wanted to scar her with my existence.

I grabbed the duvet and covered her with it before sitting back on the window seat.

I was in a predicament, one I didn't know how to get out of. "What do I do with you now, *anima mia*?"

I must have dozed off because the vibration against my thigh jarred me awake.

I patted my thigh, finding the source of the buzz before pulling my phone out. "What?"

Rubbing the tiredness from my eyes, I looked over at the bed. *Empty*.

"*Don*, your wife is outside demanding to leave."

I narrowed my eyes and stood. "Don't let her out. I'll handle it."

In no time, I was halfway across the lawn, finding Aurora shaking the gate as if it would magically open.

Thunder rumbled above us, the clouds darkening into shades of gray.

Grabbing her by the elbow, I pulled her to me. "What are you doing?" I yelled; my patience no longer existent.

She yanked herself free from my hold and stepped a few feet back. "What do you *think*? I'm getting away from you. I *hate* you for what you did to me. To my brother."

"And I hate you for what you did to me. To my

cousin," I spat out. Heat simmered deep within me, overriding the nighttime breeze. "For what you *continue* to do to me."

"You had intent," she snapped at me. "I didn't. There's a difference."

My gaze lingered on her, assessing any lies. "Is that so?"

Aurora narrowed her eyes at me. "Yes." Turning away, she muttered, "I could never do such a thing."

"Because you fear blood," I stated, knowing it to be true.

Her head snapped back up at me, eyes glossed over with weary. "How did you..."

A storm brewed within me, remembering her earlier appearance. "You passed out in my arms after you were covered in blood. I put two and two together."

Fear crossed her features as she shook her head, conjuring up anything to make me believe otherwise. "No, no. That wasn't why I passed—"

I cut off her lie. "Then it was your fear of me? Is that it?"

"I'm not *afraid* of you," she seethed.

My lips tipped up, knowing I had goaded her successfully. "Then don't lie to me. I hate liars."

"And I hate you!" she repeated, flustered.

"So, you keep saying," I drawled, driving her insane with my nonchalant demeanor.

"*I do.*"

The first drops of rain fell on us as we stared at each other. Her nose flared, my own anger mirroring hers as I tried not to act on impulse.

"Why did you come back then? If you were planning to leave anyway, why come back?"

She closed her eyes, took a deep breath, and looked skyward. "Did you kill Enzo?" she asked.

I could tell her the truth, but would she believe me?

Aurora gazed at me, squinting against the rain that suddenly picked up speed.

As lightning struck in the distance, I realized I *wanted* her trust. I *wanted* more of her. *All of her.*

She was mine and I didn't care if she hated me. I would take her anyway.

"I didn't and neither did my men."

Her hair was plastered against her distraught face and my chest pinched involuntarily seeing her in agony.

The rain pounded against the pavement, and I strained to hear her when she said, "I can't stay. My father believes you did it, which means the contract is void."

My heart picked up speed at what she confessed without saying it. *She believed me.*

Thunder boomed again, charging the tension in the air.

My need for Aurora at this moment blinded me from all morals and judgment. I was done thinking. "Come here."

Rain came down faster and harsher, cooling the heat radiating off me before the sound of thunder rumbled around us.

Aurora didn't budge from her spot, but the way her cheeks warmed in color, I knew she was losing this round.

I pushed back the tendrils of hair that had stuck to my

forehead. "Come here, baby," I soothed, even though I was a second away from grabbing her myself.

I was never one for endearments, but with Aurora they came naturally.

Her tongue ran along her bottom lip. "The contract. And—and I don't want to stay here."

Yes, the contract that she was using as an excuse to resist her urge, but I was in no mood for games tonight. "Did you think it would be so easy to leave me? You're *my* wife, Aurora. The contract is void when I say it is," I growled. "Come here. I won't ask you again." Indulging her, I took a step forward.

My heart skidded to a stop when she did the same, her eyes wide and taut.

She was breathtaking in the rain. Rain that could never dim that fire within her.

"I still hate you," she panted, taking another step toward me.

Holding back a grin, I bit the inside of my cheek. "I know."

"This doesn't change anything." *Another step.*

My body buzzed with desire at every step she took. *I was going to ruin her.*

When she stood in front of me, her chest grazing mine, she said, "You may have my body, but you'll *never* have my heart. You'd be wise to remember that, Roman Mancini."

Never, huh?

I wrapped my arm around her waist, pressing her wet body against mine before reaching up to push a lock of hair behind her ear. Piercing green eyes consumed me in all their beauty.

Her eyelids fluttered when I caressed her cheekbone with the tips of my fingers, making a path to the bridge of her nose and down to her plush lips.

I wanted to trace and memorize every inch of her.

Gripping her black curls, I pulled her up to me.

She gasped, struggling to reach my height, her breath skating across my mouth as she exhaled shakily.

My eyes drifted to her lips, flushed, and parted before I brushed my own against hers in a tender swipe, smiling against her. "I must warn you, *anima mia*, I'm not familiar with that word."

CHAPTER 21

AURORA

I needed him as much as he needed me—frantic and incessant.

The thread had snapped and there was no coming back from the inevitable.

Somewhere between the front gate and bedroom, our clothes disappeared with each touch.

The pace gave me no time to think or question what I was doing, but I didn't *want* to think—thinking led to other things... such as my morals.

I stumbled taking off my underwear, the act causing me to chuckle.

"For someone who hates me, you're *so* eager." Roman hummed in satisfaction.

Eager to choke him to death, sure.

I discarded the last article of clothing from my body and wrapped my legs and arms around him.

He held me by the backs of my thighs, his calloused

hands eliciting goosebumps along my skin. I grinned against his mouth. "Shut up."

Kissing Roman was like drinking water. No matter how long you go without it, it's the one thing you need to survive. But me? I wanted to *drown* in his kisses.

What was hidden in the dark, I felt between my legs, and it was thick and hard.

I rocked back and forth along his length, a pleasurable sensation building at the base of my spine with each grind against my hardening clit.

"*Fuck*," Roman hissed, pulling away with a groan, stilling my movements with a tight grip on my ass. "Keep doing that and this will be over sooner than I want."

My forehead rested against his, our breathing harsh, mingling in the air between us. "Then take over," I panted, taking his top lip between my teeth with a hard pull.

A screw must've been loose in my brain if I willingly gave Roman free rein over me, because he exuded dominance in every aspect of his life and he did it meticulously.

At this moment, I didn't care about any of it—who he was, why I was here, and what I felt. I wanted *all* of him.

His eyes locked on mine. "As you wish, baby."

If I wasn't nervous before, I was now.

What I hadn't mentioned to Roman was that I was a virgin. While Raphael and I had intimate experiences together, we had never had sex.

I didn't have time to stop my pulse from skyrocketing before Roman threw me on the bed.

With a huff, I leaned up on my elbows, ready to wrangle him. Instead, my mouth gaped open.

From my position on the bed, the moon lit up Roman in a dimmed spotlight. He was glorious, a sight to behold.

The shadows dancing on his tattooed skin emphasized his thick veiny arms and defined chest, down to his tight stomach where his large cock waited.

I swallowed the last bit of saliva left on my dry tongue. That might have fit partially in my mouth, but I didn't know how it would fit inside of me.

His knee landed on the edge of the bed before his fists settled on either side of me, caging me in.

I sank further into the mattress, my skin warming from his nearness.

He leaned down, flicking my top lip with his tongue. "On your knees, facing me."

His raspy voice vibrated through me, down to the pulse between my legs.

Roman stood, waiting for me to obey his order and so help me, I *did*.

I hated being told what to do, but I wasn't backing down from what *I* had given him permission to do.

My hands rested on my thighs. "Is this how you want me?" I asked, batting my lashes at him. I said he could take control, but I never said I'd make it easy for him.

His eyes darkened, hungry and feral, but if his clenched jaw was anything to go by, he was onto me. "You're toying with me."

I smiled, feigning innocence. "I don't know what you're talking about."

He stepped forward and ran a thumb over my bottom lip, causing my smile to fall. "When I fuck you hard enough to feel me for weeks, then you'll know what I'm talking about, yes?"

I knew Roman had a filthy mouth from our last rendezvous, yet I was stunned in place by his subtle threat.

The pounding of my heart reached my ears, the vibration exuding body tremors. I licked my lips, flicking his thumb in the process. "Is that a promise?"

A slow, wicked smile spread across his face, baring his teeth. "Tap my thigh if it gets too much."

When his meaning registered, a flush crept along my body, leaving a path of burning desire in its wake.

He lifted a brow, waiting for my consent, the gesture making me weak in the knees.

I nodded through my heightened nerves and blurred vision.

Roman's hand glided across my face and into my hair, grasping me at the scalp and tugging forward.

My hands landed on his hips at the abrupt movement, his cock mere inches from my face.

Pain pulsed from where strands of hair stretched and broke as his grip held firm.

"Open your mouth."

I gazed up at him through hooded eyes. "Are you always this domineering?"

His head tipped back, a low chuckle rumbling from his chest. When he looked down at me again, the heat of his stare was an inferno, ready to consume me.

"Only in the ways that matter," he drawled as his lips curved in a wicked grin. "Shall I demonstrate?"

Words caught in my throat when he seized the opportunity and slid his cock into my mouth, silencing me.

"Even better than the first time," he moaned, pushing in another inch.

I clenched my thighs together to relieve the maddening ache building there. *I'd never been this turned on in my life.*

My jaw tensed further as he pushed another inch, forcing me to widen my mouth.

This wasn't easier than the first time.

When the tip hit the back of my throat, I gagged, tears springing to my eyes from the sheer size of him.

"Suck, baby," he punctuated his words with a thrust, causing the tears to spill down my cheeks from the force.

I'm going to ruin him.

Keeping my eyes on him, I hollowed out my cheeks before pulling back and swirling my tongue around the head where pre-cum was dripping.

Despite how hard he was, the skin was as soft as silk.

I wrapped a hand around the rest of his length and licked the veiny muscle.

Roman was flushed. The wet sound of him in my mouth mixed with his satisfied grunts created an erotic symphony around the room.

I sucked the tip before flicking the sensitive head.

He broke our stare, head tipped back in pleasure. "Just like that," Roman whimpered, tightening his hold on my hair.

Seeing what I was doing to him had my arousal dripping down my thighs.

His approval was something I never thought I'd want, but here I was, taking him deeper into my mouth and twisting my hand around the base of his cock faster, feeling him thicken against my tongue.

I held power over him, making him lose himself in pleasure and control.

Unable to resist, I spread my knees wide and brought my other hand down between my slick folds.

I rubbed my clit slowly and firmly, moaning around Roman's length from the friction.

My eyes closed of their own accord, as I continued to chase my orgasm when he suddenly slipped out of my mouth with a loud pop.

I stared up at him in confusion.

Roman's face was slacked with lust, rooted desire, and passion. "You'll get off when my cock is deep inside your tight pussy. No sooner."

Beautiful bastard.

I scoffed, cleaning the side of my mouth with the back of my hand. "Is that so?"

Without waiting for his reply, I moved up the bed, resting against the headboard.

His chest moved in shallow breaths when I spread my legs wide, allowing him to see what he wanted most.

My teeth sank into my bottom lip from the sight of him watching me. He was incandescently beautiful, and it *hurt* to look at him sometimes.

I brought my hand to my neck, where I traced my fingers featherlight along my collarbone, down to the dip of my breasts before pinching and tugging a nipple between my thumb and forefinger.

A whimper escaped me, wishing it was his hand instead.

Moving further down my body, I cupped myself, grinding against the heel of my palm. "Is this what you want, *anima mia?*"

His eyes darkened further from the use of his nickname for me. I never understood why he called me that when we were constantly at each other's throats.

He crawled up the bed like a predator eyeing their prey, eating up the space between us.

Before reaching me, I stopped him with my foot against his chest, taunting him with words he'd said to me before. "You want it? You *beg* for it. Care to *demonstrate?*"

Roman gave me one of his earth-shattering smirks as he grabbed me by the ankle and yanked me down until I lay flat on the bed.

"Begging is for those who don't have. But *you're mine,* baby," he said roughly. "I have you right where I want you."

My heart thumped against my chest wildly, wanting him so badly I couldn't stand it.

He leaned down, peppering kisses along my inner thigh, never breaking eye contact.

I panted when he reached the crease of my thigh, blowing against my pulsing core.

His tongue glided against my slit, electric waves reverberating through my veins.

"I'm going to make you feel good, baby, and you'll take everything I give you, won't you? My fingers, my tongue, and my cock."

I clenched at his words, the rise and fall of my chest erratic. I felt like I was floating—and he hadn't even done anything yet.

Roman placed a single kiss at my core before bringing his tongue up and around my swollen clit, sucking it into his mouth, long and hard.

I arched off the bed, willing him to give me more. Anything. *Everything.*

His hand reached up and cupped my breast, squeezing and kneading my nipple.

When his tongue entered me, I couldn't contain the sounds that slipped out of my mouth.

I grasped his black hair with my hands as he took his time, swirling and gliding his tongue over my pussy like a starved man.

"I missed the taste of you. *Never* deprive me of this," he ordered, giving my clit a rough lick before grazing it with his teeth.

Staccato moans slipped free from my lips when he increased his pace and applied more pressure on the bundle of nerves.

Spots formed in my vision from how close I was to coming as he teased me to oblivion.

I unashamedly spread my legs wider, tugging his hair harder against me, causing Roman to hiss in response.

"Have you already forgotten my command? You're not coming until my cock fills and stretches your sweet cunt. Don't make me repeat myself."

The pulse between my legs increased in response to his words, wanting him to dull the ache.

He kissed my hipbone, and up my abdomen, each one wet with my arousal.

"*Roman,*" I pleaded. He was taking his time worshiping my body, leaving me lightheaded and feverish.

When his lips closed around my nipple and took the sensitive peak between his teeth, I yelped at the sharp pleasure before he soothed it with his tongue.

More kisses on my collarbone and throat before his face was above mine.

Something passed across his features, so tender and intimate, I closed my eyes from the force of his sentiment.

A single kiss was placed on one cheek and then the next, onto the tip of my nose and to the lids of both eyes.

My heart soared at his gentleness, and something cracked in my chest.

I opened my eyes to find him staring down at me, his presence overwhelming.

"You're irrevocably beautiful," he whispered, a crease forming between his brows, as though he was surprised by his own words. Words that seeped into me like molten lava, obliterating any notion that this was merely physical attraction.

I didn't like it.

I wrapped my legs around him, pulling him closer. "Fuck me with all your hate."

Roman searched my eyes, his alluring obsidian ones darkening, sensing what I was doing.

In the blink of an eye, his mask of Mafia *Don* slipped on again and *this* was what I needed.

Suddenly, I was turned over, hands gripping my hips and pulling me up on all fours.

"*Fuck,* these dimples." He emphasized by kissing each one on my lower back.

I panted when he ran the tip of his cock along my folds, teasing me.

This probably wasn't the best position to lose my virginity, but I was too prideful to say anything.

Without warning, Roman thrusted into me with such force that a shrill scream tore through my throat from the intrusion.

My head fell onto the pillow as my hands clenched the sheets to refrain myself from pushing him off, trying to ignore the burning sensation of being stretched.

"You're so tight," he groaned, buried in me to the hilt.

Tears slipped free from the corners of my eyes from the foreign feeling of him inside me. I took deep breaths that were shaky enough for Roman to notice the change in my body language because his hand squeezed my hip. "Aurora?"

I didn't answer him, waiting for the discomfort of being filled to subside.

When he pulled back an inch, I winced and knew he saw the evidence of his question.

"You're a virgin?" The surprise in his voice didn't mask the hint of concern in his tone.

Words failed me. All I could focus on was the roaring beat of my heart and the overwhelming ache between my legs.

Roman had stilled entirely, his own breathing sounding ragged from behind me. "Have you lost your *fucking* mind?" he snarled. "I *hurt* you."

Despite my silence, we stayed this way for a few minutes, knowing he was waiting for me to adjust to him until the burn subsided into a sliver of pleasure.

I wasn't vexed because he took one more piece of me.

His *exact* reaction was why I hadn't told him—he'd think I was incapable of handling pain, *weak.*

I eased forward an inch and thrust back against him, humming at the friction. "Do virgins scare you, or have you gone all sensitive on me?"

"Don't manipulate me right now." His anger was tangible.

I laughed mockingly, knowing I was goading him. "Sensitive, got it."

Provoking him was not smart of me, but I didn't like the vulnerable position I was in. I'd rather have the cruel and malicious Roman than the one who cared about my pain.

At least I knew what to expect from the first one.

"Don't say you didn't ask for it, baby."

He eased out, stopping at the tip before slamming into me harder this time, my body flattening out onto the bed.

Incoherent words spilled out of my mouth as I moaned, enjoying the mixture of pain and pleasure.

With his chest pressed to my back, he delivered each thrust viciously, fast, and hard.

My breasts rubbed against the bedsheet from his force, the sensation increasing my arousal.

Roman reached between my legs, his punishing pace causing his calloused fingers to rub my clit, building my climax.

Then his arm wrapped around my abdomen, pulling me up with him.

His hand circled my throat, turning my head to face him. Beads of sweat lined his forehead, face twisted in tension.

Leaning down, he kissed me with compelling ferocity. All I could focus on was my breathing as he sucked the oxygen from me, his hot tongue swirling around my own.

He broke the kiss with a tug on my bottom lip. "How does my hate feel?" he asked, each word emphasized with the savagery of his thrusts.

"It feels pathetic," I challenged him, whimpering when his free hand pinched my sensitive clit.

He stopped his harsh movements, sliding in and out of me at a torturously slow pace, depriving me of my need to come.

"How does it feel now?" He slid into me achingly slow this time, giving me every thick inch of him.

I bit my bottom lip, relishing at how perfectly he filled me, all while edging me toward my orgasm but unwilling to push me over.

"I *can't*," I gasped, riding back on his cock, needing more friction.

His hiss morphed into a curse when I clenched around him, knowing he needed to come as much as I did.

He pushed me forward, flipping me on my back, and entered me again so swiftly that I didn't feel the emptiness between my legs.

"Do you feel that, baby? How fucking needy your pussy is for my cock?"

He held both my hands above my head with one of his as the furious slaps of our bodies drowned out our sounds of pleasure.

"*Yes.*" I met each of his unhinged thrusts, my clit rubbing against his pelvis, numbing pleasure racing through me.

His lips closed around my nipple, teasing it with his tongue and teeth, causing me to buck my hips upward.

I squeezed my eyes shut, feeling the brink of my climax.

"Open your eyes, Aurora. I want to see what I do to you."

My eyes flew open at the same time my orgasm washed over me in blinding euphoria from his words.

"You drive me *crazy*," he panted, pushing back my hair from my face. "Give me one more."

I was a mess, hair sticking to my forehead with sweat, tears running down my face, worn out and quivering.

My legs shook violently, high off endorphins. I shook my head at him. *I didn't think I could come again.*

He planted his mouth on my neck, sucking, biting, and licking, leaving his mark on me.

When he wedged his hand between us and applied firm pressure on my swollen clit with his thumb, I cried out from the sensitivity.

I cursed, feeling another orgasm building as he rocked me harder into the bed.

When he shifted slightly, moving into me at a different angle, my eyes rolled to the back of my head, threatening to cross as he hit a certain spot repeatedly, and sent me over the edge.

I clenched around Roman so tightly that he grunted, pushing into me without restraint.

Wrapping his strong hand around my throat, his movements quickened. I felt him thicken inside of me.

"Fuck, Aurora, *fuck*," he cursed through clenched

teeth, his cock twitching as he gave one final thrust before his movements stilled, and he came inside of me.

I wrapped my arms around his neck, pulling him down on me. He molded into my skin as if it was his own.

Time passed as our breathing evened out and he slid out of me, causing me to bleat from the loss.

I laid there as he stood up without a word and walked into the bathroom.

The sound of running water drifted to me, and I suddenly was cold all over.

What did I expect him to do? We were far from being lovers.

When I pushed myself up in discomfort, he re-entered the room, holding a towel.

"Don't move." He leaned down, gently cleaning between my legs.

My eyes were locked on him the whole time, wondering why he thought he needed to do this.

"The bath is running; it should help with the soreness."

"You didn't have to do that," I whispered.

An indecipherable shadow flitted across his face. "I know," was all he said.

The crack in my chest widened, leaving room for Roman Mancini.

CHAPTER 22
AURORA

I woke up this morning, sated and in the arms of Roman.

My head lay on his warm, bare chest, holding him close as he snored lightly.

I didn't dare move. I didn't *want* to move because if I did, he'd wake up and I would be smacked back into reality.

Last night was surreal.

It made me question everything I thought I knew about him.

He wasn't the cause of Enzo's death, and I *believed* him when he said so. I knew it in my gut.

It didn't make sense for him to have jeopardized the contract, not when it included me.

Tilting my head up, I took in his snoozing form.

His face was smooth, free of worry—something I rarely saw while he was conscious.

I slid a finger down his chiseled jaw, his beard pricking it.

His face twitched and I immediately pulled my hand away, closing my eyes.

The urge to laugh was strong at my childish act of faking sleep, but it would've been mortifying if he found me staring at him like a creep.

When his breathing evened out, I peeked up at him and the boisterous laugh slipped out.

Roman was already staring down at me with a mischievous grin.

As my laugh died down, his grin slipped, replaced with a look of awe.

"You laughed."

A small smile adorned my face. "Yes. It's a reaction humans have when they find something humorous. You should try it sometime."

He shook his head. "You laughed because of *me*."

Then it dawned on me. I'd never laughed, let alone smiled out of joy during the time I'd been with him until now.

Heat peppered my cheeks.

His thumb caressed the apple of my cheek, where it undoubtedly bloomed with color.

"Do you always stare at people while they sleep?" he asked playfully.

That same heat traveled down my whole body from further embarrassment at his bluntness.

"Only ones as hideous as you."

"You let hideous men pound your tight little pussy?"

My eyes rounded at his crudeness. "Your mouth is filthy, Roman."

The air charged with tension, and I was still sore from last night, so I cleared my throat and sat up.

In one swift movement, he leaned up, grabbing me by the arms before laying me back on the bed.

"You love my mouth." He hovered above me, caressing my arm with a ghostlike touch, evoking goosebumps.

My heart thumped against my ribcage. "Who said anything about love?"

It was an overused word that people threw around thoughtlessly.

His only answer was a knowing grin and fingers that dug at my sides.

I threw my head back, laughing, attempting to swat his hands away from the ticklish assault.

This wasn't the Roman I knew. This was a completely different person, who was blurring the line of physical and emotional boundaries between us.

A sudden spark of panic washed over me. "*Stop.*"

And he did, staring down at me with a worried expression.

I needed to understand what was going on. Not only with him but with myself. I felt confused, but my heart had a mind of its own, beating because of *him*.

"Did I hurt you?"

My body continued buzzing under his fingertips where it touched my skin.

"Wh-what? No. I—" He was insufferable and I was frustrated. I groaned, holding the heel of my palm to my forehead. "We need to talk."

"We do," Roman agreed.

I froze and stared into obsidian eyes that mesmerized me. "We do?"

He smiled, head tilting to the side.

I was losing it, completely.

The silence was excruciating, and I didn't know how to start the inevitable conversation.

Roman and I had finished breakfast and now sat in the manor library.

It was beautiful, with large bay windows and bookshelves that adorned each wall with a ladder attached to reach the higher shelves.

I made a mental note to come here more often.

Despite the summer breeze easing through the windows, I was cold to the bone.

I sat facing Roman in a plush leather chair. His legs were sprawled out, his elbow leaning against the armrest with his fist beneath his chin.

"You're nervous," he pointed out, eyeing me skeptically.

My palms were clammy, sweat dripping down my back because I *was* nervous.

I jumped into bed with someone whom I wasn't sure I hated, and I had no idea where we stood from this point on.

Picking off invisible lint from my sweater, I inhaled deeply. "We shouldn't have done that last night."

Roman didn't miss a beat before answering. "Have sex? Isn't that normal between a married couple?"

My breath hitched at his words, unsure of why he wasn't the arrogant bastard I'd met months ago.

I glared at him. "I wouldn't use the word normal to describe whatever this is," I said, gesturing between us with my hands.

"Fair," he sighed. "How would you describe this then?" he asked, mimicking my movements.

"Dysfunctional?" I laughed humorlessly. "Don't play oblivious to our situation. Our families hate each other, and you *forced* me to be your wife."

I was way over my head and if my father knew I had doubts about my goals, he'd have my head.

Roman leaned forward, elbows resting on his knees, holding my gaze before speaking. "And you? Do you hate me?"

I pondered on his question, noticing he didn't deny anything I'd said but also didn't acknowledge it either.

The answer should've been yes, but the word refused to slip from my lips, lodged in my throat.

I didn't trust myself around him. Not when I couldn't understand the turmoil going on inside of me. I felt like I was being ripped apart, conflicted.

Somehow, with each conversation, Roman continued to learn more about me—like my fear of blood—and I didn't like it one bit.

"I hate you for what you did to me."

"I'm not sorry," he uttered. "If you're not satisfied with my answer, then you're free to leave, Aurora."

He was bluffing, I knew he was. But his nonchalance angered me.

A growl ripped through my throat as I got on my feet and went toward one of the bay windows, turning my back to him.

I didn't expect an apology from him, but a little remorse would have been appreciated.

Even so, I couldn't leave. Whether I wanted to or not, didn't matter.

I was here because I was stupid enough to make an alliance with my father. If I left empty-handed, I feared the consequences of my actions. Knowing my father, I wouldn't go unscathed.

Neither would Roman, and that terrified me more than I cared to admit.

I needed more time to figure out a permanent solution and *maybe* Roman could help me find answers to Enzo's death while I did.

Turning back to him with my arms crossed, I asked a question that petrified me to hear the answer to. "Is that what you want? For me to leave?"

CHAPTER 23
ROMAN

I was fucked. Thoroughly and utterly fucked.

Last night was my breaking point and I caved in.

Something was happening to me, and I didn't know how to cope with the loss of control. All I knew was I couldn't get rid of *her*.

The fact that Aurora believed me when I said I didn't kill her brother shifted our dynamic into something *more*.

Wide, green eyes stared at me, waiting for me to answer her question.

Did I want her to leave?

There was a raw ache in the pit of my stomach that I'd never experienced before.

She didn't kill my kin with malicious intent and that was new information for me to process. It only led me to believe her father really was the most vile man to roam the earth for putting her in a situation she had no fault in. Fault that more likely than, not was her father's.

There was a vulnerability to Aurora, and she thought I couldn't see past her sheltered barrier, but I did.

Last night hadn't felt real and I was waiting for the unfortunate moment I'd wake up to realize it never happened at all.

All I knew was *no*, I *didn't* want her to leave. But if I admitted that, I would be admitting that she held power over me.

"You can do whatever you want," I spoke with ease.

That only enraged her. Nose scrunched up; Aurora stepped closer. "That doesn't answer my question."

"I don't know what you want me to say," I said with an exasperated sigh.

My heart jackhammered against my chest from the possibility that she could walk out of here at any moment and I was too prideful to stop her despite my body screaming at me not to let her go.

"I want you to tell me the truth. Do you want me to leave, Roman?"

Fuming, I stood up and strode the few steps to her. "What do you want from me, Aurora?" I snarled. "*You* came here. *You!*"

Her face paled as she took a step back from the force of my harsh words.

We both knew she didn't have to come back.

We both knew she could've left after she had her answer regarding Enzo.

Yet she came and *stayed*.

"I don't know," she strained out, looking down at her feet.

"You don't know?" I scoffed, raking my hands through my hair in aggravation.

"No, I don't!" Her bottom lip trembled as she gaped at me with lonesome eyes.

It *hurt* to look at her. Every time I indulged myself and did, I felt these emotions invading my senses that were foreign to me. It completely threw me off guard.

Time stretched along with the potent tension, neither one of us speaking what was clearly obvious.

She didn't want to leave, and I didn't want her to either.

My phone rang, slicing through the air and I squeezed my eyes shut, reining in my temper before pulling it out and answering.

I kept my eyes glued on Aurora, who fidgeted with her nail between her teeth, deep in thought as I talked to Luca on the phone.

After hanging up, she stared at me with a weariness that made me clench my fists. All I wanted to do was wipe away anything that distressed her.

I couldn't deny it anymore. Not to myself. It was driving me insane knowing she meant more to me than I had led myself to believe.

If I allowed myself to let Aurora into my life, I knew it would be a grave decision, one that would have backlash and consequences.

The thing was though, I didn't care for any of it. Not until I needed to. All I cared about was *her*.

"I have to leave for a few days for work."

Luca informed me we needed to take care of an urgent

business matter out of town, and it was the most inconvenient interruption.

Aurora tucked a curled strand of hair behind her ear. "Oh, okay."

I should've walked out the door and left before I dug myself a deeper hole, but my feet were rooted in place.

It wasn't right to leave her this way, not after last night and not after this chaotic conversation.

Internal conflict tore at me, a silent battle of how to proceed.

Without contemplating further, my body moved before my mind could catch up, closing the distance between us and cupping her delicate face in my hand.

Her eyes widened, pupils dilating and almost drowning out the green in them.

Her soft skin against my fingers elicited a spark of energy that radiated through me like a shockwave.

"I don't understand what's happening between us. For the life of me, I can't conjure up an answer." I locked eyes with her, a warm cloak of fierceness radiating off me, trying to speak the unknown with my eyes. "I know I did wrong by you in the beginning and while I don't regret it, I'm giving you a choice here. Whatever you decide to do is in your hands." I stroked my thumb across her cheek. "But I know what I want, *anima mia*." *You.*

Before she had a chance to respond, I placed a kiss on her forehead, savoring the intimacy of it and walked away.

CHAPTER 24
AURORA

It had been a week and two days since I last saw Roman.

And I was still here, in his house.

My head pounded profusely from replaying our last conversation.

I don't understand what's happening between us.

I did wrong by you in the beginning.

I know what I want.

I couldn't fathom the mess that was my life and the tangle of webs that were my feelings. I felt things that I shouldn't have been, like missing Roman's presence.

The past week had gone by dreadfully. My father called me continuously, asking if I found any incriminating information or files regarding his assets and the answer was always no.

Not that I'd been searching anyway.

"Mrs. Mancini, what do you want for dinner?" Gianna

asked, walking into the library all bright and cheerful, interrupting my shambled thoughts.

We had become acquainted since Roman left, more so because I was alone and needed to focus on something other than the six-foot and six-inch man that occupied my mind.

I helped her around the manor even though she swatted my hands away whenever I went near the dishes or laundry.

Glancing up from my book, I smiled at her. "I wouldn't mind eating lasagna again."

She gave me a pointed look. "You've had that for three days in a row now."

"Yet I can't seem to get enough." I hummed in satisfaction, already tasting the savory dish in my mouth.

Her grin was nurturing and warm. "*Va bene.* I'll call you when it's ready."

I shut my book closed and stood up. "Can I help? I've been cooped up in this room all day." Batting my eyelashes dramatically, I pouted. "Please?"

"Only because you didn't clean the dishes this morning," she sighed.

My grin was wide as I strode to her, wrapping an arm around her frail shoulders as she led us out of the door. "I'll stop trying if you stop calling me Mrs. Mancini, as I've told you countless times."

Her only response was a playful grunt as she patted my hand.

It had been a month since my mamma's funeral, and I was a walking corpse. Unfeeling and soulless.

The house was quiet when I reached my parents' bedroom door and pushed it open, the action causing a slight creak to tear through the silence.

No one was home and it was the only time I had to rummage through my mamma's belongings and engrave every part of her into my memory.

I walked to her vanity and sat down, staring at my reflection in the mirror.

I didn't recognize myself, not when my eyes were sunken from sleep deprivation and my cheeks hollowed out from loss of appetite.

I guess that's what grief did to someone. It left them feeling foreign in their own skin.

Mamma's shawl sat on top of the dresser, and I reached for it.

The material was soft as I brought it to my face, closing my eyes and inhaling deeply.

Her scent was all over it, soothing me from the inside.

And then I opened my eyes, brought back to the reality of her being gone and that I'd never see, hear, or smell her again.

"Aurora!" My father's voice boomed through the house, forcing me onto my feet.

I put the shawl back in its original position before scurrying toward the door, but not before my father burst through.

I shook violently, fearing for myself and what punishment I'd receive today.

"I've told you countless times to stay out of this room!"

"I'm sorry, Papà," I croaked, stumbling over my words.

He reached for me, grabbing my left arm roughly with his large hand. "You will be."

"You're hurting me," I whined, feeling fresh tears stream down my face.

He dragged me out of the room and down the stairs.

I tried grasping onto the walls, furniture, anything to get away from him, but it was useless.

We reached the kitchen, where Enzo sat perched on a stool.

His face twisted in confusion and underlying anger.

Dread swarmed my stomach. What were we doing in here?

"Papà, please! I won't do it again," I begged him when he reached for the knife by the stovetop.

"Stop!" Enzo intervened, grabbing ahold of our father's shoulder.

I saw the panic flash in my brother's eyes, knowing he couldn't stop the inevitable.

He could never stop it.

"Oh, I know," my father sneered at me before grabbing my hand and slicing my palm open.

Blood gushed, out and I—

I jerked awake, my heart racing and my body slick with sweat.

Disoriented and paranoid, I frantically looked around the room.

There was no one there, only me and the black abyss.

Then the nausea hit me full force, bringing me to my feet.

I made it to the toilet two seconds before throwing up my dinner.

Hot tears rolled down my face, along with the sobs that racked through my body.

I wept. For Enzo. For myself and what would happen if I stayed with Roman.

I had tried blocking out my hurt because if I didn't acknowledge it, then it couldn't affect me.

Grief was a funny thing. Time didn't heal all wounds; it only made them easier to bear. But nothing was getting easier.

My body trembled, coiling tight with anxiety as my emotions suffocated me with an overwhelming force.

Dry heaving through the pain, all my thoughts swarmed in my mind, demanding attention.

What would happen if I gave into these indescribable feelings toward Roman?

Who murdered Enzo?

How far was my father willing to go for his revenge?

After making sure I wouldn't vomit again, I stood up and washed my mouth.

With shaky hands, I grabbed my phone and dialed the only number I knew by heart.

"Hello?"

"Irina." I sobbed anew, hearing a familiar voice, wishing she was here to comfort me more than anything.

"What's wrong, Aurora?"

"Everything *hurts*," I whimpered.

My heart felt as though it'd been scrubbed raw with sandpaper, and it was unbearable.

The sound of rummaging came down the line before Irina spoke again, "I'm taking the next flight out."

"*No!* Please don't do that. Just—" I inhaled deeply. "Just talk to me."

And she did. For the next hour, I bared myself to my best friend.

About Roman and every unfiltered thought I had—including how each one made me feel—before I dozed off to sleep.

CHAPTER 25
ROMAN

"If you wanted to talk to me, all you had to do was ask for my number, *piccola ribelle*," Luca said, a smirk playing across his lips.

I rolled my eyes, snatching my phone from his hand before bringing it up to my ear. "Who is this?"

"Your wife's one and only love."

Irina.

"How did you get my number?" I asked, rubbing my jaw in confusion. *Why was she calling me?*

"You're asking the wrong question," she huffed. "What you should be asking is *why*."

My body drained of blood, replaced by icy needles. "Is she hurt?" I demanded.

"No, not physically, at least," she sighed. "She'd have my head if she knew I called you, but she's not okay, Roman."

Gnawing pain tore through my chest. "I'm on my way home."

"At least you have a conscience unlike that heathen who answered your phone," she sneered.

I stifled a laugh. *I think I liked this girl.*

"Agreed. Thanks for the call."

"I know all about you, Roman Mancini, and if you hurt her in any way, I'll come for you. So don't thank me," she said before hanging up.

I definitely liked the girl.

I turned to Luca, who was as disheveled as me. "Can you take care of the rest? I need to head out."

"Sure thing. It's not like I need help hauling these dead assholes."

What was supposed to be a quick trip turned out to be longer than expected.

Apparently, disloyalty was circulating within my associates, and I had to scope out the damage and get rid of the culprit.

The last thing I needed was the feds breathing down my neck because people didn't know how to keep their mouths shut about my business.

"Luca, I trust you." I patted him on the shoulder as I walked past him. "Call me when it's done," I ordered, exiting the abandoned building.

The only thing on my mind was Aurora and how she hadn't left.

My lips curled into a smile. *She chose to stay.*

CHAPTER 26
AURORA

The calming smell of sandalwood and mint was the first to invade my senses as I awoke from a restless sleep.

Tearing my eyes open took more effort than I expected, but when I did, I was met with a beautiful face.

"*Anima mia*," he whispered those two words that made my insides melt like warm honey.

"You're here," I sighed in contentment, my heart somersaulting in my chest.

Midnight eyes searched mine, that same worrisome line etched between his brows. "I am."

I swallowed the dryness from my throat. "You took longer than a few days."

The back of his hand caressed the side of my face tenderly, his eyes trailing my face. "And I wish I hadn't." He blinked, hesitation peeking through his features. "You're still here."

The feelings from last night unfurled in the pit of my

stomach. "I'm going to be sick." I made a beeline for the bathroom.

I flushed the toilet when I sensed Roman enter the bathroom. His presence never went unnoticed, not by me.

"Please, go away," I pleaded, bile rising in my throat again.

From the corner of my eye, I saw him haunch down beside me. "In sickness and in health, remember?"

I turned and glared at him. "As if that meant *anything* to you when you said them."

"Shh," he coaxed, gathering my hair in his hands as I vomited once more. "I'm not arguing with you while you're like this."

"Then *leave*," I heaved, embarrassed that he was seeing me in this state of distress.

My heart and mind were at war.

My heart longed for Roman. I knew it the moment I opened my eyes this morning, staring at his cavernous ones. But my mind was logical, understanding the consequences of what would happen if I allowed myself to have this—to have him.

He was patient, rubbing circular motions across my back as I emptied the contents in my stomach until it was hollow.

"Why are you sick, Aurora?"

I leaned back against the tub, watching him through hooded eyes. I was completely out of it, my energy depleted.

I shook my head.

I couldn't exactly tell him that my body was fighting

against me because even *thinking* about my feelings for him sent me spiraling.

His gaze bore into every inch of my body with an intensity that startled me. "Are you pregnant?"

I waited for the aggression or hostility but found none in his magnificent ebony eyes.

"I'm on birth control," I strained out.

A clipped nod was all I received from him as he crossed his arms against his chest.

"Can you give me some privacy?" I asked without meeting his gaze. "I need to clean myself up."

The side of my face bore the heat of his stare before the sound of the door clicking shut echoed through the four walls.

Hurriedly, I hopped into the shower and lathered myself up with soap.

I was drained and didn't have any vigor to navigate the situation I found myself in.

My mind was a black hole, all-consuming yet nothing.

When I stepped out of the bathroom after freshening up, I didn't expect to find Roman sitting on my bed, elbows resting on his knees, staring down at the floor.

"You waited for me."

He looked up, still slouched and I hadn't noticed the dark rings around his eyes until now.

I know what I want.

His words replayed in my head, sending my heart skipping beats.

When Roman spoke, his voice came out rough. "What are we doing, baby?"

I stood still as a statue, unsure of how to answer him.

"Hm?" he urged on. "Tell me..." He stood, closing the distance between us in slow strides. "Why can't I get you out of my head?"

His words slammed into me with such force that I didn't know whether to cry or scream.

He appeared drawn as if it truly pained him to be near me.

I swallowed thickly, unsure of what to do with his confession.

If he was mad at me, then I was mad at him, for the exact same reason. He was the center of every thought I had, and I hated it.

I gathered my wits before answering him, "I don't know."

His laugh was a deep rumble, causing my entire body to vibrate from the sound before his hand shot out, wrapping around my neck, and pushing me against the wall, knocking the breath out of me.

Pain seared through my back from the assault, but I didn't say anything.

Pain numbed all else, a way to dull my thoughts and emotions.

"*You don't know,*" he mocked.

Our eyes locked in a silent battle.

Despite his aggression, I saw warmth in the depths of his eyes, a soft contrast to what he was.

I panted as his fingers dug into my skin, unwilling to squirm under his scrutiny.

"Then let me enlighten you," he rasped. "I don't only want you; I *crave* you."

My pulse picked up erratically, heightening my senses, and making me absorb his words intensely.

He couldn't want me. I was a pawn in his game. *He didn't want me.*

Tears threatened to slip free, burning the backs of my eyes. "You're lying."

Roman's thumb caressed the pulse point on my neck as he shook his head. "No, *anima mia.* You're the liar here and I hate liars."

A tear escaped from the corner of my eye and he leaned down, kissing it away, causing another to slip free from his affection.

That familiar wrinkle between his brows appeared in worry.

I couldn't keep up with him.

One second, he had my throat in a death grip and the next, he kissed my tears away.

When I stayed silent, he slapped the wall beside my head, making me jump and mold into the surface. "*Fuck you,* Aurora."

"I can't do this," I admitted, choking on the next word, my heart breaking. "*Us.*"

CHAPTER 27
ROMAN

Aurora's eyes were a window to her soul, and I would sit behind that sill till she succumbed to the truth.

"Pathetic statement. Try again," I whispered, coaxing her to admit what I saw clearly in her emerald-doe eyes. "Tell me what I already know."

Her tear-stricken face reddened in color, bringing on a furious scowl. "*I hate you.*"

Words I'd already heard before, each time sounding less convincing than the last.

Holding her gaze, I wanted her to understand neither of us were leaving this room until she spoke the truth. "Humor me."

A silent cry tore from her throat as a mixture of emotions flashed sporadically across her slowly blanching face. "I'm feeling sick again."

I tilted my head to one side. "And why do you think that is?"

I grasped her hair and with a calm voice, I confirmed what we both knew, "You *want* me and it's eating you alive."

Immediately, her head shook in denial. "And if I say I don't?" she asked, voice shaking from the lie.

Her breath hitched when I leaned forward, my lips hovering above her ear. "Then I'd say your mouth is deceitful."

"You've etched yourself into every crevice of my mind, body, and soul. I have no intention of removing you, *anima mia.*"

Green eyes widened in shock and trepidation. "You have to let me go," she whispered.

Her words slammed into me.

"What did you say?" Uncertainty crawled up my spine. "Do you think I don't see right *through* you?"

Her answer was immediate. "This won't end well for either of us," she snapped.

I could feel the stifling heat of my anger radiating between us. "I told you once that leaving me wouldn't be so easy, Aurora. That's not in the cards for you." *Not since she decided to stay.*

"And I told you once to stop commanding me." She grabbed me by the jaw, bringing my face close to hers. "You have a target on your back, Roman Mancini, and this one isn't from me."

She let go, the fire in her eyes burning brightly.

You have a target on your back.

"And how would you know that?" I sneered.

Who? What did she mean? I replayed our last few conversations, picking up any related hints.

My father believes you did it.

Clarity dawned on me.

Aurora's father believed that I executed Enzo's murder. Of course, he was out for his son's revenge, which meant Aurora...

"Is that why you're here?" I wrenched her hair back, wanting to see what lie she'd spew this time. "To spy on me?"

How could I have let my guard down so easily? Over a girl who I wasn't even supposed to be fond of in the first place.

"From what you've told me, it wasn't hard to guess that you have daddy issues. My only question is, why help him? Why protect him?"

Aurora might've killed my cousin, but she didn't do it on her own, not with that fear of hers.

I was certain her father had ordered the murder of my cousin if he confessed to his daughter's crime all those years ago.

It made me wonder why he hated her to that extreme, knowing she'd have a target on her back.

Aurora bared her teeth at me. "Screw you."

A humorless chuckle escaped me. "You already have."

The murderous rage inside of me grew tenfold when she shoved me. "You say that you can see right through me, but you *can't*," she yelled, nostrils flaring. "I'm not protecting *him*, you bastard."

None of it made sense.

"Then tell me!" I released her, raking my hands through my hair. "What am I not seeing?"

She appeared worn out, her fight diminishing along

with the light in her eyes as she leaned her head against the wall, watching me with a stillness that arose goosebumps along my flesh.

No. I couldn't believe it.

The air rose ten degrees, thawing my chilled heart. "You're protecting me?" I asked incredulously.

She nodded lightly and I almost missed the gesture, but I saw the moment her shielded wall crumbled, eyes gleaming with resolve.

All the blood in my body rushed toward my heart, increasing in pace.

When she took a step forward, her gaze leisurely swept across my face, lingering on my mouth for a beat longer.

A moment's hesitation before she grasped me by the collar, pulled me down, and captured my lips in a fervent kiss.

Teeth clashed and tongues glided, all while an everlasting fire burned deep inside my tainted soul.

My hands wrapped around her waist, bringing her flush against me, terrified that at any moment she'd disappear.

Aurora broke the kiss with a nip at my bottom lip, cheeks flushed. "Take off your pants," she uttered while taking off her own pajama bottoms.

My cock stood to attention when I followed her order.

Hooking my hands beneath her thighs, I lifted her up, and wrapped her legs around my waist.

I pushed her against the wall, lining myself up with her cunt, *needing* to feed into this new sense of urgency to be inside her.

When her eyes locked on mine, I slowly eased in, causing us to moan in unison.

Inch by inch, I deliberately took my time savoring this moment.

"You were made for me," I breathed, relishing the way she squeezed around me.

This was different. I couldn't explain the fullness I felt in my chest, but it was there, intense and potent.

"I need more," Aurora gasped, digging her nails into my shoulder blades.

I gripped her hair, exposing the column of her neck and planting wet kisses there as I picked up speed, pumping into her relentlessly.

"Tell me what I already knew," I repeated, sucking on the skin between her shoulder and neck.

The sounds of her pleasure ricocheted off the walls and straight to my thickening cock. "I want you."

"*Fuck.* Say it again," I groaned, knowing I could come from those three words alone.

Aurora gripped my hair, pulling me in for an ardent kiss. "I want you, Roman Mancini."

I never knew how desperate I was for someone to want me until I met this hypnotizing siren.

"Good, because I was never letting you go." I wedged my hand in between us, applying firm pressure on her clit with the pad of my thumb, stroking her in slow circles.

With one hand gripping her hip, I thrust into her, each one hard with promise.

She moaned, circling her arms around my neck for support.

The harsh sounds of our breathing grew as did the savagery of our touches.

"*Yes,*" she cried as her pussy clenched around me tightly.

"Are you going to come for me, baby?"

Her mouth grew slack, her eyes rolling back as waves of pleasure washed over her trembling body.

That look was all it took for me to come undone.

My cock twitched and with one final thrust, I bit into the crevice of Aurora's neck as I came, marking her mine, forever.

CHAPTER 28

ROMAN

"You know I was surprised when you called for this meeting," Uncle Stefano pointed out.

"It's an urgent matter."

He leaned back in his chair, the leather groaning under his weight, waiting for me to continue.

I didn't know how favorable this meeting would end, but I couldn't ignore that my uncle had a vendetta against my wife. He had to know where I stood, even if that displeased him.

"I'm excluding Aurora from this scheme. No harm will come to her, physically or otherwise."

He hummed with a continuous nod of his head. "Are you finally admitting to me that you've fallen in love with the girl?"

I wish I'd heard him wrong, but the silence in the room was eerily still as my uncle stared at me with unsettling ease.

"I'm not in love with her," I retorted, the sentence not sounding quite right to my own ears.

"Yet your eyes tell a different story, Roman."

My eyes?

I glared at him, unwilling to give him an extreme reaction to his comment.

"You want to exclude the person who pulled the trigger on my son?" he scoffed bitterly. "No, I don't think so."

"She had no choice," I bellowed, rage simmering beneath my skin.

He pinned me with a hard stare. "Did she tell you that herself?"

"She didn't have to." I'd never tell him about Aurora's fear of blood, not because I didn't trust my uncle, but because that was a vulnerability of hers. If she had kept it from me, I knew she wouldn't want others to know. "It was her father's doing, I'm sure of it."

"Even if that's true, it doesn't excuse the fact that Aurora Bianchi held that gun to my son's head."

My jaw ached from grinding my teeth. "I loved Milo as if he was my own brother. Do you think I won't inflict pain on the person who executed his death?"

His view on the situation was understandable and I sympathized with him, but this was nonnegotiable.

"You raised me after I lost my parents and I'll forever be grateful for you, but don't make me choose."

"Why? Because you'll choose her?"

Yes.

Taking a sip of the amber liquid in my hand, I let him answer his own question.

"I see," he said with furrowed brows before a hint of a smile adorned his face. "You're as stubborn as your *papà*."

A warm sense of nostalgia seeped into my chest at the mention of my father.

Uncle Stefano stood from his chair, buttoning his suit jacket. "I love you, Roman, but I make no promises." He walked toward my office door, his hand circling the knob, but before turning it, he glanced back at me with uncertainty. "I hope you know what you're doing."

The door clicked shut, leaving me alone with my thoughts.

Thoughts that should've centered around whether my uncle was going to go against my command. Instead, they centered around someone who never left my mind. Green eyes and long black hair.

You've fallen in love with the girl.

I could deny it all I wanted, but the way my blood pumped faster around her, the way my eyes searched for her in every room, the way I longed for her presence when she wasn't near proved otherwise.

I was in love with Aurora Bianchi.

CHAPTER 29
AURORA

I didn't know why I decided to do this.

I mean, it wouldn't be the first time I cooked breakfast, but the knowledge that Roman would be eating something I made had me questioning my abilities.

"It's not too late for Gianna to make breakfast, you know."

I turned my attention away from the turkey bacon cooking on the pan and stared at Roman with narrowed eyes. "It's not too late to put on a shirt either," I mocked, sizing him up with my spatula.

His laugh raked along my skin in a rough caress, making me hyperaware of his naked torso. No one should be *that* attractive.

He tilted his head in feigned innocence. "I don't think so."

I chuckled at his arrogance, turning back to flip the bacon when strong arms wrapped around my waist. "I enjoy watching your cheeks turn pink every time I catch you gawking at me."

My knees threatened to buckle against his hold when his soft lips landed on the apple of my cheek, giving it a peck.

"I don't *gawk*." *I so was.*

He nuzzled the crook of my neck, inhaling deeply. "It'd be okay if you did. After all, I unashamedly do it to you."

I cleared my throat. "Can you, uh, set up the table?" If he continued touching me, I'd eat *him* for breakfast.

He squeezed my hip before moving toward the cabinet to our right, grabbing plates.

"Might want to explain the meaning behind each tattoo while you're at it."

"They're all meaningless," he answered, opening the fridge, and pulling out cranberry juice.

I opened the oven, took out the frittata, and set it on the island between the pancakes and fruit medley.

"You're telling me, you inked yourself from head to toe and none of it has any significance?" I asked, surprised by his answer.

Roman sat on a stool, grinning at me with an arched brow. "Head to toe?"

"You know what I mean," I huffed, taking a seat next to him.

Before I had a chance to reach for anything, he began gathering a bit of everything onto my plate.

Immediately, I grabbed his forearm to stop him. "You don't have to do that."

"I know," he affirmed before piling food onto his own

plate. "Thank you for breakfast, *anima mia.*"

Butterflies took flight, fluttering in my stomach from his words. "You're welcome."

After Roman coaxed me into admitting my feelings for him a few days ago, I couldn't help but hate myself for it.

I needed to talk to my father and convince him Roman wasn't behind Enzo's murder. But even I knew it would be useless, or I would have done it already. With the loss of his son, my father finally had a motive to go against Roman and I knew he would do everything in his power to take him down.

And now that Roman knew my father had a vendetta against him, I knew I couldn't stop the inevitable blood-bath waiting to happen.

I took a bite out of the frittata and despite my sudden loss of appetite, it was delicious.

He cleared his throat, earning my attention. "Can I ask you something?"

My heart thudded. "Sure."

"What happened that day?" His voice was low, cautious. "I need you to tell me."

I swallowed against the bile threatening to rise. I knew what day he was referring to. It was the same day I'd tried to forget for ten years.

"What do you want to know?"

He turned to face me. "Everything."

I exhaled shakily, not knowing where to start but doing so anyway. "Losing a parent at a young age is never easy. I thought after losing my mother, my father would pick up the pieces of my broken heart and mend it, but he didn't. Instead, he let it rot into nothing."

Tears welled in my eyes, but I swallowed the strain in my throat, needing to continue for my own sake.

I needed to revisit the past that haunted me.

"You see, I was holding onto something that was never there." The sting of my tears warmed my face as I recalled the memory. "That day, my father had asked me to go to the stables with him and I thought, wow, he's finally trying to spend time with his only daughter."

I sniffled, biting back a smile. "I've always loved horse-back riding." Though, it'd been years since I last rode.

Roman watched me with a hard expression, the irises of his eyes deepening into a darker shade of obsidian. He stayed silent, allowing me to tell the story at my own pace.

"I should've known better, but the little girl in me held onto that sliver of hope." My palms grew clammy from nerves. "You need to get rid of that stupid fear of yours, he'd said, as if he wasn't the reason I had it in the first place."

He grabbed my arm, bringing my attention back to him. I hadn't even noticed I zoned out. "What do you mean?"

I blinked, realizing I'd never told anyone about how my fear of blood started, not even Irina.

"It happened after my mother passed away. I think he despised me because I resembled her so heavily." I clenched my fists, feeling my rage come off me in waves. "When he would punish me unjustly, he'd make me bleed."

Dismay flickered in his gaze before it clouded with something sinister. "You do understand that your father will die, yes?"

His tone of voice snaked down my bones, deadly and promising.

I didn't answer him. Instead, I continued unraveling the events from that day.

"It was *horrible*." My voice cracked on the last word. "I tried to stop it from happening, but my father threatened me with the life of a loved one if I didn't..." I pinched my lips together to stop the sob from tearing through. "Kill him," I whispered, looking at Roman with regret. "And when I disappointed him by retching right after, I ran."

"Right into my arms."

I nodded. "I didn't know who you were or who *he* was to you, but then I stood there, watching as my own father outed me for something he'd forced me to do."

The urge to touch him at this moment was powerful. I lifted my hand, cupping his cheek. "I'm so sorry, Roman."

I didn't expect him to forgive me, but I hoped he understood the position I had been in.

His only response was a kiss to the palm of my hand. "I want to take you somewhere."

I laughed in shock at his sudden change of topic, wiping away the tears that clung to my cheeks. "What? Like a date?"

"If that's what you want it to be then yes, a date."

The seriousness of his expression made me falter.

Going on a date with Roman was so out of the ordinary, yet I couldn't help but savor it. "Okay. A date."

"Meet me in the foyer in thirty. Wear something casual."

"Was the blindfold necessary?"

"Might as well get used to it," Roman chuckled with dark amusement.

"I see you're back to being crude."

"I never stopped." He kissed the back of my head while guiding me with firm hands on my waist.

We stopped walking after two minutes, a familiar smell wafting through the air.

"Take it off."

Excitement buzzed to the surface of my skin as I peeled off the blindfold.

I stared in awe at the massive green field before me with a stable smacked dab in the center of it. "This is yours?"

"It's *ours*. Come on." He grabbed my hand, pulling me along.

As we neared, I could hear the neighing of horses coming from inside. "Are we riding?" I squealed.

He shot me a sideways glance with a huge smile adorning his face, showcasing his perfect teeth. "When you said you loved horseback riding, I had one of my men drop these off." I didn't realize his free hand was behind his back until he pulled out a pair of black riding boots.

My chest caved in, my throat constricting from emotion. "I haven't done this in years."

"In that case, you're definitely wearing a helmet."

I laughed, rolling my eyes at his concern.

"*Ciao, Don*"

Roman turned and I peered behind him where a lanky man stood. "Charlie." He nodded. "How's the family?"

"You know how it is. Are you riding today?"

"I am." Roman moved to the side, putting me in Charlie's view. "With my wife, Aurora."

My wife. I'd nerve get used to that.

"*Signora*," he greeted me shyly.

I smiled. "*Piacere*, Charlie."

"Bring out Knight and Winter," Roman instructed, nodding his head toward Charlie.

Then he grabbed my hand, walking us toward the side. "Sit." He pointed at the haystack.

I sat, confused as to what he was doing, but then he got on his knees, grabbed my ankle, and slipped off my sneaker.

"And they say chivalry is dead."

Roman took off my other shoe. "Yes, getting on my knees for you is quite chivalrous of me," he drawled, voice dripping in sin.

I was burning up and it had nothing to do with the summer heat.

He slipped on one boot before zipping it up.

"So, Knight and Winter? Are those names meaningless like your tattoos?"

He slipped on the last boot, zipping it up before gazing up at me. "No."

I stared at the intensity of his midnight eyes, completely enthralled before something moved from the corner of my eyes, catching my attention.

"Wow." I stood, moving toward the enchanting white horse.

"Winter is her name," Charlie informed me, handing me the strap before disappearing inside the stables again.

"Aren't you precious," I crooned, caressing the long

strands of mesmerizing white hair.

Charlie reappeared, holding onto a stunning black horse that neighed loudly.

Suddenly, the names made sense now.

"I've saddled them up already, as you can see," he laughed, handing Roman a helmet.

I scoffed, frowning at Roman. "You were serious?"

He walked toward me, setting the helmet atop my head, fastening, and clasping it at the bottom. "Deadly."

"Okay, you wear one too then." I crossed my arms at his blank stare. "I'm serious. If you make me a widow at this age, I'll find you in the afterlife and wreak havoc on you."

Roman's laugh was throaty, a sound I wanted to hear repeatedly. "Oh, I hope so." Without breaking eye contact, he called out for Charlie. "Bring an extra helmet. The bane of my existence demands I wear one."

"The words that come out of your mouth," I gasped sarcastically, feathering the back of my hand against my brow. "I'm swooning."

"Bane of your existence she may be, but she's rather lovely if you ask me," Charlie interjected, handing Roman the helmet.

I smirked at Roman's murderous glare toward Charlie, who hurried away from his scrutiny.

"At least *he* thinks I'm lovely," I muttered, turning back to Winter, who leaned into my touch.

Warm hands grabbed my waist, the touch searing through my clothes. "*I* think a lot of things about you," Roman whispered in my ear, biting the lobe. My eyes fluttered shut as I leaned into his chest. "Right now, I'm thinking..." His hand moved south, where he cupped me through my jeans. "How I can dissuade you from this date so you can ride me instead."

I bit back a moan, wanting to grind my pulsing clit against his hand.

Without warning, he lifted me, forcing me to swing my leg until I sat securely on the saddle. "On second thought, I love the way your eyes light up too much in this moment."

My mouth gaped open as he strode toward Knight and lifted himself gracefully on the horse before putting on his helmet.

He winked at me, jerking his head to the side, signaling for me to go.

Beautiful bastard.

I grasped the reins, tapping Winter gently on her side with the heel of my shoe to get her moving.

The sun beamed on my face along with the slight breeze skating across my skin, creating the perfect moment.

I pulled on the reins, signaling to the precious horse to pick up speed. There was a vast field before me, and I'd use it to my advantage.

Leaning forward, I savored the adrenaline coursing through my veins from the thrill.

Roman caught up fast, calling out to me. "Take it easy, beautiful!"

Giggling at his command, I pulled on the reins a few more times, riding through the greenery and loving every moment of it.

I glanced sideways, amused by his struggle to keep up

with me. "You're not fast enough!"

He smirked, eyes ablaze with challenge. "I'll have to rectify that when we get home."

The adrenaline erupted into a fiery buzz, pumping in my bloodstream. "You'll have to catch me first."

I pulled the left side of the reins, heading toward the lake.

The wind whipped across my face; the feeling of freedom was so foreign that I forgot what it felt like.

Tilting my head back, I laughed aloud. *This* was freedom. *This* was the reality I yearned for.

Roman caught up to me when I hopped off Winter.

I waited for him with my hands on my hips, grinning because I outran him.

"I hadn't done that in a while," he grumbled, grabbing the back of his neck.

"Mhm, neither have I."

He reached for my hand and pulled me to him. "Are you teasing me, *anima mia?*"

Splaying my hands across his broad chest, I felt the heat of his body radiate through my palms. "Maybe."

His eyes narrowed in on me, gleaming with amusement before his fingers dug into my sides, tickling the sensitive flesh.

I laughed, trying to swat his hands away, but it was useless. I fell to the ground, flat on my back as I cried for mercy.

When Roman stopped torturing me with his fingers, I relaxed, catching my breath. "I'll refrain from calling you profanities because today was perfect, so I'll thank you instead."

He stared at me intensely, with a vivid emotion that could have made me burst into flames.

Before I could decipher it, he lowered his head, capturing my lips in a long and deliberate pull.

Instantly, I wrapped my arms around his neck, pulling him down on me. I melted against him, savoring the taste of his mouth against mine.

This kiss was different. It was overwhelming in the best way possible, the feel of him sending my brain to short circuit from drug-induced pleasure.

When he pulled back, I saw that same emotion reflected in his features and this time, it was clear, glowing in his black eyes.

He opened his mouth, but before he could utter the first word, I cut him off, "Don't say it."

He inched back. "Why?"

I swallowed against the tightness in my throat, finding the courage to say what I needed to. "Because I don't think I'll be able to say it back."

His gaze traveled the length of my face, hand caressing the strands of my hair before leaning down and locking eyes with me. "I'm desperately in love with you," he proclaimed with a pained smile.

Hearing him say it aloud was different, rendering me speechless.

Those six words seeped into me, becoming a part of me. "You love me?" I asked in wonder.

"Infinitely," he murmured. "And if all you ever did was hate me, I'd die a happy man knowing you felt *something* for me."

CHAPTER 30
AURORA

And then, I was sucked back into my reality.

"Either you come willingly, or I will send Pip to get you."

"*No*," I rushed out, my heart skipping a beat. "We both know you sending someone over here would end badly."

"I know," my father said indifferently. "Figure out a way to come to the house. We have much to discuss."

I hung up the phone and turned off the faucet that had been running to drown out my voice.

Roman didn't know I was on the phone with my father, and I wouldn't tell him either.

It had been weeks since he confessed his love to me and while I hadn't said it back to him, I had these strong emotions for him that I wasn't ready to name.

A part of me feared that if I did and something terrible happened, I would be left with irreversible pain.

A knock came through the door, startling me in place.

"Aurora, I'm leaving soon."

Taking a deep breath, I looked into the mirror once more. *It would be one white lie.*

Opening the door, I found Roman shirtless, wearing those gray sweatpants that drove me insane, with his hands resting above the doorframe.

Crossing my arms, I avoided the bottom half of his body and how low his sweats sat on his hips. "When will you be home?"

A smirk played on his lips as he tilted his head. "Why? Are you going to miss me?"

I scoffed, rolling my eyes. "Someone needs to humble you and fast."

In an instant, he reached out and pulled me to him, my chest crashing into his. He leaned down, nipping my top lip playfully. "Can that someone be you? I would be most humble for you, baby."

Roman had been the source of all my smiles recently and it was a fact that I would've thought absurd months ago.

Wrapping my arms around his neck, I pulled him in closer. "Is that so?"

He hummed, staring at my mouth. "'Tis so."

I giggled, pressing my lips once against his, savoring the taste of him.

Pulling back, I cleared my throat. "Actually, I also need to go out today."

He raised his brows. "Oh?"

"The cemetery." Unwrapping my arms from his neck, I fidgeted on my feet, hoping he wouldn't sense my lie. "I haven't visited my mother's grave yet or Enzo's," I said weakly.

"I'll come with you."

"*No!* I mean," I inhaled sharply. "I don't want to keep you."

Uncertainty creased his brows. "I'll tell Ricardo to take you."

Shaking my head, I took a step back. "I want to go alone."

Indecision was clear in his eyes, and I knew I needed to play my cards right to get what I wanted, even if it hurt him.

"Unless you still consider me as an object and not a person."

His jaw clenched tightly, the muscle protruding and I knew I had won this round.

"I'll text you when I'm back home." I forced a smile. "I need to do this on my own, okay?"

He stared at me with narrowed eyes as if he wanted to refuse me, but then he nodded his head and sighed. "Okay."

Giving him a swift kiss on the cheek, I grabbed my wallet from the dresser and left the room.

Taking one of Roman's cars wasn't ideal because he could easily track me. If I was being honest, he could have someone follow me without my knowledge, but I knew he wanted to build our trust.

It made my stomach coil tightly. I wanted the same thing, yet here I was, tearing down the foundation.

Once again, I stood in front of the black wooden door—my father's office.

Except this time, there were soft voices seeping through it.

Like before, I knocked once before entering.

I made it past the threshold when I stopped in my tracks, staring at my father and the man occupying the seat in front of him.

"Raphael?"

"Hello, Aurora."

Blinking a few times to rid the image of my ex-boyfriend, I asked, "What are you doing here?"

"Sit and find out."

The command was from my father and for a split second, I had forgotten he was here.

If Raphael and my father were in the same room, I knew something terrible was awaiting.

My body drew taut, urging me to turn away and run, but my feet were rooted in place.

Instead, I closed the door behind me and walked further into the office.

I peered at my father while sensing Raphael's eyes trail over me, making me squirm from his attention.

"What did you want to discuss?" I stole a glance at Raphael before staring at my father again. "I thought this was a private matter."

"It is." He took a sip of the clear liquid sloshing in his glass. "One that includes Raphael Mancini."

A sudden weakness settled over my limbs, forcing me to sit on the chair beside Roman's brother. "What do you mean?"

"It's quite convenient actually." He shrugged. "Raphael has decided to give a helping hand and offer his *assistance*."

"Assistance?" My brows furrowed in confusion before a cold hand touched my forearm, pulling my gaze to him.

I clenched my hands into fists, wanting to shrug off Raphael's touch, but refrained from doing so until I knew the reason for his presence.

"It'll all be over soon."

The crazed look in Raphael's eyes was something I hadn't noticed before, but up close, I could see the manic sparkling in his dilated pupils.

Swallowing against the rising bile, I slowly pulled my arm away from his touch. "What does that mean?"

A wide smile spread across his face, sly and wolfish.

"Assistance as in he has offered his men to work for me until things smooth over."

My head snapped to my father's voice, not understanding a single thing spiraling inside this room. "*His men?*" I shook my head. "*Smooth over?* What exactly are you talking about?"

He huffed, impatience evident on his wrinkled forehead. "Raphael informed me of the history between you two."

"And you don't have to worry about being married to my brother any longer," Raphael cut in.

The thunderous beat of my heart threatened to leap out of my chest.

"It's clear that you haven't been successful with our original plan. Therefore, we're changing it."

Changing it.

My mind raced with excuses to spit out, knowing whatever his second plan was, it would be worse.

"I need more time," I lied.

My father's hands slammed on the desk, his focus sharpening in on me. "I don't *have* more time."

I stared at him cautiously as he cleared his throat and loosened his shirt collar.

"Now that I have a crew to stand by me against Roman, I need you to do something."

Swallowing the dryness in my throat, I found my voice to utter one word. "What?"

"Get him alone and I'll take care of the rest."

Even the most soulless man learns how to love.

Earn his trust.

"He doesn't trust me yet."

My father lifted his chin. "You cruising around town with him the past few weeks has proved otherwise."

Roman had been insistent on making up for lost time and while I knew it would be a bad idea for this exact reason, I hadn't been able to reject him.

"Do this one thing and you can be free from him, Aurora." Raphael leaned in, forcing me to stare at his roguish expression. He was plotting his brother's death as if it was normal. "Then we can be together."

The taste of blood burst on my tongue from biting the inside of my cheek too hard.

This was Raphael's motive. He didn't care to help my father. He only wanted to have *me*.

The need to prove to my father that my husband was innocent gnawed at me. I couldn't allow him to 'take care of the rest' when I knew it meant death.

"He didn't kill Enzo," I fired back. "I can't prove it, but he had no reason to do so. He wouldn't jeopardize the contract, not when I was on the line."

Surprise flickered in my father's gaze. "You're defending our enemy?"

"*Your* enemy!"

The displeasure I felt on the inside must have shown on the outside because my father chuckled, wiping a hand down his face.

"Oh, *cara*." His smile was ominous. "You've fallen in love with him."

My father had the resources now to hurt Roman and whether I agreed to his plan or not didn't matter, he would move forward with it anyway.

Maybe that was why I hadn't cared if I wore my heart on my sleeve, finally putting a name to these emotions thickening inside my chest. *Love.*

"I have never asked you for anything. If you ever loved me at all, you won't hurt him." The desperation in my tone was horrid, but I couldn't lose Roman. "Please, *Papà*."

The silence dragged on and I could feel the daggers shot my way by Raphael, who hadn't uttered another word since my father last spoke.

"As you wish."

Though relief washed over me, easing my tension a sliver, my father was never one to negotiate.

"But I still want him alone. He needs to sign over everything that belongs to me."

"Let me talk to him," I argued. "He might listen."

"If I use you as leverage to lure him here, I don't trust that he won't bring backup." He clicked his tongue, shaking his head. "No. We're doing this my way. You trust me and I trust you. That's how this works."

But I didn't trust him, not even a fraction of the word.

In fact, once I left this office, I would tell Roman about what my father was up to.

"If you risk my plan by not doing what I told you." The determined gleam in my father's eyes was vicious. "Well, you know how vile I can get."

A shiver slid down my spine, knowing what he was capable of.

Standing from my seat, I stepped toward the door but stopped short when my father spoke again. "I will send you the details of when and where to meet me."

CHAPTER 31
ROMAN

A weight had lifted from my shoulders when I told Aurora I loved her, but it settled deep into my heart knowing, she didn't feel the same.

No matter, I'd keep her regardless.

It was past midnight when I headed out of the Underground Club. I had needed to release the pent-up tension from Aurora's lack of 'I love you' and my uncle's refusal to leave her out of the plan.

I unlocked my car door, itching to go home and crawl into bed with my wife, to hold her while she snored lightly in my arms.

Her demeanor was odd earlier this afternoon, but it could have been because she was visiting her mother and brother's graves.

It had taken everything in me not to order Ricardo to follow her.

I wanted Aurora's trust and her loyalty to me.

Suddenly, I lurched forward when a strong force hit

me in the back of the head, pain blooming and disorienting me.

I blinked rapidly to get rid of the black spots forming in my vision when I felt the sharp jabs everywhere.

The men attacking me grunted as they pummeled me to the ground.

There must've been a group of them, continuing their assault, and not allowing me a moment to stand or move.

The pain radiated throughout my body until it numbed me from their repeated blows.

It was over as soon as it began, or maybe I'd lost sense of time as I laid on the gravel, my mind drifting to green eyes and curly black hair.

"This is only the beginning," one of them said, the voice unrecognizable.

I coughed, tasting the metallic tang of blood, unwilling to move until they had left.

When the silence echoed in the still night, I slowly pulled myself up, wincing from the discomfort.

I wasn't unaware of the many people who'd love to see me six feet deep into the ground, but I cursed myself for not being more cautious.

Despite the last-minute plan, I should've alerted Ricardo and the team that I was at the club tonight.

As a Made man, I constantly had a target on my back.

I dragged myself into the car, needing to get home to check the damage done to my body.

During the short drive, the adrenaline wore off, replaced by the burning ache of my wounds.

I stepped out of my car and walked up the pathway to the front door.

Quietly, I unlocked it and entered, not wanting to wake Aurora. The last thing I wanted was for her to see me this way.

Pain erupted in my abdomen, increasing with each step. I grunted, clutching my side, and feeling a damp spot on my shirt.

"Roman?" Aurora called out.

I glanced up and saw her standing at the end of the dark hall, her silhouette outlined by the lamp nearby. *Shit.*

"You're up." It was all I could say without hinting at my discomfort from standing.

When she took a step toward me, I tensed.

"I couldn't sleep without you."

How could I not be helplessly in love with her when she said things like that?

"What happened to humbling me?" I joked through the searing throb in my side. "I'll be up in a minute."

I waited for her to round the corner and walk up the stairs, but dread filled me as she took another step and flipped the switch to the ceiling light on.

Her face blanched, switching between agony and aversion. "What happened to you? You're bleeding *everywhere!*" She was frantic and I was scared that at any moment, she'd faint.

"Look away from me, *anima mia.*" The dull ache vibrated along my entire body, causing me to clench my teeth. "I'll call my doctor."

Her gaze was fixated on me, ignoring my command.

The rise and fall of her chest turned rapid as she took another hesitating step toward me.

Insufferable woman.

"Aurora," I warned.

She shook her head, her jade eyes widening the closer she got to me.

What was she doing?

Multiple emotions passed across her features as she stood before me. Her throat worked in a hard swallow. "Let me help you," she choked. Her hands gingerly touched around my injured areas. "Please."

She gazed up at me, her brows dipped in distress upon her watering eyes.

My energy was depleting fast and I didn't have it in me to argue with her, so I gave a brisk nod, leaning into her touch.

"Hold on to me," she instructed, slinging my arm around her neck before I completely lost all balance.

She walked us to the living room, gently laying me on the leather couch. "I'll be right back."

As I waited for her, I looked down at the blood seeping through my shirt in multiple areas. In a struggle to get it off, I cursed, barely lifting an inch.

"*Stop.*" Aurora reappeared at my side again. "Let me help you."

My gaze drifted to the first aid supplies she held in her hands. "What are you doing?"

She knelt at my side, her face blotchy and red, as if she'd been crying during the few short minutes she'd left me alone. "Where's your phone?"

"In my pocket."

Aurora made quick work, pulling it out from my sweatpants. "Here," she said, handing it to me. "Call your doctor."

So I did because the lightheadedness I was experiencing felt like I would be dragged into the dark abyss soon.

"He's on his way."

She gave me a small nod before grabbing the scissors by her side. "I'm going to cut your shirt down the middle. I need to see..." She paused, inhaling a shaky breath. "I need to see your injuries."

I grabbed her wrist when her fingers grazed the end of my shirt. "I can't let you do that, *anima mia.*"

She lifted her gaze at me, green eyes piercing and fervid. "You're my husband, Roman. Don't expect me to sit here and watch you writhe in anguish."

I grinned from her words. "You admit it then?"

If it weren't for the inconvenient condition I was in, I'd spread her legs and show her how much I enjoyed hearing those words come out of her mouth.

"What?"

"That I'm your husband."

Aurora stared at me blankly. "You're serious right now?"

I shrugged, wincing from the gesture. "You've never said it before."

She sighed in frustration before continuing her previous action of cutting the fabric.

The beat of my heart thumped loudly the closer she got to the neckline, and it had everything to do with how Aurora would react. "All I'm saying is, I wouldn't mind you calling me your husband every so often. Turns me on." I tried to lighten the mood and ease the tension radiating off her in waves, but she wasn't paying attention.

When she pulled apart the shirt, her hand flew to her mouth as her eyes brimmed with tears. "Who did this to you, baby?"

I followed her line of sight, finding open wounds surfacing the front of my body, oozing with blood. "I don't know."

"Don't lie to me."

"I'm not." But I was intent on finding out.

Aurora grabbed a cloth, pouring water on it from a bottle before slowly dabbing it around the wound to the left of my rib. "You're firing your security team."

"Yes, *anima mia*." I wasn't, but I didn't have any desire to upset her further.

I stared at her determined face as she carefully cleaned the wounds as much as she could.

I was completely bewildered at how she could stomach the sight of me right now. I knew it couldn't be easy for her.

"Why are you doing this?" I grated when she rubbed at a sensitive area.

Time stretched for what seemed like an eternity as I waited for her to answer.

When she sat back on her heels and finally focused her gaze on me, a tear fell from the corner of her eye. "Because I love you, too."

My heart threatened to beat out of my chest. "Don't say that because of the condition I'm in," I whispered.

Aurora shook her head, brows scrunched. "*Seeing* you like this confirmed what I knew all along." She reached out and cupped my face in her delicate hands, easing my discomfort with that single touch. "*Seeing* you like this replaced my one fear with something far scarier. Losing you."

A sense of euphoria welled up inside of me, and I knew if death called for me at this moment, I'd go peacefully with the knowledge that I had the one thing I yearned for—Aurora's love.

"I'm helplessly in love with every single part of you, Roman. The good, the bad, and everything in between."

Taking a deep breath from her direct words, I fought with my body to lean up on my elbow.

Instantly, my muscles screamed at me, disabling me from the action.

"Stop moving," she bit out.

Aurora didn't know the only *good* part of me was her being my wife.

"Then kiss me."

Her eyes rounded, darting between my face and chest, hesitation clear in her doe eyes.

"You won't hurt me." It would only hurt if she deprived me of it.

She gave a subtle nod before leaning down and bracing her elbows on either side of my head, cradling it in between the crook.

Her nose touched mine in a featherlight touch, causing me to lean up and crash my lips against hers.

The softness of her mouth was a contrast to the urgency with which I kissed her.

With a shooting sensation slicing up my arm, I grabbed the small of her back, bringing her down on me, chest to chest.

If I was doing more harm than good, it didn't feel like it.

Her body molded against mine to perfection and when I slipped my tongue inside her mouth, I couldn't feel anything other than pure bliss.

The light sound of a knock came from the other side of the house, jolting Aurora to rip herself off me.

"The doctor," she panted with bruised lips.

Yes, the doctor I might fucking kill for intruding on the best medication I could take.

Aurora was gone for a moment before returning with Dr. Aldo in tow.

He appeared the same as he usually did, with gray hair and lines etched across his aging face, except this time, his eyes were red from being woken up in the middle of the night.

He pushed up his glasses, looking at me pointedly with a frown creasing his forehead. "What have you gotten yourself into now, Roman?"

CHAPTER 32
AURORA

"No concussion, but it could've been worse, right? It's not like fractured ribs and multiple wounds decorating not only your chest but your back is a big deal!"

The morning rays of sun slowly seeped in through the arched window, illuminating the room.

Dr. Aldo had left not too long ago, patching Roman's wounds, then prescribing him medication, and scolding him to take it easy for the next few weeks.

"Stop giving me a headache and come here."

My sigh was audible. I wasn't finished yelling at him for telling me his current condition could've been worse, but I stopped my shuffling, drew the curtains closed, and climbed into bed next to him.

Flat on his back for comfort, he turned his head to look at me instead. "Come closer."

I didn't move. "No. You already inflicted more damage on your ribs when you kissed me."

A lopsided grin adorned his face. "And I'd do it again, *anima mia*," he admitted proudly.

If it weren't for his current state, I might've kissed him again to knock some sense into him.

"Why do you call me that?" I asked. *"Your soul?"* At first, I had thought he used it maliciously, but it stuck with him even after our relationship grew out of hatred.

Roman's face took on a solemn expression as he fixed his tender, dark eyes on me. "Because even in my sleep, it yearns for you." He reached out and grabbed my hand, beckoning me to move closer. "You've not only stolen this heart that beats for you." He placed my palm on his chest, allowing me to feel the thrum of his heartbeat. "But this soul that attached itself to you in that dark corridor all those years ago." With a glint in his eye, he sighed in relief. "And I don't ever want it back."

Hot tears streamed down my face from the gravity of his words.

"Your tears hurt me more than the wounds on my back."

I shook my head, bringing his hand to my lips, where I placed kisses against his knuckles. "The love I carry for you consumes me. These are happy tears."

A pained expression marred his face. "You were all I thought of when I was attacked and how I needed to get back to you."

My heart squeezed at his confession. *"Roman."*

He shook his head, his eyes blurred with tears. "Then, when I got to you, all I could think about was how to avoid you. I didn't want you to see me that way. The *blood.*"

It hadn't been easy. I had cried for ten minutes in the bathroom, for him, but mostly for myself.

This fear had burdened me for far too long and knowing he was attacked had terrified me more than the crimson color.

"I could have lost you," I whispered. "And if that had happened, I would have cursed you for all eternity for dying too soon."

He laughed at that, deep and hearty.

"I'm not joking."

"I know, baby. That's what makes it funny." He yawned then, sleep weighing down on his eyes. "I forgot to ask you how your visit to the cemetery went."

Forcing a pinched smile, I pushed back his tousled black hair. "We can talk about that in the morning. Right now, you need to sleep."

The painkillers had kicked in because he nodded and closed his eyes.

I laid beside him, hearing his breathing turn even and heavy.

If someone had told me that I would fall in love with this beautiful bastard, I would have deemed them insane.

Now, every breath I took ached for him wholly.

There was a feeling in my gut that told me my father had everything to do with what happened to Roman tonight—a reminder of what was at stake if I didn't follow through with his command.

Sliding out of bed, careful not to wake him, I grabbed my phone and stepped outside of the bedroom.

Scrolling through the call log, I clicked on the number that sent my heart racing in angst and rage.

"The sun has only now risen. This better be important, Aurora," my father irately groaned.

"Oh, I'm sorry," I feigned sincerity. "Did I interrupt your sleep? Because you sure as hell interrupted mine when you sent out your men to ambush Roman."

Resentment carved its way further inside my chest at my father's ignorance.

"I take it you received my message."

"You didn't need to do that. Not when I already agreed to help you." Even though I had lied.

"Yes, but now you understand the seriousness of which I spoke earlier. Jeopardize my plan and your husband won't live to see another day."

"Your plan will have to wait. He has fractured ribs and multiple wounds." My jaw hurt from gritting my teeth tightly.

He sighed. "You have two weeks and then I'll send you the details of the whereabouts."

"Two weeks isn't enough time for him to heal."

"*Two weeks* is me being generous. Don't take it personally, *mia cara*."

The edges of my phone dug into my palm from squeezing so hard. I hung up on him without another word.

I was torn between telling Roman about my father's plan or not.

The thought of him dead sent my heart pounding with anxiety.

If I kept this secret, he would hate me for breaking his trust, but I cared more about him taking his next breath.

I dragged my feet back into our bedroom and laid next to him again.

That constant furrow between his brows had finally smoothed out.

Two more weeks was all I had with Roman. I swallowed the sobs that threatened to release.

Breaking his trust once was by force.

Breaking his trust twice was a choice.

He would never forgive me.

CHAPTER 33
ROMAN

Being bedridden wasn't how I wanted to spend my days.

It felt like I had lost every bit of control in my life, and I *hated* it.

The only perk was my wife, who seemed to have glued herself to me since the attack like a second skin as if I would disappear into thin air.

It was odd because I knew I should be grateful for her presence, yet when she was near, there was something off about her that I couldn't pinpoint.

Meanwhile, I had asked Ricardo and the rest of my crew to search for any leads on the night I was ambushed, but none were found yet.

The cameras from the Underground Club weren't angled at my car. Whoever targeted me was smarter than I had thought.

"Do I have to continuously remind you to take your medication?" Aurora threw her hands in the air, glaring at me with a flare of her nose. "What if I wasn't here one day?"

"Unless you've conjured up a secret plan to leave me, then your argument is mute."

She scoffed, grabbing a glass from the cupboard before filling it with water. "You're hopeless."

Her concern hadn't diminished even though I was magnificently better than I had been two weeks ago.

The wounds on my body were merely bruises or scabs and the ache in my ribs had dulled.

"Open."

Aurora stood between my legs, my hands resting on her hips.

With a twitch of my lips, I did as she asked. She put the pill on my tongue and brought the glass to my lips, letting me drink the cold liquid.

My hands glided against her backside before giving a squeeze. "Maybe, I like it when you're in charge."

"Is that so?" she asked, saddling herself on my lap, the heat of her cunt hardening my cock.

"'Tis so." I pulled her in for a kiss by the back of her head.

We moved our mouths slowly and heatedly, breathing each other in and tasting each other with every swipe of our tongue.

She moaned in satisfaction when I lifted my hips a fraction, thrusting against where she wanted me most.

Her tongue explored my mouth, hot and ardent. We were in sync with more than just our mouths as she ground against me in quick and firm movements.

I pulled her hair back, trailing kisses along the column

of her slender throat. She continued to rock against me, taking her pleasure unashamedly.

Biting her ear, I felt her shiver. "Show me what you want."

We probably shouldn't be doing this in the kitchen where staff could walk in, but the noises slipping free from her mouth were all I could focus on.

Her hands trembled as she worked the knot on my sweatpants. Simultaneously, I pulled down the strap of her camisole, baring her breast.

"*Roman,*" she gasped when I took her nipple in my mouth, nipping and sucking the peak.

Her hands stilled, fisting my waistband.

I smirked against her skin at the way her head lolled back, whimpering against my touch.

Pulling the other strap down, I kneaded her other breast, feeling the weight of its perfection.

It was clear her initial intention of taking off my pants had been forgotten.

Her moans echoed around the kitchen straight to my thickening cock when I pinched her nipple between my thumb and forefinger.

"Are you going to come like this, baby?"

"*Yes.*" Her voice shook, her lips parting slightly as she moved back and forth against my length.

A growl ripped through me, ready to rip off the rest of her clothes when Ricardo's voice boomed through the foyer. "*Don?*"

In an instant, Aurora shot up from her position, adjusting the straps of her camisole a second before he walked into the kitchen.

He halted mid-step, eyeing us suspiciously.

"What is it?" I snapped, adjusting myself.

He shook his head, regaining focus. "Sorry. I'm here for *Capo Donna*."

I quirked a brow at him, but then he signaled to Aurora, who looked like she had seen a ghost.

Moments ago, she had a flush creeping along her skin and now she was pale, void of any color.

Ricardo leaned forward, his arm extending to her. "It's parked out front."

She reached out and took the key that he dropped in her palm.

Turning on his heel, he left the room, the sound of the main door shutting behind him.

Even then, Aurora's attention hadn't faltered from where he once stood, holding the key tightly in between her hands.

I walked toward her and she didn't seem to notice until my hand circled her elbow, pulling her out of whatever trance she was in.

She smiled, one that didn't reach her eyes. "I have a surprise for you." The key dangled in front of us, the sound of it jingling from the shake of her hand.

Grasping her wrist, I leaned down, catching her striking green eyes. "What kind of surprise is this that it has you wanting to jump out of your own skin?"

"You haven't been out in a while, so I'm just nervous."

"Is that all?"

Her demeanor had changed within the span of two minutes. There was something wrong with my wife and I hated that I couldn't figure out what.

"Yes." Her chuckle was small, fake. "Or maybe I'm eager to get back home and finish what we started."

She was lying.

I pulled her to me, kissing her cheek. "How about we finish it now."

Her shove was lighthearted. "Later."

"Are you lying, *anima mia*?" In a silent battle, I held her stare, trying to reassure her that she could tell me whatever was on her mind. "You know I hate liars."

"I know."

"You haven't been the same since you visited the cemetery."

Her eyes narrowed in on me, a spark of anger blazing within them. "What does that mean?"

"It's like you're here, but at the same time you're not."

It was true. Aurora had tended to my every need while injured, but she was withdrawn.

"I'm sorry that visiting the graves of my dead mother and brother weren't a joy ride for me. Next time, I'll be sure to throw a party."

Her words planted a seed of guilt in me. "That's not what I meant."

"It's fine, Roman." She removed herself from my grasp. "I'll be in the car."

When she walked out of the kitchen, the pressure in my chest threatened to crush me from the inside out while my mind and heart raced in opposite directions.

I slipped my phone from my pocket and dialed my head of security.

Moments later, I sat in the passenger seat of the car

Ricardo had parked out in the front, Aurora occupying the driver's seat.

"Here," she said, handing me a blindfold.

I stared at her blankly, waiting for an explanation as she fanned the black cloth in my face.

"For the surprise. Wouldn't want to spoil it."

Taking it from her, I wrapped it around my eyes. "Care to give me a hint?"

"Nope."

The car rumbled to life, the vibration humming beneath me.

The drive was long, each passing minute more excruciating than the last.

Aurora's energy radiated off her in waves and it was palpable. If I reached out, I could grasp it between my fingers.

Every harsh inhale and exhale of her breathing sent my own pulse to thump heavily, and I didn't even think she noticed that she was doing it.

When the car slowed and crunched beneath gravel, curiosity swarmed in my mind once again.

"Are we here?"

The ignition cut off, the silence stretching between us.

She exhaled sharply. "We are."

"Why don't you sound excited, *anima mia*? Tell me what's bothering you and I'll fix it." *Just tell me.*

"I'm afraid you won't like it."

I chuckled because even if the surprise were a piece of charcoal, I would cherish it.

Reaching to snatch off the blindfold, I felt her soft hand rest on mine. "Not yet."

The sound of the car door opening and closing permeated, leaving me alone in the suffocating stillness. Then, the light summer breeze drifted in, feathering along my face as the door to my right opened.

Knowing my footing, I stepped out, colliding into her.

"Woah, there," she giggled, holding me by my biceps to steady herself.

The sound lulled my unwelcome thoughts, a calming melody I longed to hear when it was gone.

Even with my eyes covered, every inch of her being was etched into memory. Her every emotion radiated off her deep into my chest and right now, it tore me apart, limb by limb.

"I love you." It was a promise, a plead, and forever.

Instead of returning the sentiment, Aurora's breath skated across my mouth, her enchanting essence enveloping my senses.

She planted her lips firmly on mine, her hands cupping my face as if it were the last time she would do it.

One fleeting kiss.

It was only when she pulled back that I tasted the salty liquid on my lips—her tears.

Fuck this.

I slipped off the blindfold, slowly turning and taking in my surroundings.

We were standing in the middle of an abandoned warehouse, the silence eerie, chilling the beginning of my splintered heart.

"Aurora?"

"Forgive me," my wife croaked, unwilling to meet my gaze.

Then, the sound of clapping boomed in the air, diverting my attention to the source.

Just like that, the one person who filled my once hollow heart, drained it.

"If I didn't see it with my own two eyes, I would have never believed that *the* Roman Mancini fell in love," Aurora's father mused. "Nonetheless, with *my* daughter."

My attention drifted to the woman who singlehandedly fooled me into submission.

She was clutching her stomach, pain evident on her features as she glanced at me for a moment.

Anger churned in my chest, my hands trembling with rage. "What is this?" I ground out through clenched teeth.

"You'll find out soon enough."

On signal, several men approached me, Aurora's shrieking scream slicing through the thick air. "*No!*" Her step faltered when an arm wrapped around her torso, pulling her back.

My eyes darted to the man who stood behind her.

Motherfucker.

Raphael smirked at me as he held firm around Aurora.

It was a reflex to reach for her and when I did, pain seared through me as the first fist flew right under my injured rib.

I growled, ready to pounce on the fucker in front of me when my arms were held back by two men on either side of me.

"See, I could have ended your life in that parking lot two weeks ago, but what would be the fun in that, huh?"

There it was, my suspicion confirmed.

If he thought my death would be on his hands, he was not only going to die, but he was detached from reality.

Leveling a look at Angelo Bianchi, I bared my teeth, giving him a fierce smile. "You're not going to do shit. Did you forget I possess everything in your name?"

He waved a single hand in the air, signaling to one of his men before a fist slammed into my jaw, bringing out a dark chuckle from me.

"Seems that I struck a nerve." I spat out the blood that pooled in my mouth.

A strangled noise sounded, diverting my attention back to Aurora, ready to pass out with the way her face carried a yellowish tone.

Her hair stuck to her sweaty forehead, and she trembled despite the summer air.

I ran my tongue across my teeth. She wasn't my problem anymore, not when she betrayed me.

"Stop hurting him! *Please,*" she pleaded, looking at her father with eyes welled in sorrow.

Her words vanished before they could reach me, lacking the sentiment they would have had.

Her cries meant nothing to me, not when she was responsible for the position I was in.

The only person who had ever managed to hurt me was *her*.

Angelo's eyes crinkled into slits, disregarding his daughter. His chin tipped up. "Tie him up."

As if on cue, multiple explosions boomed through the stiff air, low and deep.

The men holding me loosened their grip, giving me

the leeway to elbow one in the face before taking out my gun from my hoister and shooting them both.

Shouting erupted along with the black smoke that spread faster than I anticipated.

Squinting my eyes, I scanned the expanse of the warehouse, searching for curly black hair.

Death would come to her when I decided and only then would I deliver it myself.

Waving an arm through the cloudy air, the first person who appeared was Ricardo, coming straight for me. I shook my head, immediately shouting an order. "Fucking find her and take her back to the manor."

He nodded, going back in the direction he came from.

The fumes of the smoke invaded my lungs, making it hard to breathe, but I would suffer through it until I did what I should have done a decade ago.

Put a bullet in Angelo Bianchi's skull.

"*Let go!*"

My head snapped at the recognizable voice coming from my left.

Swiftly, I stepped in that direction, pointing my gun in front of me.

"*Don't!*"

The thunderous beat of my heart was steady, roaring in my ears rhythmically.

Through the foggy air, I made out two silhouettes. A glimpse of curly hair appeared before it disappeared through the haze.

Snarling through clenched teeth, I walked straight through the smoke, finding myself right between Raphael and Aurora.

I aimed the end of the barrel to the side of my brother's head, my finger on the trigger. "Take your hands off her."

His breathing was harsh, eyes flashing with cold hatred.

When had my own flesh and blood begun to loathe me so deeply, he plotted my downfall with my enemy?

I pressed the gun firmer, emphasizing the seriousness of my words.

He relented, releasing a trembling Aurora.

It physically hurt to look at her, the one who had crushed my soul within the palm of her hands.

I *couldn't* set my gaze upon her.

"*Go*, Aurora," I ordered, holding Raphael's stare.

She didn't listen.

It was getting harder to breathe with each passing second. "*Go!*"

"*Where?*" she cried, her voice cracking.

Fuck. She didn't know where we stood and despite wanting to leave her alone in her misery, I couldn't.

Fits of coughing echoed nearby before Ricardo appeared, covering his mouth with his arm.

"Get her out of here, Ric."

Enduring a small piece of torture, I snuck a glance at Aurora.

My head of security pulled her in the opposite direction, but her emerald eyes were trained on me, eyebrows drawn in an anguished expression.

We had shared many unyielding stares, yet this was the one I broke away from first.

Raphael turned; his forehead pressed into my gun. "Kill me, then," he seethed.

"Why did you do it?" I asked, frowning in disbelief.

"You *took* her when she wasn't yours to take."

A burning trickle coursed through my chest, tightening it.

"I'll never stop," he snickered, manic rage evident on his features.

I cocked the gun, setting my finger on the trigger again.

"At least I'll die knowing you're a tortured son of a bitch."

"You're no brother of mine," I whispered.

Bang!

CHAPTER 34
AURORA

Numbing pain racked through my body.

Everywhere ached: my muscles, my bones, my head, and most of all, the gaping hole in my chest.

"You can't leave him in there!"

Ricardo ignored my protests, pushing me inside the backseat of the car before shutting the door.

There was a coldness that had claimed me since I stepped foot into that warehouse, and it hadn't thawed since.

Not knowing if Roman was okay seized my lungs from working.

Would he make it out?

Had my father escaped, or would he kill him?

Nicolai occupied the driver's seat, gripping the steering wheel, his knuckles white. "Why did you do it?"

His question lingered in the confined space of the car

before Ricardo opened the passenger door and sat, shooting out a command to drive.

The ignition hummed to life, charging the beat of my heart to escalate.

I couldn't figure out why they had come or how they knew our whereabouts, but I was *relieved.*

My father would have killed Roman if his men hadn't interfered.

It was all my fault. I had become naïve and held onto the hope that my father could be civil.

Images of Roman's face flashed in my mind. Every hit he took back there, I had felt.

Even now, it tore me apart from the inside, starting from the cramping that twisted in my stomach.

I groaned, clutching my stomach, a light coating of sweat forming on my skin.

"Are you okay?" Nicolai asked, eyeing me wearily in the rearview mirror.

"She's fine. Eyes on the road."

Ricardo's tone was stern, but the edge carried underlying dismay.

When we pulled into the driveway of the manor, the pain in my body eased a fraction. "You brought me home?"

The two men spared a glance at each other before opening their doors and getting out of the car.

I followed suit, pulling on Ricardo's sleeve. "You have to go back."

He faced me, eyes murderous, the intensity of them downright frightening.

When he looked to where I still held his arm, I let go.

"Do yourself a favor and shut the fuck up."

He disappeared inside the house without another word while I tried not to fall into hysteria over when Roman would be back.

"He's coming back."

I then noticed Nicolai standing beside me, his blonde hair longer than when I last saw him.

Swallowing the nausea that suddenly washed over me, I nodded my head at the olive branch he spared me.

"As Roman's salvation, you really disappointed me."

The branch snapped in half, and I couldn't even blame him. I hated me, too.

Out of Roman's men, Nicolai had shown me kindness from the start and maybe that's why I felt so alone when he disappeared inside the house.

An excruciatingly slow half hour passed before Roman entered the house.

Ricardo, Nicolai, and I waited in the sitting area. That too, was excruciating. Their anger consumed me, nearly tangible.

"Where is she?" Roman's voice boomed throughout the house, echoing straight to my pounding heart.

The sounds of his steps neared until he stood in the doorway.

My heart lodged in my throat. For the first time since I met him, I was *terrified* beyond belief.

His eyes held no ounce of warmth within them, pinning me in place with an inhumane expression. I sucked in a sharp breath from the harshness of it.

When he charged for me, I took a step back, my body coiling tight from anxiety. "Roman."

He grabbed my wrist and without a word, tugged me after him.

My feet tripped over itself along with the abnormal beat of my pulse.

"*Roman!*" I scratched at his arm, the pressure of his fingers digging into my wrist, aching.

He ignored me, dragging me through the halls before swinging a black door open, and pulling me inside.

Tears welled up in my eyes, my broken heart pummeling to my cramping stomach.

It was dark and cold as I fumbled down the steps to the unknown.

"*Stop!*"

More silence, his grip threatening to pierce through my skin.

"You're *hurting* me!" I sobbed.

The farther down the stairs we went, the more panicked I became.

With my free hand, I clawed at the wall, trying to free myself, and breaking my nails in the process.

The pain from my fingertips didn't compare to the horrendous ache originating in my stomach that crept all the way to my chest.

My energy depleted when I took the last step.

It felt like I had been beaten with a baseball bat. The pain was all I could focus on. It was agonizing and overwhelming.

"*Wait!*" I pleaded when he pushed me onto the hard floor with little effort.

He turned on the small bulb hanging from the ceiling, the light casting dimly on his shadowed face.

It shook me to my core to find his stare blank. No anger or fury was present in those obsidian eyes.

"*Please.*" I wept when I heard the clanking of chains erupt.

The cold metal bit into my skin, binding my wrists.

"I'm *begging* you, don't do this, Roman."

He tightened the shackles further, eliciting a broken whimper from my lips.

Yet, a part of me wanted this. I deserved whatever punishment was awaiting me. I betrayed his trust.

He hated liars and I had become the biggest of them all.

When he came down on his haunches in front of me, I couldn't even recognize him. Not even the Mafia *Don* was present.

Fresh tears mixed with my sweat streamed down my face in scorching beads.

Roman stared at me for a long moment, and I held my breath the whole time before he pushed my face away roughly in disgust.

It was the first emotion he had shown, and it ripped me apart, right down the middle.

He stood, staring down at me as he reached for the bulb switch. "When you acted unusual this morning, I hoped I was wrong, but you turned out exactly like the one person you hate."

When darkness surrounded me, the cold grasp of terror assailed me.

The sound of his footsteps fading away from me was the last thing I heard before the door slammed shut and I sat in the unbearable silence of my thoughts.

The ache in my lower abdomen that had begun earlier in the evening contracted to excruciating levels.

My body tightened as the pain gripped me in a vise all around my stomach and back.

Horror rolled through me when the feeling of warm liquid pooled between my legs, flowing free and heavily.

My body trembled, muscles spasming to the point that I was afraid they would snap.

With a shaky hand, I touched the front of my jeans with my fingers before bringing it up to my nose.

The smell of metallic hit my nostrils and I recoiled, vomiting onto the cold floor beside me.

This wasn't happening.

It was impossible.

Regret and guilt clawed at my throat.

Pressing a hand to my mouth, I bawled, the hurt of today's events consuming me.

CHAPTER 35

ROMAN

"Roman, if you don't release that girl... so help me, God."

"For fuck's sake, she's only been down there for ten minutes." Yet it was an agonizing eternity.

I released a steadying breath, raking a hand through my disheveled hair.

"It could have been for five seconds," Gianna scolded. "Go get her. *Proprio adesso.*"

Pacing around the kitchen island, I glared at her. "You can't tell me what to do."

"I *can* and I *will*. Don't disrespect me by forgetting who I am. Once upon a time, I changed your diapers."

My tone was venomous when I spoke my next words. "She *betrayed* me. *Lied* to me."

Saying the words aloud splintered my heart further, something I didn't think it could do after what had happened.

Gianna stared at me with her warm brown eyes, her face scrunched up in pity.

"Don't look at me like that."

"You didn't even ask her why she did it."

How could I have asked her when I couldn't even stand to look at her? Let alone be in her presence.

"You might not be a saint, Roman, but you are just."

Resting my hands against the cold countertop, I bowed my head. "I'm *drowning*."

It wasn't that I was oblivious to Aurora's pain. It was that my own had overpowered all else.

Locking her in the basement was to give her an ounce of what I was feeling, but all it did was leave me with a slab of regret in the center of my empty chest.

When Gianna's frail hand rubbed my back in soothing motions, I jerked to meet her gaze. "Love isn't easy. It never has been and never will be. *You* decide whether it's worth it or not."

That was the problem.

Loving Aurora *was* worth it. No matter how battered and bruised my heart was, she was worth every tear and scar.

But it didn't make it hurt any less.

I gave her a slight nod before brushing past her.

If Aurora wanted to hurt me, then she had succeeded. She held that power in the palms of her hands.

It was deathly quiet as I descended the stairs. It unnerved me.

Switching on the bulb above, I stared down at Aurora's fetal form. The small amount of light cast on her tear-stained face.

Hiking up my pants by the knees, I lowered down to my haunches.

Her eyes were closed, but by the way her breathing escalated, I knew she was awake.

I gently grabbed her by the arm and pulled her up.

She winced, staring at me through bloodshot eyes. Her distraught features stole my next breath, rendering me speechless.

Even if she deserved to be down here for disloyalty, I shouldn't have done it.

Reaching into my pocket, I retrieved the key to the chains and unlocked them from her wrists.

I massaged her skin with my thumb, touching the grooves of where the shackles bit into. *Fuck.*

"I'm sorry," she whispered, pulling my attention to her face again.

Her tears released anew. "I'm so sorry, Roman."

"Why did you do it?"

She brought her knees to her chest. "It wasn't supposed to turn out that way."

I stayed silent, waiting for her to continue.

She never did.

Reaching for the gun on my holster, I switched the safety off.

Aurora's doe eyes widened further when I reached for her hand, wrapping it around the handle with my own, pointing the end of the barrel to my chest.

She pressed further into the wall, trying to free her hand from my grip. "Wh- what are you d- doing?"

I stared deep into the window of her soul as the gun

dug into my chest, the erratic pounding of my heart vibrating against it.

"When I told you my heart was yours, I meant it. And I know I was undeserving of yours, but the last thing I expected was for you to shatter mine into a million pieces," I breathed. "Pull the trigger, *anima mia*." My finger curled against hers over the trigger.

Tears ran down her face, a steady stream until it dripped down her chin.

"Pull it and free me from this agonizing torment. I am *nothing* without the heart that beats for you."

"*Please*," she screeched, baring her teeth. "I don't want this. *I love you!*"

"Did you love me when you betrayed me?"

"It's *because* I love you that I betrayed you." She squeezed her eyes shut, head tilted upward. "It's because I love you that I'm willing to accept whatever punishment you see fit. " Then her face crumpled, another piercing sob escaping her lips. "God knows, I already am."

My eyes fell to our joined hands, my heart thumping once before halting when I noticed the blood covering hers.

Dropping the gun, I grabbed her hands, pulling them to me. "Aurora, what is this?"

She cried harder.

I gripped her face in between my palms. "*Anima mia*, what did you do?"

She choked through her weeping, and I didn't wait another second.

Wrapping her in my arms, I picked her up and strode up the stairs.

When I reached the top, I called for Gianna.

She came hurrying behind me as I rushed my way up the main stairs. "Call Dr. Aldo."

"What's wrong with her?"

"*Call!*"

Opening the door to our bedroom, I laid Aurora down on the bed, finally being able to inspect the rest of her body.

Blood stained the front of her jeans—so *much blood*.

My body went slack, numbing all senses as I dropped to my knees, staring at the crimson color.

"It's okay, Roman," Aurora whispered.

Tears welled in my eyes, blurring the image I so badly wanted to erase from my memory.

"Did—" I paused, swallowing down the thick restraint in my throat. "Did *I* do that?"

She shook her head, pinching her lips together as the pillow under her head became drenched with her tears.

"I didn't know," she bawled, covering her face with her hands. "I- I di- didn't..."

Her sentence went unfinished when I climbed into bed next to her, bringing her trembling body close to mine.

I caressed her hair, kissing the top of her head repeatedly, trying to make her understand that I knew.

"I'm sorry I lost our baby."

Her words were a piercing cry, gnawing at my skin, pulling it until it stretched and ripped apart.

Our baby.

Grabbing her chin, I tilted her face toward me, staring into the purest shade of green that made me fall in love with her.

"Don't you dare apologize to me, *anima mia.*" The burn in my eyes increased until a lone tear trickled down my face.

If I hadn't locked her in the basement, this wouldn't have happened. "I'm the one who's sorry." I pressed a kiss to her cheek, nuzzling my nose against it. "Please, forgive me."

My body was visibly shaking. Becoming a father wasn't something I had wanted until I met Aurora and I realized I wanted all *her* children.

My wife brought her arm around me, pulling me to her chest, her touch breathing life into me when all I felt was dead.

"There's nothing to forgive." Her voice quavered, breaking my entire being with each word. "I was experiencing unusual stomach pain this afternoon, but I brushed it aside thinking it was anxiety."

She pulled my head back, her eyes traveling the length of my face before settling on my eyes. "When I said I betrayed you because I love you, I was being honest. Your life was on the line, and I would rather have lived with your hatred for me than live without you at all."

"I would have done anything for you if you had told me. *Anything.*"

She closed her eyes, face twisted in grief.

We were silent for a few moments, embraced in one another's touch before she spoke again.

"Do you hate me?"

I could never, even if I tried. I don't even think I had ever hated her when I was supposed to.

"The word hate doesn't exist on the same spectrum as to how I feel about you, Aurora."

"Roman?"

"Yes, *anima mia*?"

Her inhale was sharp. "Please leave the room when Dr. Aldo comes. I don't want you to listen."

I peered down at her, narrowing my eyes. "Aurora..."

"*Please.*"

She was saving me from suffering further. If I sat here and listened to the details of what happened, I would lose it.

Aurora Mancini was the strongest woman I had ever met, and I fell in love with her more with each passing day.

A knock came through the door, bursting our bubble, and we both knew who it was.

"I love you." Pressing a firm kiss to her forehead, I leaned my head against hers. "I'll be right outside the door."

"I love you, too."

CHAPTER 36
AURORA

Sunrise to sunset, time had passed, the days blending from one to another.

It might have been three, seven, or maybe ten days since I had left my bedroom. I couldn't remember.

"You need fresh air, Aurora. I'm trying to be patient, but being within these four walls for one more day is *not* healthy."

Roman looked at me with apprehension. His hair was unkempt and his beard had grown out. Even with the bold bags beneath his eyes, he was beautiful.

"Do you think you could do that for me?" he asked, stroking my hair.

There was an emptiness in my body where my soul might have been. It was as if I wasn't in control, watching myself from a distance. I was rooted in place by this invisible anchor.

"One more day." My voice was hoarse, my throat dry, making it hard to speak.

My husband who had experienced the same loss as me in a different way, didn't believe for one second what I said to be true.

It was apparent with the way he pursed his lips.

I turned over on the bed, my back facing him before the first tear slipped from my eye.

His disappointment and pity made me want to die.

He sighed. "Okay, *anima mia*. One more day."

When the door shut, I let the self-loathing settle.

Dr. Aldo had examined me and asked numerous questions regarding the miscarriage.

He concluded that even though being on birth control lowered the chances of getting pregnant significantly, it wasn't impossible, especially if I wasn't consistent with the time.

I was muddled. I hadn't missed a day of taking my pill. Or so I thought.

Having nothing else to do but drown in the recesses of my mind, I realized I must have missed some days. I was under stress and pressure during the past few months that it hadn't become a priority.

It hadn't become a priority and now I was suffering the loss of a child. *My* child.

I killed my baby.

Silent cries filled the room. Every day, death brimmed to the surface, close to overflowing with my sorrow until it destroyed my essence.

Zoning in and out of sleep, one more day had turned into a few more. I think.

Gianna had left breakfast or maybe dinner on my bedside table when the door opened again.

I didn't turn to look at who entered the room because more likely than not, it was always Roman.

"One more day, Roman. Please just..." I sighed, burying my face into the pillow.

"I don't know which is worse, the smell in this room or you assuming I'm that ogre you call your husband."

The voice rendered me immobile. It belonged to someone who I thought I wouldn't hear or see again.

Impossible.

Somehow, I mustered enough energy and courage to turn.

A dam broke inside of me, bringing me to my feet as I lunged forward.

"Enzo," I bawled, wrapping my arms around his shoulders and my legs around his waist. I clung to him as if he would slip away at any moment.

Had I truly gone off the deep end and started hallucinating my dead brother?

He held me close, falling to his knees as he caressed my back. "Shh, it's okay. I'm here now, *sorella mia*."

I cried even harder, burying my head into his shoulder, my body shaking from the force of my sobs.

"Is it really you?" I shrieked, my tears hot on my skin.

"I'm so sorry for leaving you," he whispered. "I'm so sorry about your baby."

I choked, the pain in his voice cloaking me. It was raw and intense.

When I opened my eyes, Roman was standing by the doorway, leaning against the wall with his hands deep in his pockets.

My gaze locked on his and the crease between his brows smoothed out for the first time in days.

He gave me a small smile, a mixture of pain and relief crossing his features.

I hiccuped, fresh tears blooming. I was overwhelmed.

"Aurora," my brother coaxed, leaning back.

I stared at his face, trying to memorize every inch in case he really was a figment of my imagination.

He was different yet the same.

He had the same long hair, thick beard, and chiseled features. But there was a cold glint in his eyes that wasn't there before.

It made my heart squeeze in worry not knowing what happened to him. My lip trembled. "I thought you were dead."

He removed me from himself and stood. I followed suit, Roman coming to stand beside me.

"I need to talk to you both." He eyed me and my husband.

Roman's hand gripped my hip, giving it a reassuring squeeze.

When the two most important men in my life left my bedroom, I made quick work to bathe and clothe myself.

Nothing could take away my suffering, but my brother had come close to it.

Seeing him had mended a piece of my heart, giving me the push I needed to finally get up and leave my room.

I stared into the mirror, and I looked like death.

The bags under my eyes were puffy, my face blotchy and red.

Trying to force a smile on my face, I failed.

Sighing, I switched the light off and went in search of Enzo and Roman.

They were seated in the library, deep in conversation.

The smile I had failed to plaster on my face earlier, reappeared in its genuine form.

My heart soared at the sight of them.

"Hope I'm not interrupting." I sauntered into the room, their conversation coming to a halt.

I sat across from my brother, beside Roman on the leather couch. Immediately, his hand came to rest on my thigh.

There was no right way to jump into the inevitable conversation, so I ripped off the band-aid.

"What happened to you, Enzo?" I asked. "Our father said you were shot dead... executed by the Mancinis."

Enzo flicked his gaze to Roman before settling on me. "I *was* shot," he clarified. "Not dead." He gestured to himself. "Obviously and definitely *not* by the Mancinis."

This wasn't new information to me. I had known Roman had nothing to do with what happened to my brother. However, him confirming that he *was* shot, sent a jolt of dread through me.

"Who did it?" It was Roman who asked because I suddenly forgot how to speak.

I waited for Enzo's reply, the ringing in my ears deafening.

"Angelo Bianchi."

Ice rolled through my veins, freezing my entire body.

My father was a heinous man who had traumatized me from a young age, but his son? It was nearly unbelievable that he would do that to his golden child.

"He ambushed me, but I wasn't surprised," he continued, shaking his head. "I refused to support him in all aspects until he saved you, Aurora." Then his mouth tipped up slightly. "But you didn't need saving though, huh?"

My cheeks flushed with heat. The irony of it was not lost on me. I had fallen in love with Roman.

"Don't be embarrassed. You could've done worse than this ogre."

"Care to get shot again?" Roman deadpanned, though his tone carried a hint of sarcasm.

It was then that a petite woman entered the room, heading straight for my brother with her head bent low.

My eyes narrowed on her, trying to figure out where I had seen her before. She looked familiar. Red hair and freckle faced.

Then it hit me. She was the young housekeeper I had met when I first came back to Italy.

She took the seat next to Enzo, fidgeting with the sleeve of her shirt.

"Aurora, you remember Sofia?" Enzo asked, staring at her as if she held the world in the palm of her hands.

"Yes. *Ciao*, Sofia."

When she lifted her head, her eyes were bloodshot, pupils dilated, almost drowning out the green in them.

There was something broken about this girl. I could see the empty void in her eyes, and it unsettled me.

"Thanks for letting us stay over the past few days, Aurora." She appeared fragile, but her voice was firm.

Confusion creased my brows. "You've been here for a few days?" I turned, glaring at Roman who didn't look the least bit regretful. "They've been here, and you didn't care to tell me?"

"In your condition? No, *anima mia*, I didn't care to tell you."

All I could do was huff and cross my arms. I couldn't be mad at my husband for taking my mental state into consideration, even if it made me angry. "It wasn't your call to make."

He pulled my hand to him and caressed his lips across my knuckles, kissing each one.

"You might have forced her into marriage, Roman, but she's got you wrapped around her finger like no other."

"Did you want the bullet between your legs or through your fucking skull?" Roman shot back at my brother.

"Thinking about what's between my legs? Sorry, but you're not my type." Enzo's rough chuckle elicited a scowl from Roman and it was an odd thing to see.

These two people who had loathed each other were now on civil terms, throwing around playful insults and threats.

They must've had a few days to hash out their business while I was unaware.

I didn't want to diminish the lightness of the conversation, but there were far too many questions I still had for my brother.

"Why would our father tell me you died when you didn't? I don't understand."

Enzo shrugged. "He must've wanted to make you believe your husband was responsible for my supposed death. Knowing our father, he tried using you to scheme against Roman, didn't he?"

I nodded because that's exactly what had happened.

"He said... he buried you." A tremor racked through my body, and Roman squeezed my hand, reminding me I wasn't alone in this. "Where were you, Enzo?"

My brother remained silent, the coldness in his eyes darkening the green in them.

He didn't respond, waiting for me to figure out the answer to my question.

Our father didn't bury him, which meant he hadn't taken his body...

My breath caught in my throat, horror realization settling in. "He left you for dead?"

"I had enough strength to dial Sofia's number and tell her my location." He paused, closing his eyes in refrained temper. "I was in the hospital for a while, recovering from the multiple gunshot wounds. That's why I couldn't come to you sooner." My brother's eyes searched mine. "I would never leave you."

His words were a sharp knife, slicing me where it hurt most. It gutted me that he went through that.

"I wish you would have told me. I would have come to you."

It wasn't lost on me that Sofia must have been with him, but I didn't know the particulars of their relationship.

If I had been there with him, then he might have felt a sliver of ease to know I was okay. He hadn't known what conspired between Roman and me while he was gone.

"There were too many unanswered questions for me to have contacted you. I couldn't risk it."

He clarified my thoughts and I hated that he pretexted me even on the brink of death.

"And that was his opportunity to take me down. Or try to. The fucker knew how much you meant to Aurora," Roman added, bringing us back to the root of the discussion, stating the only sensible conclusion to it all.

My father had used me to try to gather information on his enemy.

Not only me, but my brother. Enzo had always been loyal to our father and had a better relationship with him than me, yet that left him with nothing but bullet wounds.

"I'm so sorry."

"It's not your fault, Aurora. It's my own for continuing to believe that he could change into a better man."

Sofia put her hand over Enzo's and that act alone parted my brother's lips in what might have been shock.

He turned to her, looking between where their hands connected and back to her face, his features turning soft as she gave him the smallest of smiles.

There was something painfully raw between these two. It was palpable and anyone within their presence could attest to it.

"Where do we go from here?" Roman asked, breaking the trance that had fixated upon my brother.

"We?"

"You're my brother-in-law, much to my dismay. That means we're family." Roman smirked. "But don't think I won't shoot you if I find it convenient."

Enzo scoffed, turning his attention to me. "This is who you fell in love with? Are you sure you don't have Stockholm syndrome?"

"Even if I did, I'm too far gone. I love everything that makes him, him."

Appearing slightly uncomfortable, he stood, bringing Sofia along with him. "If you don't mind, we can continue this conversation at a later time."

Neither I nor my husband objected because we knew it must have been difficult for my brother to reminisce on the horrific memory of my father shooting him on top of his recovery at the hospital.

It was overwhelming and I knew the feeling all too well.

"That's okay." I gave him an encouraging smile as if he needed it.

Enzo had been broken by our father far worse than me. At least, I had known what to expect but my brother hadn't.

The air sparked brighter when they left, and it was only Roman and me.

We hadn't had a proper conversation since before that horrible night and I knew I owed it to him and myself.

"I'm sorry, Roman."

He turned on the couch, facing me. "For?"

"For... everything."

It was hard to put into words how badly I felt for hurting him in more ways than one.

"For losing your trust. Shutting you out." I exhaled heavily. "Our baby."

He pulled me on his lap, bringing me close to the warmth of his solid chest.

Tangling my fingers in his wavy hair, the smell of him invaded my senses, soothing me instantly.

"You're a fighter, Aurora." He clutched my shirt in his fist as if he were afraid I would slip from his grasp. "You had to do what you needed to do to survive. I can't put blame on you for that."

He leaned back, searching my face with intense compassion. It made my heart soar for him. "As for the baby, you couldn't have known. You were thrown into a situation that jeopardized your mental health." His obsidian eyes seared through me. "I need you to understand that I don't blame you for any of it. *Any of it.*"

I clung to the words coming from his lips.

He tipped my chin up with his forefinger. "Do you understand what I'm saying?"

I wanted to, but it was hard when I had spent enough time blaming myself to truly believe I hadn't had choices.

Yet, he never used it against me and the way he was looking at me with yearning had me whispering the word, "Yes."

CHAPTER 37
AURORA

Jumping back into work in what seemed like forever had become a form of therapy for me—an outlet to focus on other people's troubles rather than my own.

It had been over two weeks since Enzo and Sofia had come into our lives. They continued to stay at the manor after further discussion.

Angelo Bianchi didn't know that Enzo was alive, and we intended to keep it that way until we had a set plan in place.

Ricardo informed us that Angelo was in hiding. The team was out searching for him and if I knew one thing, it was that Roman wouldn't give up his hunt until my father was six feet underground.

"Are you still with me?"

Irina's voice brought me back to the present.

Glancing down at my laptop screen, her perfectly groomed brow arched in question.

We had finished a meeting with a potential client and decided to stay on the video call to catch up.

"Yes, sorry. It's been a whirlwind of chaos these past couple of weeks." I shrugged a shoulder.

"I know," she sighed. "I'm sorry I wasn't there when you needed me."

"Don't apologize. I was a wreck, and nothing could have helped me come out of it."

"Except for Enzo."

My smile was pained. "Except for Enzo," I agreed. "I thought I lost him, Irina."

That familiar swell of emotion built inside of me. No matter what, my brother never gave up on me. He dealt with the cards he was given and helped me in his own way.

He had done what he needed to do to survive.

"But you didn't. He is with you, *always*. Maybe not in this moment because he's probably doing sinister things to that redhead."

That visual twisted my features into a grimace.

"Sorry, but it's true. From what you've told me, they definitely have something going on."

"Doesn't mean I want that image in my head!"

I had gathered absolutely nothing about Sofia in the short few weeks she'd been here.

The girl was reserved and the only time she appeared somewhat stable was when Enzo was around.

"Anyway," she drawled. "Before I go, I need to tell you something."

My heart dropped to my feet. I hated that sentence because it usually led to nothing good.

Irina's expression didn't ease my concern either. She twirled a strand of blonde hair around her finger, gnawing at her bottom lip.

"Spit it out!"

Then her face split into a huge smile. "I'm visiting you this summer!"

I suppressed my excitement and scoffed. "I never agreed to that."

"Oh, uh." She appeared worried; her brows scrunched up.

Irina's hurt expression almost fooled me until she laughed. "That's too bad!"

I joined her, squealing. "I am *so* excited! You're staying the whole summer, you hear me?"

"You're so dramatic, but yes, I hear you."

"I'm swooning."

"Oh, shut up."

My best friend visiting me the whole summer was exactly what I needed.

Being without her after not spending a day apart was harrowing and that was putting it lightly.

The door of my home office creaked open, my attention diverting from my best friend.

"And that's my cue to go."

Turning back to the screen, I huffed. "You don't even know who it is."

"With the way your face glowed, there's only one person I know who could have that effect on you."

My cheeks burst with heat at her observation.

Immediately, I lifted my gaze back to the source of my "glow."

He looked devastating.

Dressed in all black as usual, shirt stretching deliciously against his chest from his crossed arms, he waited for me to end the call.

"Hi, Roman!" Irina called out.

My husband drew closer to me, rounding the desk before standing behind me. He bent low, one hand resting on the desk and the other on my chair.

His hovering awakened goosebumps to rise on my skin.

This reaction to him would never cease. Even when I had hated him, I wanted him.

"Always a pleasure, Irina."

"It is when that dog of yours isn't present," she sneered. "Hopefully, he's learned not to answer other people's phones."

I arched a brow, eyeing the two of them. "What exactly are we talking about?"

"Goodbye, Irina." And with that, Roman shut my laptop.

He turned my chair, hands resting on the armrests. "Are you finished with work?"

"Not until you tell me what Irina meant."

Who was the dog, and why would they need to learn not to answer other people's phones?

"Luca."

"Luca?"

"*Luca,*" he repeated with feigned astonishment.

There was a whole conversation to be had about that later. Right now, the smell of sandalwood and mint engulfed me, heightening my nerve endings.

Roman and I hadn't been intimate in almost a month, and I knew it was because of his fear of hurting me.

He thought I was fragile and while I understood his concern, I didn't want him to walk on eggshells around me.

Standing up, I closed the distance between us, pressing my palms on his chest, and feeling his heart thrum against my fingertips. "Touch me, Roman."

His eyes narrowed in on me, confusion creasing between his brows.

"Touch me," I repeated, my fingers digging into his shirt.

His hands circled my wrists, an action to stop me from continuing.

Leaning up, I pressed a gentle kiss to his cheek. "Touch me."

"Aurora." My name was a plea and a warning on his tongue. The roughness in which he said it caressed my skin, increasing my lusted haze.

"Touch me." I brought his hands down to my hips.

His skin was hot to the touch, feeding this burn inside of the pit of my stomach.

Roman gazed at me with a darkness that made me shudder.

It was only a matter of seconds before he snapped and took what was his.

I would forever be his.

And he would forever be mine.

"Touch me," I choked, my throat tightening with emotion. *"Please."*

A growl ripped through his throat before he squeezed, picking me up by the back of my thighs.

I wrapped myself around his waist as he discarded everything from the desk with his arm in one swift motion.

He dropped me on the glass table, spreading my knees apart roughly, causing me to gasp.

"You want to provoke me?" he asked, kneading my flesh. "Mission accomplished."

A deep and content sigh escaped me when he slid his calloused hands up my thighs.

The tweed mini skirt I had on gave him easy access to where I wanted him.

He hooked two fingers in the center of my underwear, moving them up and down.

I whimpered when his knuckles brushed against my clit for the briefest of moments.

"I've hardly touched you and your pussy is soaked."

He pulled, the fabric digging into my skin before it ripped off me.

The anticipation of his next move was killing me slowly.

"Lay back," he instructed.

Through hooded eyes, I watched him as I leaned back on my elbows.

Pulling my knees up, he spread me wider, setting my feet on either side of the desk.

Exposed bare, I fought the urge to close my legs.

I wanted him to see me, *all* of me.

Roman's gaze traveled the length of my body, stopping at my pussy.

Biting down on my lip, my clit throbbed from the feral expression on his face, full of desire.

My need for him was fierce and I couldn't think straight with him standing there, watching me with unrestrained desire.

His head lifted, pinning me in place with the intensity of his midnight eyes as he stepped between my legs.

Dropping to his knees, he wrapped his hands around the front of my thighs, pulling me forward until I sat on the edge of the desk.

It should've embarrassed me that in broad daylight, Roman had a clear view of my arousal dripping from me, but it didn't.

A sweat broke out on my skin at how erotic this image of him on his knees was for me, all while I was spread out on the table for him to take.

The first glide of his tongue had me arching my back and dropping my head on the table.

With one hand splayed across my chest to hold me still, he took his time, lapping at me with precision.

"I could *survive* from the fucking taste of you."

The noises coming out of my mouth were loud and incoherent, but I didn't care. He worked his tongue, nipping, sucking, and licking me to oblivion.

Clutching onto the edge of the table, I ground myself against his perfect mouth, riding his face.

He groaned, squeezing my thighs to widen my legs further.

"Did touching yourself satisfy you these past few weeks?"

My mind was clouded from pleasure, his words not making sense.

When his teeth grazed my clit, I yelped. "Did it?"

"I- I haven't..."

Another graze sent my eyes rolling to the back of my head. "Don't lie to me, baby."

"*No.*" Sweat ran down my forehead from his teasing and taunting. "Fuck."

Pleased with my answer, he swirled his tongue against my folds before plunging it deep inside me.

Tremors racked throughout my body from the in-and-out glide of his tongue.

The familiar spark of an orgasm started at the base of my spine, my brain short circuiting from the sensation.

Moaning through the pleasure, I held onto Roman's hair, urging him to go faster and harder.

His tongue was warm, the feel of it burning me up from the inside, edging me toward release.

It didn't take long for me to shatter, my legs trembling around his head.

He dragged out my orgasm, sinking two fingers inside of me. I clenched around him when he curled them to hit that spot that darkened my vision.

I had only come out of my euphoric high when I was flipped over, my feet on the floor and front pressed against the table.

The coolness of the glass didn't do anything to dim the fiery desire within me and when the sound of Roman's zipper ripped through the air, it further increased.

He nudged my legs open with his knees, pushing my skirt further up.

When I felt the thick head of his cock slide up and down my folds, I whimpered, pushing back to take him inside me.

"Roman, are you in there?"

My body locked tight. The sound of Stefano Mancini had me scrambling to free myself from my husband's hold.

Before I had a chance to move an inch, Roman's hand covered my mouth. His breath feathered my ear when he whispered, "Keep quiet and take my cock like the good, obedient girl you are."

My muffled protest was cut short when he slammed into me in one thrust.

Stretching me in burning pleasure, I bit down on his palm to refrain myself from moaning.

He moved in me savagely, fast, and hard, pushing me further up the desk.

Reaching out to grab ahold of anything, I whimpered from the feel of him filling me from behind.

"Roman, did you hear me?"

His uncle was still there, clueless about what was happening behind the door.

I thought Roman would at least answer back, but he only picked up his pace, pounding into me repeatedly.

Knowing that at any moment, his uncle or anyone else could walk in here sent my heart racing and my body coiling tight.

Every brutal thrust brought me closer to my orgasm, his length reaching that spot inside me that had me recip-rocating his movements.

"Do you like knowing someone could hear your screams as I fill you with every inch of my cock? Or maybe because they could walk in and see how fucking good you take me."

His words had me clenching around him.

"You're a very bad girl, Aurora," Roman grunted, removing his hand from my mouth.

Without it, I had to bite my lip to suppress the noises wanting to slip free from my lips.

Beautiful bastard.

"Answer me."

His heavy palm came down on my backside, the sting of it pulsing on my skin.

"Do." *Slap.* "You." *Slap.* "Like." *Slap.* "It?" *Slap.*

Each smack was met with a thrust.

Sweat ran down my face, the mixture of pain and pleasure overwhelmingly blissful.

Withering in need, I replied hoarsely, *"Yes."*

With that answer, he pulled me up by my hair, the angle making him go deeper.

Reaching in front of me, Roman stroked my clit, slow and firm, the slick sounds of him entering me growing louder.

That was all it took for my body to tighten and shake violently as I climaxed.

Flattening me back on the glass, he lifted my knee, thrusting as his cock grew thicker and twitched seconds before spilling in me with a suppressed growl.

He collapsed on top of me, our harsh breathing evening out before it went quiet.

The mortification set in when he eased out of me, our mixed come dripping down my legs.

"Is he still out there?" I asked. I couldn't move from

my spot, scared that my legs would give out if I tried to stand.

A soft material brushed between my legs and around my thighs before my skirt was pulled down, and I was lifted from the table.

"Maybe, maybe not." Roman shrugged, kissing my cheek. "Guess we'll find out."

"What? *No!* Don't you dare open that door."

Zipping his pants up, he gave me a smirk before heading toward the door.

All I could do was brush through my hair with my fingers and hope that the air didn't smell of sex.

Stefano's visit was unexpected and the last time I had the displeasure of being in his presence, he reminded me that I was less than human—their property.

With a quick glance in my direction, Roman opened the door.

CHAPTER 38

ROMAN

"To what do I owe the pleasure?"

Uncle Stefano ignored me, walking past me into the office.

With his hands behind his back, he assessed his surroundings, as if he was searching for something.

The look of curiosity etched on his face before his gaze landed on Aurora.

I suppressed a chuckle, noting how she was smoothing down her tangled hair.

She stopped her movements, dropping her hands to her sides.

A silent battle was happening between my wife and uncle as they stared at one another, neither one backing down from each other's gaze.

The awkward silence broke when Uncle Stefano cleared his throat. "How are you feeling?"

"*Zio*," I warned, taking a step toward him.

His intentions were unclear. For all I knew, his question could have been malicious.

He knew of Aurora's condition and if he thought he could use it against her, then his next breath would be his last.

He gave me a sideways glance with one brow arched. "I'm only asking the girl how she is."

"I'm better, considering all things," Aurora replied, bringing his attention back to her. "*Grazie.*"

As if I had entered an alternate universe, my uncle smiled a fraction. "Sounded like it."

Shame was an emotion I never felt, but as my wife's cheeks turned a deep shade of red, I felt a sliver of it for her.

"It will take time to grow fond of you, but I *trust* my nephew, and if he loves you, be rest assured that I have no intention of harming you."

Despite Aurora's embarrassment, her posture didn't falter from its strong state. "That's good to hear because the saying 'may the best woman win' would've been said if your intention was otherwise."

That evoked a chuckle from him. "A girl with a backbone is exactly what you needed, Roman."

Understatement of the century.

"Was there a reason for your presence today, *Zio?*"

"Indeed."

There was only one topic of discussion that had been our focus on the business side of things, and it had started when Angelo Bianchi went into hiding.

If my uncle showing up unannounced went anything to go by, it led me to believe it was to our advantage.

"You've found him," I concluded.

"Who?" Aurora asked, forehead scrunched in confusion.

Uncle Stefano ignored our questions, heading straight for the door. "I will be waiting in the sitting room. I've informed everyone to gather there."

The door clicked shut, the silence drawing out.

"It's my father, isn't it? He's been found?"

"I don't know, *anima mia*," I muttered, pinching the bridge of my nose from the possibility.

If he was, we both knew what his fate would be.

Regardless of how much pain Aurora's father inflicted upon her and Enzo, he was still their father.

"Aurora..."

"I know what's to come if he's found," she cut in. "And I want him dead."

The steel look in her eyes was deadly. There wasn't an ounce of hesitation or regret present in her jaded orbs.

"Very well." Grabbing her delicate hand, I intertwined my fingers with hers and led us out of the room.

The sitting room was filled when we walked in.

Enzo, Sofia, Luca, Ricardo, Nicolai, and the others were lounging on furniture, whispering between themselves.

"Ah, they're here," Uncle Stefano stated, bringing everyone's attention to us. "Let's begin."

Leading Aurora to a plush leather couch, I sat and brought her down on my lap.

Uncle Stefano stood in the middle of the room, his white suit free of crease and stain.

"I'll get straight to the point as I hate dramatics." With

a clap of his hands, he announced, "Angelo Bianchi has been found."

You could have heard a pin drop from the absolute silence that blanketed the room.

"He has been hiding in Raphael's new nightclub. I had been waiting for a slip-up on their part to happen and it finally did. My men were posted all over Italy, and he was seen entering and leaving the club this morning."

"Great," Enzo spoke, sounding bored, but from the way his shoulders slumped slightly, I knew he was putting on a show. "What's next?"

He would never forgive his father for nearly killing him, that much was clear, but it didn't mean that the loss of his father wouldn't hurt him.

"His death," my uncle answered. "The club has a grand event tonight which gives us the perfect opportunity to slither in."

"As long as someone's dying, I'm in," Luca said, leaning further into the couch.

"Must you always be morbid?" I watched my best friend as he took a sip of his bourbon.

"You took me as I am."

"I regret my choices."

"And Angelo's fortune?" Enzo asked. "Will you continue holding that in your possession after he dies?"

"Consider it already transferred to your name, *brother*," I mocked. "Don't deem me so foul, yes?"

His disapproving grunt caused me to snicker which earned me an elbow to the rib from my wife.

"Extra supplies will be provided." With a wave of my uncle's hand, a bulky man entered, holding a large black box. "Change and grab your weapons. I want this execution to be clean and smooth. No. Mess. Ups."

"When we get to the nightclub, we will scatter. On my cue, shots will be fired to create a distraction as we deal with Angelo. I'll be back in an hour. I expect everyone to be ready by then."

With that, he took his leave.

Immediately, my crew went to work, strapping themselves in gear.

"Don't tell me I can't go."

Turning to the beautiful woman in my arms, I watched her nibble on her bottom lip.

I pulled her chin down, freeing it from between her teeth. "I won't be telling you anything." Grabbing her jaw, I leaned in. "But you're not leaving my side, understand? God knows you've never left my sight."

"*So* possessive."

"Among other things when it comes to you."

She laughed for the first time in what seemed like forever, making my heart somersault in my chest.

Leaning into my touch, I kissed her forehead when the voices to our right rose.

We turned to watch Enzo and Sofia in a heated argument.

"You're not going, and that's final."

"Then you can't either," Sofia argued. "You almost *died* the last time you were near your father."

"You *cannot* be there." Enzo pulled at his hair, his face scrunched in affliction. "From the moment I've met you, you've lived in my head. I cannot focus on my task if I'm too busy thinking of your safety."

As if his words had struck her, Sofia remained silent despite the evident displeasure slashed across her features.

It was intruding to listen in on them and while others were busy getting ready, Aurora and I had front row seats to their public conversation.

"Perhaps we should get ready instead of eavesdropping?"

"Huh?" Aurora asked distractedly, fixated on her brother and the redhead.

"Aurora."

She gaped at me, her cheeks flushed. "Sorry. It's just interesting to see my brother... like that."

Interesting for her, odd for me.

It wasn't a hard guess that Enzo loved that girl, but it was also evident she had something strange about her.

Though it was none of my business to interfere.

Pulling Aurora up by the waist, I walked us to the black box and reached inside.

I grinned, handing her the short blonde wig. "This might be more fun than I thought."

CHAPTER 39

AURORA

"Hold still."

I watched as my husband went down on his haunches in front of me, pushing the slit of my red dress to the side.

"If you had let me put it on at the house, you wouldn't be on your knees right now."

Roman strapped a gun around my thigh, a smirk carving his devastating mouth. "I love getting on my knees for you."

I suppressed the urge to laugh at his playfulness because we were in a *not* so very playful situation. "I'll hold you to that later."

He tightened the strap further. "I count on it."

He had spent the past hour teaching me the basics of how to use a gun while reminding me never to leave his side tonight.

He must have forgotten that I had used the same object on his deceased cousin.

"Everything is set." Enzo appeared beside me, fixing his gun on his holster. "A few of Stefano's men slipped in as security to get us in."

My stomach twisted into knots knowing it was almost time.

"That easily?"

"With Raphael dead, their management has been... less than stellar."

The crew had been keeping cover in the back alleyway for the past fifteen minutes, waiting.

The sound of excited crowds busted to life, heightening the anxiety gripping me in a vise.

It wasn't because I feared for Angelo Bianchi's life.

It was because I feared for my *family* and how wrong this could go.

We were going in blind, hoping that our plan of distraction and execution would work.

"Don't tell me you're getting cold feet."

My smile was pinched as I shrugged my shoulders.

He palmed my face reassuringly, bringing me away from my pessimistic thoughts. "I've always got your back, *sorella mia*."

Words he had said to me once before and meant it too.

A tightness in my chest formed. "And I've got yours."

That was all that needed to be said between my brother and me as we exchanged a meaningful look before he walked toward the rest of the group.

"Are you?" Roman asked, pulling me to him by my waist. "Getting cold feet?"

For the first time in my life, I was sure of what I

wanted when it came to the man who was supposed to be my father.

He had let me down countless times, hurting me repeatedly as if I wasn't his daughter.

"I meant what I said. I want him dead."

Roman tilted his head to the side, eyes assessing me, and lip curled between his teeth.

Whatever he was thinking, he didn't verbalize it.

Instead, he squeezed my hip and bent his head, placing a firm kiss on my lips.

Too quick for me to enjoy his touch.

"This isn't goodbye," he whispered against my mouth.

I swallowed the doubts that resurfaced and gave him another fleeting kiss.

"Gather around, everyone."

In seconds, we were surrounded by our crew and the night breeze that chilled my bones.

"Inside, we split up," Roman asserted. "Enzo, Aurora, and I will take one corner. Luca, Ricardo, and Nico will take another. The rest of you spread out and wait for destruction. Any questions?"

"Can we celebrate afterward?"

Leaning forward, I saw pale-blonde hair and chocolate-brown eyes.

"Nico," Roman irately groaned, rubbing his temple. "Be serious for once, kid."

"I am!" His hands flew up in the air.

"I should've left you at the house."

Nicolai scoffed, sheathing his knife inside his shirt sleeve.

It seemed that the Mafia *Don* had a soft spot for someone other than his wife.

No one else had the advantage of pushing Roman's buttons except for the young man muttering profanities under his breath.

It was then that Stefano appeared, eyes sharp and determined.

It was time.

Aside from our men disguised as security, entering the nightclub was easier than I thought with how packed it was.

The space was dark, lights strewn out on the ceiling to cast a light glow against the crowd.

The deep echoes of music blasted through the chattering of people.

The mix of body odors and alcohol were strong as Enzo, Roman, and I made our way through the crowd.

As instructed, we stood in one area, assessing our environment.

The corner we occupied was secluded enough for us to be hidden from anyone who might recognize us, which was unlikely, especially with the itchy blonde wig I wore.

"I don't see him," Enzo pointed out, lighting the cigarette in his mouth.

"When did you start smoking again?"

His only answer was the exhale of a puff of smoke.

"Over there," Roman interrupted, saving my brother from a lecture.

We turned in unison to catch his line of sight.

Angelo Bianchi stood with two men at the far side of the lounge space, laughing at something one said.

He had on a black suit, his salt and pepper hair sleeked back to perfection, and a conniving smile that made me want to hurl.

"*Motherfucker*," Enzo cursed, taking another drag of his cigarette.

If he was spotted by us, that meant the others had spotted him, too.

Adrenaline coursed through my veins, expecting the chaos that would erupt soon.

"And there's my uncle," Roman pointed out.

He stood not too far from Angelo, his eyes tracking his every movement, waiting for the right time to attack.

A half-hour must have passed before the first piercing gunshot was fired by Stefano, aimed right at one of the men sitting next to Angelo.

Immediately, the screaming of civilians fleeing the premises broke out, their bodies shoving past me.

I homed in on Angelo, who tried to escape through one of the exits.

My body moved on autopilot, shoving my way through the crowd.

"Aurora!"

I kept moving.

There was no way I would let that heinous man escape once again.

A gasp escaped me when I was spun around abruptly by my arm.

The hand came down on my face faster than I could block, the force of it knocking me to the floor.

My right cheek throbbed from the impact of the hit.

"*Fuck*." Roman was near, his voice sounding muffled to my ears.

"That was my boss, bitch. Wrong move."

Scrambling off the floor, I watched as Ricardo held the man who must have hit me in a headlock.

In one swift motion, my husband's head of security jerked his arm to the side, snapping the man's neck and letting him fall to the ground.

"Three kills within a minute? Unbelievable," he sighed in disappointment.

Ricardo was relentless.

Pressing down on my cheekbone, I winced when I touched the slightly risen skin.

If I was targeted, then we had been spotted.

"We're going to have a long fucking talk about you not following orders when we get home." Roman appeared in front of me, instantly grabbing my face between his hands, and assessing the damage.

It must have looked terrible because without breaking eye contact, he aimed his gun down and to the left before firing.

Turning my head slightly, I found a bullet lodged into the man's throat, blood running down the column of it.

My lips parted in surprise. "He was already dead."

"Not dead enough."

The music stopped, creating an eerie tension in the room.

The space was almost empty, save for the lifeless bodies on the ground.

"Come on," Luca shouted, running past us.

Searching the area, Enzo was nowhere to be seen.

Only Nicolai, who had someone pinned to the floor, two knives slashing across their throat with one swipe on either side.

The sweat pouring down my face was as rapid as the thump of my heartbeat.

Wherever Luca was leading us, I hoped my brother was there too.

I expected to have heard police sirens by now, but it seemed that Stefano had also taken care of that.

It was quiet as we descended the steps to the basement.

The heavy noise of our breathing echoed through the narrow walls.

"I don't even know why I'm wasting my time on you!"

Enzo's voice carried up the stairs, halting me in place.

"Aurora?" Roman whispered, squeezing my hand.

"I... I—" Words failed me as I grasped the realization that I would face something I wasn't sure I was truly ready for.

"It's okay, *anima mia*. I'm here."

A glance in his direction was enough for me to believe him.

His pure midnight eyes searched mine, calming something deep inside me.

With every shred of my existence, I knew that I would be okay, so long as he was by my side.

I nodded, squeezing his hand in return.

The voices grew louder until we reached the bottom step.

The room was brighter than the top level and more sophisticated.

Chandeliers dangled from a white ceiling, furnished with lounge cubicles and a bar at the end of the room.

Smack dab in the middle was Angelo Bianchi tied to a chair, a streak of blood dripping down his nose.

Enzo was standing before him, sleeves rolled up to his elbows, his face a mixture of pure torment and anger.

The instant Angelo's eyes landed on me, he laughed boisterously.

I flinched from the sound, mentally kicking myself for taking a step back.

"It wouldn't have been quite a family reunion without the *whore* showing up."

My brother moved fast, landing a punch on Angelo, and knocking his tooth out. "Don't fucking talk about her." He grabbed his face. "Take your eyes off her. *Right now.*"

With a sneer, he spat blood on the floor in my direction and averted his eyes from me.

The energy in the room was palpable.

Heat and unreleased tension emanated from both Roman, who had a murderous aura to him and Enzo, who was two seconds away from going on a rampage.

"I'll ask you again and this time, I expect an answer. What was your motive in killing Milo Mancini?"

Milo must have been Roman's cousin and underboss.

Shivers racked through my body, having put a name to the man *I* killed.

"I didn't kill anyone," Angelo snarled. "I thought *that* much was clear."

"It's also clear that you weren't man enough to execute it yourself, having your daughter do it." Stefano appeared from behind the bar, swirling the drink in his hand. "Seems like you weren't a father either."

My mouth gaped open at him defending me. Intense emotion swirled through me and I could have burst into tears.

"Both of my children are alive, Stefano. Where's yours?"

With those harsh words, the air chilled, hairs rising to my exposed skin.

It was Roman who aimed his gun at Angelo, his hand shaking from unrestrained fury.

Enzo held his hand up at him. "Put your gun down, brother."

Roman's nostrils flared, his breathing uneven before he let out a pained growl and dropped his hand.

"Don't think I saved you from death, Angelo," Enzo clarified. "You will die today. And when you do, no one will care. You're worthless in this life as you will be in the next."

This seemed to have caused Angelo distress as he swallowed audibly. It was clear he cared for his son despite what he had done to him.

"If you hadn't been persistent in saving that girl, I would have never shot you, Enzo."

"That *girl* is my sister. Your daughter!"

A disgruntled sound slipped from his lips, his displeasure evident.

Stefano swirled his drink once more, taking slow strides until he reached Angelo. "Why did you kill my son?"

Impatience wore thin as Angelo spat out, "Because he had an affair with my *wife*."

Stefano's face twisted in unbelievable shock.

I swallowed, my heart thumping against my ribcage. "He's lying."

I couldn't believe what he said to be true. My mother could have never been capable of doing that.

"Am I?" Angelo asked. "When she died, I couldn't bring myself to go through her belongings for a few years... but then one day, I did."

His expression turned dark and wild. "There was a photo tucked deep into her jewelry box. I thought it was odd, but then I flipped it. Your mother and Milo in a *loving* embrace."

My brother's fists clenched at his sides before his eyes caught mine, forehead creasing in disbelief.

"If you don't believe my words, you can find the photo back at the house. I kept it as a reminder that she was nothing but a whore, like her daughter."

"I think it's time a bullet found its home between his eyes, isn't it?" Luca said, pulling the safety off his gun.

The reason Angelo Bianchi created a dispute between the two families was because of an affair—my *mother's* affair.

"No."

I hadn't realized I was the one who spoke until I felt all eyes on me, whereas mine were glued to Angelo.

Everything made sense now. Angelo not only hated me because I looked like his deceased wife but also because that *same* wife cheated on him.

He made me kill Milo and then outed me to the

Mancinis because he knew it would bring me torture and affliction.

But I wasn't my mother.

Ignoring Roman calling my name, I walked toward the man who caused me more suffering than anyone I had ever met.

"Here to defend my behalf, *mia cara?*"

It was a nickname that lodged a knife within me, shredding me into pieces from the inside out.

He didn't deserve my words. Nor did he deserve my gaze, but I found the will to stare into his eyes which were the same shade of green as mine.

I wanted to watch the light leave his eyes as I took his life.

Holding his stare, I reached under the side of my dress, feeling the cold metal graze my fingertips as I pulled the gun from my thigh.

"You?" Angelo asked mockingly with a laugh. "The little girl who fears blood is going to *shoot* me. We both know you can't."

He didn't know the first thing about me, and I was glad for it. That fear that began because of him would die with him.

With a steady hand, I rested the end of the gun to his temple.

If anyone in the room wanted to object, they didn't.

They knew as well as I did, that I needed to be the one to do this.

I needed to do this for myself.

Utter fear crossed Angelo's face when I pulled the safety off, an emotion I hadn't seen before.

He deserved to feel even an ounce of that emotion, the same emotion I had felt on countless occasions because of him.

"Au—"

My name was cut short when I pulled the trigger.

Bang!

EPILOGUE
AURORA

One Year Later

"Are you ready for tonight?" Roman whispered in my ear, pulling me back against his chest.

Staring at our reflection in the mirror, I smiled, content with my life and knowing this was the happiest I had ever been.

"I'm nervous but excited to share the news."

It was our first Christmas together and we had decided to throw a small party with our closest friends and family.

He rubbed the growing swell of my stomach soothingly. "It's the best news, *anima mia*. There's nothing to be nervous about."

But nerves were unavoidable when I had been through an awful experience.

Roman would scold me for stressing if I continued to go back and forth with him so I turned, wrapping my arms around his waist.

He eyed me precariously when I gave him a cheeky smile. "That beautiful smile of yours won't work on me."

"Oh, come on!" I batted my lashes and pouted my lips. "Show me."

He silently contemplated, his obsidian eyes searching my desperate expression.

Patience was not a virtue of mine, and I had only lasted a full six hours before I nagged him to tell me what my Christmas present was.

With a heavy sigh, he stepped back, his fingers reaching the top button of his black dress shirt and undoing it.

Tilting my head in confusion, I laughed in shock. "I said show me my present, not your North Pole."

Roman tipped his head back, laughing loudly and candidly. The sound warmed every inch of my mind, body, soul, and most of all, my heart.

His rough timbre was infectious, the sound of my own laughter joining his.

"You never cease to amaze me, Aurora."

"I would..." He continued undoing each button until his shirt was completely undone. "Hope not..."

It wasn't his sculpted chest that stole my breath away this time, it was the tattoo decorating his heart.

Stepping forward, I placed my hands across his bare chest, moving them up to his broad shoulders before pushing down his shirt.

The skin of his chest now bore a siren with long black hair. *Curly*.

My heart thumped against my ribcage.

Tracing a finger across the fresh ink, I noticed the small details.

The siren's front was hidden, two dimples adorning the small of its back, *just like mine.*

Eyes an emerald green, *just like mine.*

Exhaling a shaky breath, I lifted my head, locking eyes with my husband as he stared down at me with heated love and desire.

"Is this..."

"You?" he asked, finishing my question. "Yes."

Flutters took flight in my stomach, intensifying the heavy feeling in my chest that overtook my senses. "You got a tattoo of me?"

My eyes welled with tears as I traced the beautiful lines of the artwork.

Roman had inked me on his skin. Permanent. Like our love.

"Why a siren?" I choked.

Cupping my face, he leaned in, kissing the tip of my nose. "I don't think my soul was ever mine to begin with. Not since I met you."

Holding his wrists to lean further into his touch, a steady stream of tears ran down my cheeks.

"That one night in that corridor was all it took for me to surrender to you. Like a siren, you beckoned me with your presence alone." His knuckles traced my jaw affectionately down to my chin which he tipped up, staring deep into the depths of my soul. "And, *anima mia?* I don't ever want to escape your hold."

Somehow, I'd found my voice through the overwhelming

emotions threatening to consume me. "I am utterly and wholly in love with you, Roman Mancini. Even then, there aren't enough words to describe how deeply I feel for you."

A wicked smile crept across his face, eyes glinting with satisfaction.

I had trodden that path to hell and welcomed the devil in front of me.

He was mine as much as I was his.

With that, he sealed our fate together with a kiss.

For eternity.

THANK YOU FOR READING!
WHAT'S NEXT?

If you enjoyed reading Tainted Ties, please consider leaving a review!

Next up is the story of Luca and Irina in Stolen Seconds

ACKNOWLEDGMENTS

To my family: Thank you for supporting me on this journey and being my rock. I wouldn't have gotten this far without you.

To my friends: Thank you for listening to me hours on end talking about the same plot repeatedly and being excited as if it was the first time. You know who you are.

To my editor: Thank you for being patient with me, despite my midnight messages. My grammar has never been better.

To my supportive readers: This wouldn't have been possible without any of you. I hope you fall in love with my book as much as I did writing it. Thank you, infinitely.

ABOUT THE AUTHOR

Gheeti Nusrati began her writing journey a year ago. With a strong love for reading, she discovered a passion for creating stories that invoke strong emotions. She hopes to continue this new journey with the support of her amazing readers.

instagram.com/author_gheeti

goodreads.com/gheeti

tiktok.com/@gheeti

Made in the USA
Las Vegas, NV
11 April 2024

88555256R00189